H. A. Nicola

Stranger in the Wharf

Limited Special Edition. No. 18 of 25 Paperbacks

H. A. Nicola is an author whose work is infused and inspired by real life events and observations written with her unique unapologetic and humorous insight.

This work is dedicated to
all who are on the same mission.

H. A. Nicola

STRANGER IN THE WHARF

AUSTIN MACAULEY PUBLISHERS™
LONDON · CAMBRIDGE · NEW YORK · SHARJAH

Copyright © H. A. Nicola (2019)

The right of H. A. Nicola to be identified as the author of this work has been asserted by her in accordance with section 77 and 78 of the Copyright, Designs and Patents Act 1988.

All rights reserved. No part of this publication may be reproduced, stored in a retrieval system or transmitted in any form or by any means, electronic, mechanical, photocopying, recording or otherwise, without the prior permission of the publishers.

Any person who commits any unauthorised act in relation to this publication may be liable to criminal prosecution and civil claims for damages.

This is a work of fiction. Names, characters, businesses, places, events, locales and incidents are either the products of the author's imagination or used in a fictitious manner. Any resemblance to actual persons, living or dead, or actual events is purely coincidental.

A CIP catalogue record for this title is available from the British Library.

ISBN 9781528926171 (Paperback)
ISBN 9781528964586 (ePub e-book)

www.austinmacauley.com

First Published (2019)
Austin Macauley Publishers Ltd
25 Canada Square
Canary Wharf
London
E14 5LQ

To Peach Ri and Pepa

Chapter 1
22 March 2017

An explosive situation is unravelling on the streets of Westminster, Central London—the seat of British Parliament—culminating into a frenetically charged atmosphere. Running, shouting, bloodcurdling screams.

High above the commotion, way up on the 13th floor of the Westminster Park Plaza Hotel erupts a torrent of raised voices, more gut-wrenching, high-pitched howls, hands outstretched and deep-seated groans.

Below, Big Ben chimes aloud, stating his authority over the capital, calling for it to stand to attention in an attempt to detain the pandemonium, countering the confusion with its regal stance, shortly followed by a weighted solemnity in the air.

Up above, a combination of commandeering directions and bated breath resume, pushing and shoving, and forceful impact can be heard from beyond the presidential suite walls. Uncertainty fills the air; the atmosphere is clouded with sensual anxiety. Backs are pressed against the wall, arms are arrested and legs bound.

Below… sudden screeches as a vehicle is thrust to a complete stop. A hive of erratic activity follows. Frenzy and mayhem ensue.

Unaware of the travesty outside as they continue their own euphoric ascent, hands are groping aggressively behind heads, pushing down and forcefully demanding surrender.

The energy builds; the tension is almost unbearable.

Loud sirens. Emergency sirens, everywhere. The city is in the grip of abject fear.

Finally… it shoots… powerfully. The acceleration is Herculean; the substance emitted—substantial—splattering against the wall, the bed, the sheets and her.

Suddenly their phones begin to ring incessantly, punctuated with the sounds of constant notifications, competing for attention to form a continual symphony.

He picks up his phone and edges towards the corner of the room; his broad white undefined back, dotted with liver spots, facing her. He listens and then spins around—his face ashen. He strides quickly toward the window and looks down onto the streets, eyes darting, taking in whatever was unfolding—getting paler by the second. The accustomed rose pink of his complexion fading to a patchy oatmeal.

He reaches for the hotel remote on the large, ornate oak desk and switches on the flat-screen television hanging from the facing wall and sits down on the edge of the bed; his naked buttocks still damp with orgasmic perspiration.

The reporter on the screen looks tense with apprehension as she faces the nation with the dreaded news—the imposing structure of Westminster forming the formidable backdrop.

"You are watching a BBC news special. Reports are coming in of a shooting at the Palace of Westminster outside the House of Commons.

A policeman has been stabbed, and his apparent attacker shot by police officers in what is developing into a major security breach outside the Houses of Parliament. These live pictures are of Westminster Bridge, where eyewitnesses say a car mowed down several pedestrians. The indication is that there are as many as 12 people injured. The car was then said to have driven into the railings of the Palace of Westminster. Many people are being treated at the scene, as you can see from these pictures…"

He reduces the volume of the television, sighs, runs his fingers through his hair and turns back to look at her. She sits huddled, like a chocolate whirl, still wrapped in the sex-sodden sheets, eyes wide, dazed and in shock.

He crawls across the bed and pulls her to him as they try to take in more of the events unfolding, both on the screen and on the streets below the scene of their torrid encounter.

His phone rings again. He is reassuring someone that he is okay, but that he can't talk, and he will ring them when he gets the chance.

Her phone buzzes loudly. She clasps it to her ear just as a vehement voice bellows. She could hear the combination of fearful anticipation and relief in her son's voice as he demands to know why she hasn't been responding to his calls.

"Oh … I'm sorry, son … It must have been the signal. I didn't hear it ring. Yes, I'm okay. I'm okay…"

They both place their phones down and embrace each other again, needing each other's reassurance.

Their hearts are thundering in their chests as they pull apart just enough to glance into each other's eyes. His gaze softens as he sees the fear and immediately moves to strengthen his hold. Their lips clasp together, as though they could not be separated. He tenderly places her back into the imprint of her body still visible on the bed. He couldn't begin to explain why, even now, at a moment like this, he feels consumed with wanting. His private parts testify of his intention.

The condom had been long since discarded. She couldn't quite pinpoint when, but it had been somewhere between the heavy petting and the fumbling. The built-up suspense was too great, for she had chided and teased that he was missing out, and that he needed to experience her fully—unprohibited by a thin rubber sheath. He too needed little convincing that he must observe closely the soft folds inside her, first hand. To feel them hug his manhood in a warm embrace as he pushes them open to stretch and mould them around him.

He is compelled to find the origin of her intoxicating wetness, to see the response on her face to the sensitivity of his touch.

He reproaches any hindrance to him finding her G-spot, wanting to pervade her clitoris, to infuse and embody the organs that he had thus far only tasted of.

She had promised to allow him to feel her vice-like grip from the contracting of her vagina. She had taunted him that he would not have experienced it in quite the same way before. The dangerous excitement had been untenable.

Yet still, he needed more of her, but just managed to resist the compulsion to press himself against the entrance to her rectum.

Just as he senses her euphoria mounting, he pulls out and waits for the tension to dribble out of his body and soil the sheets for the second time.

They lie still for a moment until their awareness of where they are slowly returns. Conscious that he is lying heavily upon her, he lifts his torso away, panting and dripping, totally spent.

She lies motionless, lost in her own delirium, eyes soft and blurred.

She hears the volume of the television rising again as the reporter continues her horrific account.

"... *A car, likened to a Hyundai Tucson, was witnessed to accelerate over Westminster Bridge at approximately 2:40 p.m. before suddenly and deliberately veering to the opposing lane, mounting the pavement and ploughing into several pedestrians, leaving 12 people injured. Eyewitnesses confirm that one man was seen to jump off the bridge into the River Thames to avoid the impact.*

Emergency services are arriving as bodies lay strewn on the streets. The vehicle was then said to have crashed into the railings outside New Palace Yard, where the assailant was seen heading through the Carriage Gates entrance, presumably undetected by armed patrol. Shortly, thereafter, he was confronted by an armed officer who, it has been confirmed, later died from fatal stab wounds..."

He switches the television off abruptly—angrily. His face contorted with concern and guilt. He takes her hand whilst avoiding her eyes and leads her out to the large terrace of their suite, high above the aftermath of the massacre and wraps his arms around her from behind, as if to protect her from the late-afternoon chill. Adorned with their hotel bathrobes, the cool concrete beneath their feet rapidly reducing the balmy temperature of their bodies, they gaze out at the flashing lights and the chaotic scenes below. He presses her head into his chest, shielding her from the full impact of the horrific scenes unfurling. Kissing her forehead gently, bewildered, as he tries to absorb the fact that at the exact moment terrorists plotted outside, they had been lost in their own bubble, intricately uniting their own diverse nations and navigating a harmonious collision.

Chapter 2
The Start

The winter lights in London were some of the most spectacular and innovative in the world, as far as Cayenne was concerned, and the weeks and months leading up to Christmas wouldn't be the same without them. She loved how they made the trees twinkle, and how they filled up seemingly every household window with a welcoming glow; and she couldn't fail to be in awe of how they set the famous streets alight with Christmas spirit. Just when you thought the streets of the capital couldn't get any busier, the ushering in of festivities brought with it hordes of visitors, eager to sample the dazzling spectacles and elaborate installations.

Cayenne happened to have first-hand knowledge of this, having been fortunate enough to see the festive lights across the globe from New York to Sydney, from Tokyo to Paris whilst travelling the world with British Airways during her cabin-crew days. So enchanted was she with this festive tradition, that she made a point of ensuring she was always on shift over the Christmas period which inevitably made her popular with her fellow crew members, most of whom longed to be home with their families; and they were only too pleased to swap their work pattern with hers. She was there several times when New York was magnificently transformed into a sparkling winter wonderland immediately after Thanksgiving. She had witnessed more than once, the City of Cape Town's festive lights switch on, on the Grand Parade, to the acoustic sounds of an array of local musicians. How could she forget the kaleidoscopic light overload at the Cascades in the south of Sydney, and the singing Santas, polar bears and frosty snowmen in neighbouring Karne Street. When she closed her eyes, she could still recall the smell of the garden inside Roppongi Hills in Tokyo, remembering gazing up at the huge glistening tree and meandering around what seemed like thousands of lights strewn over the grounds.

What she especially loved about living in Canary Wharf was that the lighting stayed on all year 'round, even the trees shone at night all year long, which inspired many late-night walks with her children.

Years later, she still had the treasured mementoes from these captured exploits in a photo album at home; and from time to time, she sought them out to recapture the magic. Perhaps what she loved most about the season was the fact that it seemed to not only bring families together but whole communities. Whatever country she found herself in at the time, she could scarcely remember being surrounded by just the local natives, but she would find herself linking arms with French travellers in Tokyo, a family from South Carolina in Sydney, a newly engaged couple from the UK on a beach in Bangkok, all joining together to bid farewell to the old year and usher in the new, singing *Auld Lang Syne* beneath a multi-coloured explosion in the sky.

But by far, her favourite illuminations were that of the London offering—the beautiful balloon bulbs on Oxford Street which looked like flames behind frosted glass, or the drop-shaped bulb lights on Regents Street which had tiny little dancing fairies inside. The Café de Paris for the last two years had a climbing Santa Claus scurrying up to a makeshift chimney with his sack of goods on his shoulder. Ever since she had moved from Torquay to Canary Wharf with her three children, she had become enchanted with the perennial lights in the business district. She was fascinated by the way fresh installations popped up every year and enjoyed the charmed open ice rink where couples often skated around looking romantically into each other's eyes. It drew crowds from many other boroughs which made her feel all the more fortunate. There was a unique buzzing energy that characterised the place she now had the good fortune to call home.

Not only had her eldest son Diego wanted to experience the big city after leaving school in the Midlands, but her second son Ocean, who had been diagnosed with severe learning difficulties from an early age, had previously been in an unsuitable school that catered for a wide variety of generic needs, both physical and psychological. Cayenne felt very strongly that Ocean required a facility that catered for his specific needs and felt that London would provide him with better opportunities for a higher standard of specialised education.

So she had urgently set to work to make it happen. She had always been a determined woman. The kind of go-getter that not only expressed her wishes but made them manifest with a confidence and determination that many would covet. She often considered that the advantage of growing up under a critical West-Indian eye was that it developed in her a resolutely thick skin and a steely determination to forge her own path.

Now here they were, with only one of their two original cats, as Tokyo—the male of the duo—had decided that a move wasn't for him and had promptly jumped out of the removal van and straight over the neighbour's fence, whereas Temple clearly sensed their excitement and stayed put, though whether the fact that she had four babies inside her influenced her decision was debatable. The boys were settled—Diego in college, and Ocean in one of the top special needs schools in London—and little Sugar, her only daughter, slowly ingratiating herself into her new class at the local junior school. Cayenne was relieved that her outwardly shy daughter had acclimatised quicker than expected, given her tendency to withdraw within herself whenever she encountered a new environment, to such an extent that the parent-teacher meetings would consist of Cayenne listening to a version of her daughter that was largely unrecognisable from the astute, determined, stubborn child that she lived with. She would smile within herself, remembering that she too had been the quiet girl in her formative years. Unsure of herself and feeling that she had little to contribute, which was an image far removed from the epitome of confidence that she saw reflected in her image today. Once she had settled the children and done her best to cosmetically update their apartment, situated a stone throw from South Quay, just across the bridge from the centre of the hubbub, she had determined that it was now her time to find fulfilment. But what would that look like? What did she see herself doing? What new direction was beckoning? Was she ready for a long-term relationship, or was it time to finally explore sexual freedom and diversity, having seemingly missed out on this part of her early adulthood? She wasn't sure. Fortunately, her children were in total agreement that their mother, who was still considered relevant considering her advanced years and had kept herself in good condition, should by all means come out from her self-induced hibernation and begin to experience life in the big city.

Unfortunately, an ill-fated attempt at online dating had ensured a furtive scurry back to relative obscurity for several months. Against her better judgement and fuelled by a sense of daring rather than an acute desire to find a mate, she had added her name to a few online dating sites, uploading a recent picture which she felt represented a woman who would like to date, rather than was desperate to date. After eliminating a few scary options, and several more dubious profiles, she had come across the details of an Asian gentleman that she knew was bound to be younger than her, probably around ten years younger by her estimation. If she was prepared to be honest, her motivation was the cute pictures that represented him whereby he was posing confidently by a pool which looked to be somewhere in the Mediterranean as indicated by the stunning sun-kissed ambience, and the brilliant blue of the sea behind him. His responses via text had been reasonably intelligent, and perhaps his quick replies had appeased her ego somewhat.

After a few days, he had offered his phone number; and following some consideration, she decided to initiate contact with Kamal; and over a period of a few weeks, they had built up a steady stream of communication. Had she been paying attention, she would have noticed that his voice was slightly jarring, but perhaps their joint enthusiasm for fitness and well-being caused her to overlook such minor details. He even offered to train her when she had told him she was considering joining a local gym. He described in detail the kind of workouts that he would devise for her according to her goals and expressed in no uncertain terms, his appreciation for women that made the effort to look after themselves. Cayenne had to admit she was beginning to feel a little optimistic about this guy, even as a possible candidate to accompany her on nights out. Any doubts that surfaced would soon dissipate with just a glance at the humble-looking, striking eastern native who peered at her from his profile photo with his piercing uncompromising eyes that seemed to say, "This is me. Take it or leave it." No apparent pretence. Eventually, he offered to arrange a meetup. Nothing too adventurous—a meal and a drink. An opportunity to continue their discussions face-to-face.

"Mom, make sure you meet him somewhere really public," Diego had admonished when she told him that a date had been set to meet Kamal. As each day passed leading up to the appointment, Cayenne noticed a tension building up with her eldest son who she suspected was beginning to experience unexpected mounting concern for his mother embarking on this new venture. On the actual date night, he could barely bring himself to look at her whilst tersely reminding her to keep her phone on, as it had always angered him when he couldn't reach her immediately. He warned her not to stay out too late. She chuckled to herself wondering when he had suddenly become her guardian and tried to determine precisely when the tables had turned. When he escorted her to the front door and waited for her to disappear into the elevator, the steely look in his eye made her feel as though she were a teenager exercising the audacity to embark on an independent social life. She could just about hear his deep monotone voice as the doors closed in front of her, and the elevator began its descent to the ground floor,

"Make sure you call me every ten minutes…"

She had arranged for Kamal to pick her up in his car outside the nearest Docklands Light Rail Station, and she had been instructed to look out for a black Mercedes. She stood in her knee-high stiletto boots, shivering slightly in the cold night air, watching the cars go by and casually observing the people milling around, crossing at the traffic lights and alighting from the latest train arrival on the rail tracks overhead, high above the main road. After around five minutes of waiting, a black rather ordinary-looking Mercedes pulled up opposite her, and the driver's side window gradually wound down, and a bronze hand emerged and waved at her. Without looking too intently at the features of her escort, her attentions temporarily diverted towards having to navigate a busy road in vertiginous kinky boots, she tried to appear demure and relaxed as she circled the vehicle and edged open the passenger door. She sat down in the comfortable leather chair appreciating how warm it felt and pulled the kinky boots in after her, in her best imitation of an actress appearing at a premiere attempting to retain her modesty in front of a crowd of waiting photographers armed with zoom lenses and flashlights. Instantly, she could see that the person sitting opposite her only bore a vague similarity to the profile picture and consequently the image that she had now built up in her mind during their month-long affiliation. His thick luscious locks that once fell attractively over his forehead were nowhere to be seen, and Cayenne could now positively date his profile by at least five years owing to the recession of his hairline. He was dressed in a plain shirt and smart trousers, which made him appear more plain rather than smart. She could confidently hazard a guess that any passion he may have had for fitness was now as challenged as the follicles that had disappeared from his scalp. He clearly hadn't seen the inside of a gym in recent years, and what a pity that talking to someone by phone and text seemed to disguise signals of any possible personality disorder that meeting them face-to-face could reveal.

They had barely exchanged pleasantries when he could clearly no longer avoid the abject shock emanating from her eyes.

"You look the same as your picture," said Kamal in a robotic voice that cast her mind back to Ocean's previous generic schooling facility. "Do I look the same?"

The extent of her shock made any thought of sugar coating the truth futile.

"No…" For some reason, she felt no compulsion to elaborate.

"I look different?" he asked revealing an astute gluttony for punishment.

"Yes…"

"Okay…"

"Bye then," she had replied in what she sincerely hoped was an empathetic voice and climbed back out of the vehicle with a speed which belied the vertigo that accompanied her entrance and disappeared into the night without a backward glance.

She dialled Diego's phone to enquire if he wanted anything from the local Tesco, which she passed on the way back to her apartment.

"Mummy?"

"Yes, it's me…"

"You okay?" his voice sounded anxious.

"Yeah, I'm fine."

"Is it really you? What's the password?"

Cayenne uttered a word from their favourite family superhero movie which they used when answering the door to their home.

Once he was reassured, Diego continued, "So where are you? How long you gonna be?"

"I'm at Tesco; I'll be ten minutes…"

Chapter 3

Cayenne eventually forced herself to join the local gym albeit with a sense of reluctance, as it had not been something she had ever envisioned herself doing. In fact, it wasn't long ago that she had made a point of running past this same glass-fronted branch of the popular Nuffield Health Chain on her early-morning jogs and tried hard not to snigger at the treadmill runners peering back at her through the huge semi-frosted windows and thinking why on earth would you pay what must undoubtedly be an expensive fee for what appeared to be an extremely high-tech, extensively equipped gym; simply to run on a treadmill when surely she was enjoying the same exercise absolutely free with wonderful views and fresh air into the bargain.

After two years in this concrete paradise, Cayenne was still enamoured when strolling around her zone-2 borough and couldn't fail to remain tickled with excitement, like a child in Lapland, at her good fortune. Not a day went by without her thanking the gods for the opportunity to live amongst the thriving energy of the inner city with its excellent transport links, which could have her in Oxford Street in 20 minutes; she often mused smugly.

She delighted that on bright, mildly cold afternoons, like today, when she was heading back towards home after attending Ocean's school assembly, that she had the time to take a wander in Canary Wharf for a coffee and a rare sweet treat from the assortment of beverage outlets and patisseries along with the masses of city workers spilling out onto the streets to escape the corporate battles taking place in hidden domains.

She found the unengaging crowds a perfect way to lose herself for a moment in the faceless ensemble and be carried along by the throngs around the elegant shopping malls with their glass walls, immaculate from the constant attention of men in smart uniform, admiring the polished escalators and secluded corridors where a lone pianist could often be found serenading passers-by with the strains of a classical playlist.

Cayenne was well-aware that her demeanour and body language could often be described as standoffish; and her fierce facial expression, a deterrent to any social interaction, owing possibly to the after-effects of some of the toxic relationships of her past and misjudged friendship choices. She now felt that she had finally made some progress on her journey to self-discovery, which the move to London had accelerated rapidly.

Diego had recalled many times how concerned he had been about his mother's increasing depression during their time on the South Coast.

"Mum, I don't think you realise how despondent you were…" He would remind her. "I remember coming in from school, and you would be just sitting there, perched on the edge of the sofa…"

"Oh yeah, I never actually sat on the sofa properly, did I?"

"No. You would just sit there like this…" She would watch with mild amusement as her eldest child demonstrated her stiff, remote posture, and her distant gaze, as he imitated how she stared at the television almost oblivious to surroundings.

Raising three children virtually alone, and with little outside support, had not helped matters. She had grown to accept that she was responsible for some of the poor choices she had made, even though she had been young and ill-equipped to know better with only vague cautionary tales and minimal words of generational wisdom to draw from for guidance; and as a result, she had determined that her own style of parenting would be considerably different.

She decided that she would bombard her own children from every angle with the lessons from her own experiences, and what she had learned, whilst allowing them the space and support to make informed decisions, to ensure that they would seldom experience the same kind of vulnerability that often left her feeling as though there was no voice of counsel in moments of uncertainty.

Her daughter's request from that morning over breakfast suddenly popped into her head. She had just happened to mention that the latest edition of David Walliam's book series had just been released, and she had just happened to wonder whether her mum had seen it yet.

Cayenne promised that she would look out for it the next time she went to Waterstones; and as luck would have it, Waterstones was beckoning as she prepared to dismount the escalator.

There was something about the institutional book store that she had always found intriguing and comforting, which went way back to her teenage years when she would often get lost whilst browsing and emerge hours later having fallen deeply into a fantasy fictional plot or become totally absorbed into someone's inspirational life story. The cavernous, warren-like ambience, and discreet, soft lighting and hidden corners always seemed to provide a welcoming contrast to the hustle and bustle of the streets outside.

The children's section was located on the middle level which opened out onto the first floor of the Cabot Place Mall. There was a friendly assistant who had clearly been accosted for the same book by other anxious parents and seemed to read her mind as she wandered aimlessly around the store. The tall thin lady, who sported shoulder-length, overly highlighted hair and a printed floral blouse, echoed her daughter's enthusiasm confirming that this particular edition was in her opinion the best book of the series so far, and that her own daughter was devouring it as they spoke.

Feeling decidedly pleased with herself at the thought of her daughter's face when she returned from school to find the book strategically placed on her brilliant white ladder desk or perhaps casually propped up on the bottom bunk, she glanced at the time on her phone and hurried back down the escalators and out of the plush glass, metal-framed doors leading out into the street, glancing furtively to her left to see if the bus was approaching. If she was quick, she would just have time to get home, change clothes and head to the gym for her yogalates class.

She had just negotiated the slow traffic under Canary Wharf Pier and spun around to await the D8 bus to Crossharbour when…

"Excuse me."

She had already subconsciously suspected that the tall, well-built man, in slightly casual business attire, that had woven into her peripheral vision where she stood had planned to approach her; but in the blink of an eye, he had clearly thought better of it and pretended to continue walking along the road.

She imagined that when his day had begun, he would have had a perfectly crafted tie, holding the neck of his now-open shirt in place, and that the blazer component of his suit was perhaps now slung across the back of his office chair; and that his tousled hair, which seemed to have a trail of finger strands running through it, stemmed from perfectly coifed origins.

His hesitation did not surprise her in the slightest. She had almost come to expect it after years of unknowingly honing a rather frosty exterior. The acerbic orbit in which she manoeuvred until recently, whenever outside of her home environment, was enough to deter even the most confident individual.

Certainly, few had made an obvious attempt at an approach in the two years since her return to London, and those who had, were no doubt still reeling from the consequent rebuttal.

From just behind her, she heard…

"Could you tell me how to get to Greenwich from here?"

The returning stranger had clearly obtained some much needed courage.

Uncharacteristically, she found herself pondering the logistics of the stranger's desired location—perhaps in part to reward him for his bravery. But before she could politely decline to expand upon her limited navigation skills, the stranger had clearly read her hesitation as a positive indication to proceed with his true intentions.

"Actually, I'm going to be honest here, I've just followed you from Waterstones…" He paused to gauge her response. His words hung in the air for a moment as her mind went from surprise to slight concern, followed by a feeling that distinctly resembled flattery.

"I was wondering whether you would join me for a glass of wine…" His hands were in his pockets, and he was smiling. Not broadly but with an air of confidence.

She was about to shake her head in an obvious refusal when he continued,

"Oh, go on. Please. I've had a really bad day at work; it's been a really rough day, and it would be nice to have some company. What do you say?"

Taken aback by both the proposition and more so by his blatant honesty, which she had to admit was refreshingly enticing, especially given the wall of hostility he had contemplated, she was aware that even though she was shaking her head, there was little conviction in her response which clearly egged him on to persevere.

"You do drink wine?"

"Yes," she replied; no doubt the sparkle in her eye confirming her partiality towards her preferred tipple.

"Just one glass won't hurt, will it?" His gaze was steady and self-assured, not at all pathetically pleading.
She reminded herself of her recent resolution to make an effort to be more open and sociable. Glancing briefly at the time on her phone, to her surprise, she tentatively acquiesced.

"Thank you," he smiled appreciatively and released a sigh of relief. "Shall we go to Bar One?"

She nodded blankly, having no knowledge of local bars owing to her hibernation and lack of social activity.
Walking one step behind enabled her to observe the stranger more closely.
His slightly-too-long floppy hair which she considered a rather youthful style for a man, who had to be in her estimation, in the region of 40, simply refused to submit, resisting the constant strokes from what she suspected were nervous hands or a formed habit; and he clearly had no real intention of taming the once chestnut strands, which were succumbing rapidly to imposing salt-and-pepper tones.
He had a good strong build, not at all athletic but certainly well-managed. He had an overly confident saunter which was designed to disguise the awkward, penguin-like plod, which she suspected would become more apparent the less self-conscious he became.
His hands were firmly stuffed in his pockets in-between hair strokes, and she could see that her acceptance of a glass of wine had delivered him a healthy dose of testosterone.
He is almost attractive, she pondered. His swagger was intriguing. He was clearly attempting to keep any sign of self-consciousness well-hidden. She wondered whether he was well-versed in this afternoon practice as aside from the fact that she did not possess the ego to assume that her flawless beauty had caused him to stray from his usual lunchtime routine; his stride was not of someone who was treading cautiously on unknown territory.

She sat at the small wooden window table overlooking the terrace of this stylish city bar, which was evidently in recovery from the lunchtime rush. She moved the uncleared debris, left over by the previous occupants, to one side to make room for the large glass of red wine that the stranger had disappeared to the bar to retrieve and gazed out onto the nearby harbour with its exotic boats varying in size from tiny, small-party affairs to large multi-deck monsters—the size of a large apartment.

She glanced around the bar where the few visible staff were busy clearing away the remnants of rush hour. The stranger was heading towards her with something thick, dark and full-bodied, and what appeared to be a bottle of his preferred ale. He placed them down in the space she had cleared on the table and ran his fingers through his hair for the umpteenth time since his approach 20 minutes before.

"Again, thank you. I really appreciate you coming. Not keeping you from anything, am I?"

"I've got some time before the school run…"

"You've got children?" He enquired without an ounce of surprise in his voice.

"Three."

"Wow. You don't look like you have three children. You look amazing."

Perhaps it was the lingering bewilderment at the fact that she was sitting across from a complete stranger in the middle of the day, enjoying good quality wine, totally unexpectedly that she found herself smiling knowingly at his compliment, giving no real indication of acceptance or denial, almost as though he was telling her something unnecessarily.

The conversation quickly changed course as he expanded on the details of the corporate matters that had played a part in the upset of his day and doubtless added to the assortment of grey running through his hair.

He made what appeared to be a strong attempt to refocus his mind by widening his eyes and shaking his head vigorously, in the same way that one does when trying to eradicate sleep from the eyes in the middle of an important conference, or when driving on the motorway at night. A slightly startled expression fell over his face.

"Yeah, I was saying it's been a rough time at work lately. Basically, I was gunning for a promotion, right? " There was a pause. "I didn't get it…"

She would learn that he often punctuated his sentences with the question… Right? With the hint of an accent that sounded suspiciously antipodean, which she concluded didn't suit him, and therefore arrived at the opinion that it was something that he had picked up from somebody else.

His face screwed up from time to time, as though he was being very careful about how much he revealed, forcing himself to hold back.

"I've been preparing for it for the past year, you know, overtime, coming in at weekends, extra hours etc."

She listened intently whilst savouring the delicious wine.

There was heavier sighing.

"There are certain individuals that, you know, kind of gave me the indication that I was doing the right thing; and that, you know, it was more or less certain. A done deal…" He was wringing his hands now and grimacing.

He fell silent, but his expression and hand gestures could clearly be interpreted as the devastating blow of the outcome.

"I can certainly imagine how you must be feeling," she offered tentatively, "but do you subscribe at all to the notion that everything happens for a reason? Perhaps this wasn't the right timing. Maybe there is something that you can take from this; and the next time you go for it, you will be more prepared…"

His eyes widened with appreciation, as though surprised by her words.

"Yeah, I guess you're right. Problem is… Now I can't be bothered…" He chuckled nervously. "Do you know what I mean? After all that hard work and then to not get the result you wanted… I just feel a bit like… oh, what's the point…"

Her forehead wrinkled in judgement, "But surely that's not the right approach. Doesn't that mean that you weren't necessarily doing that extra work for the right reasons? That it was purely to try to please other people who you thought would have some sort of influence on your promotion…"

He laughed and shrugged with resignation, "You're absolutely right. That's not good, is it?"
She smiled at him. She appreciated that he appeared to be able to laugh at himself and wasn't easily offended in a world where to be defensive had almost become a natural reaction. He was willing to own up to his behaviour and see the funny side.
She could feel herself settling more in her chair and enjoying the moment.
He paused again, and the expression of bewilderment had returned. He shook his head in disbelief.

"I mean. You could have been anybody that I approached, but you're actually making sense…" He was looking directly at her.

"So do you think you will go for it again?" she asked breaking the silence.

He sighed and teased the hair again. "There's an opportunity to go for it next year…" He shrugged nonchalantly.

"I'll see what happens. I'm an accountant, right? I work for an American company. It's a good job, I'm on a six-figure salary. So it's difficult to decide. Do I stay put even though I'm getting to the point where I dread coming in in the mornings? Or do I go and do something else. Trouble is, if I go and work for another company, surely I'm just going to encounter the same old shit or possibly risk having to work my way up again." He took a large swig from his bottle. "I think I'm going to get over this disappointment and then see how I feel…"
He drew his eyes back to her face, staring intently. His searching eyes revealing unspoken questions.

"Enough about me. I've really enjoyed your company today. Can we do this again sometime? I mean I'd be happy to just have a drink and look at you if I'm honest…" He chuckled leaning back in his chair to look over her again.
"Erm… I guess I have been thinking about going out more and meeting people; but at the same time, sometimes, I think it would be fun to actually keep things quite vague. I mean I don't want to

have to reveal everything about myself. I don't believe that that is the only way to get to know someone. I can't bear those typical getting-to-know-you questions, you know… 'What do you do? Where do you live?'"… She rolled her eyes in mock indignation… "But yeah, it might be nice to do this again…"

"Can we exchange emails, and then we can talk about what we want. We can call it 'Rules of Engagement' or something."

They both laughed.

"You can tell me what you want, and what you don't want. I mean a woman like you deserves at the very least some fine dining. Perhaps some high-end treats…"

She drained the last of the velvet wine and allowed herself to consider his proposition. She had had a pleasant time; he was fairly good company if not the most positive mindset she had come across. But he outwardly expressed his appreciation of her, and that was something that she hadn't experienced… well in a very long time. It made her feel good. She felt as though she was glowing from the inside just a little. She knew that she was generally a good judge of character and hadn't detected any insincerity. She had long since determined in her own mind that she was going to accept herself as beautiful regardless of society's depiction of beauty, and this had given her confidence and self-approval, but she had underestimated how good it felt to have someone else see it too.

He was gazing at her deeply now, as if for the first time, taking in her red-tinged hair, caramel skin; slender, elegant hands and perfectly manicured nails. She presumed he had taken in her image from behind to his heart's content whilst following her from Waterstones.

A slow appreciative smile crept across his lips, starting at one end, gradually opening up to a full smile; revealing off white, slightly-crooked teeth, which somehow added a little to his charm.

But his smile was closely followed by a downcast shadow and a glance at the time on his mobile phone, which she observed was far from the latest smartphone model, but it looked well-worn, basic and a little dated. *Perhaps it wasn't his main phone*, she thought. *Perhaps this was the designated lunchtime pick-up phone. The phone that no one else knew about and used for the specific purpose of organising clandestine lunches.*

"I've got to get back to the office. They'll be wondering where I am," he sighed with the forlorn expression of someone about to face the general practitioner, following an uncertain X-ray. "I really don't want to go. I feel as though I've dominated the conversation. I haven't even asked what you do. Oh, but you don't like those questions, do you?" he chuckled.

"I'm a carer," she offered. Suddenly wondering why she didn't feel like revealing that her autistic son was her charge.

"That's a difficult job, right? Very challenging I expect. So surely you deserve to take some time out every now and then. Are you single?"

"Yes."
He shook his head in disbelief, "I mean, why is that? A beautiful woman like you should have men queueing up surely…"

"I enjoy my life; I'm certainly not desperate…"

"Oh no, I didn't mean to imply that you were…"

"I guess I'm just figuring out what I want…"

He took a long gulp from his bottle without taking his eyes from her and leaned forward,

"And have you figured out what you want?"

She screwed her face up in contemplation. "I find myself wavering between wanting something of quality, but at the same time I feel as though I've missed out on a lot of… shall we say casual fun?"
Her comment visibly piqued his interest, and the corners of his lips twitched with gleeful anticipation.

"Now… perhaps, that's where I come in…"

"How old are your children?"
"I'd rather not say anymore to be honest. I'm not sure we need to know too much about each other at this point…"

"Absolutely. Which brings me back to our, erm… 'Rules of Engagement' policy. We can draw up an agreement that you're happy with. Your expectations, ways in which I can indulge you…"

The innuendo in his voice was palpable.

"What's your name?"

"Bethany…" She picked up her glass to hide the smirk that was threatening to seep onto her face.

He let out a huge guffaw, throwing his head back. She liked that he felt he could laugh easily around her. It made her want to relax more around him.

"What's yours?"

His eyes scoured the ceiling momentarily… "Jon…"

They were both laughing now. Somehow, their newly assigned names gave the atmosphere a decidedly arousing edge. They were both aware that once they began communicating via email, their true identities would become clear which only added to the frisson.

The very fact that he had proposed exchanging emails, as opposed to telephone numbers, led her to ponder his domestic situation.

There had been no wedding ring visible, not that that was definitive evidence. Perhaps he was attached but bored. Was he contemplating leaving a relationship? These thoughts were very brief in all honesty. She didn't much care to know any details at this point as she resolutely didn't plan on revealing many details of her own. Not because she had anything to hide. She was simply at a stage in life where she felt very protective of herself.

He waited for her to pick up her bags and escorted her to the exit, and they stepped through the half-glazed wooden door.

The winter sun was still shining onto the terrace as they re-joined the hustle and bustle of the business district.

He placed his hands on her arms protectively and leaned in and kissed her on both cheeks. *What a gallant gesture*, she thought. The few relationships that she had had in her life—namely the children's father, and some other questionable decisions prompted by loneliness rather than good judgement—were scarcely characterised by gallant gestures of tenderness.

He thanked her again, and then they turned and walked in opposite directions, much like the complete strangers that they were. It was several moments before she realised that seemingly lost in thought, she had passed the bus stop and was now half-way home. Thoughts of what had just happened reverberated in her head; the unexpected appeal of meeting a stranger and actually having more than just a banal conversation about nothing of relevance but rather establishing a fleeting connection—a basic understanding of sorts. The buzz had effectively carried her home; and before she knew it, she was crossing the street in front of the Canary Wharf Hilton Hotel and strolling determinedly past South Quay Station before weaving in and out of the lunchtime crowd outside Harbour Exchange Square in what seemed like no time at all. For some strange reason, she was suddenly overcome with bashful self-consciousness as she strolled through the walkway of the Square, which was littered with the usual lunch seekers. She found herself dipping her head as though her sordid plans would become evident if anyone caught her eye, utterly convinced that if she wasn't decidedly black, her blushes would be obvious for all to see. She often pitied those women whose very emotions could be read, like an open book, by virtue of the colouring of their chest area or cheekbones.

The builders' boards surrounding the newly erected Baltimore Tower were starting to come down, revealing beautifully landscaped designs surrounding the unusual multi-storey structure, indicating that it was clearly nearing completion. She found it incredibly exciting to see these new development blocks popping up. What to others may be considered an eyesore or a sign of overdevelopment was a symbol of progress and prosperity to her, signifying a new phase and chapter. The Tower, which according to the advertisements incorporated both apartments of varying sizes, and all the facilities of a modern hotel, was 40 storeys high and was designed with an irregular outline, so that the building appeared to spiral its way to the top. The balconies were huge and semi-circular, and she could only imagine how exquisite the interior was, and the magnificent views available from such celestial heights. She made a left turn behind the children's adventure playground and approached her own building which was tucked away in the corner of a large private square. As she was reaching for her fob that unlocked the main entrance glass door, the familiar sound of her email alert sounded several times, indicating that she had either received several messages simultaneously; or that she had just come out of a dead signal spot, and the device was now catching up.

She rushed inside willing the elevator to reach her fifth-floor abode, so that she could find out if one of the notifications was from the stranger.

She hurried along the corridor to her door, key at the ready. She never failed to appreciate the contrast from the dazzling white of the communal hallway, with its cobalt blue linoleum flooring, to the dimly lit cosy ambience that she had managed to create inside with its brown and bronze hues and clever lighting, made all the more of an achievement because she had done it all herself. Even the wall of chocolate-brown floor to ceiling curtains in the living room had been particularly challenging to execute single-handedly, as they proved to be exceptionally heavy and needed reinforced curtain fittings. The wallpapering, which she had never attempted before, evidenced to the keen eye, by uneven matching on the odd, poorly applied sheet, added to her sense of pride as she was still very pleased with the overall effect and the transformation from the stark white, and in her opinion bland apartment, to the tinted almost Moroccan feel that she stood in today. Now all she had to do was continue the theme to the rest of the apartment.

She dropped her shopping bags on the kitchen counter and reached for her phone glancing furtively at the recent notifications.

She tapped on her email app and quickly discarded of the usual daily pop-ups one by one, so that the one with the name that she didn't recognise made its way to the top of the list.

She took a deep inhale of breath and then opened the email.

It was addressed from Kenneth Halpern-Smith, associated with the email address Khs2002@outlook.com. The title read: RULES OF ENGAGEMENT. And there, in all its splendour, was a detailed itinerary of a proposed second meeting.

He addressed her as 'Queen'; and by the first sentence, she was hooked.

Chapter 4
Rules of Engagement

"…Jon intends to whisk Bethany to a secret location, one in keeping with her regal status, where he can take in her awesome beauty at close quarters and undress her first with his eyes and relieve her of the Agent Provocateur claddings that he surprised her with earlier and thoroughly enjoy how the garment, though strategically sparing, will completely emphasise the delicious curvature of her body.

He is particularly curious to discover precisely how the black-lace garment, complete with rose-red tassels, will complement the bronze of her skin.

So tell me, Queen, what can I do to enhance your pleasure? I am totally at your service.

Jon…"

She hadn't quite expected him to get straight to the point. This was a new one on her. On the one hand, it indicated that this was a man who knew what he wanted and didn't want to play games. This was a good thing surely. She had always appreciated people that were unapologetically themselves. Totally unafraid to say… this is me. But was she ready to jump head first into this new experience? Clearly, she had indicated as much. She must have somehow given off some vibe of wanting adventure. Something new. Perhaps let slip some kind of dispirited resignation that she had reached this stage in life without taking full advantage of opportunities. Not fully embraced the notion of life being short and seizing the day. He was taking her at her word.

So now she knew his real name. Kenneth Halpern-Smith. Funnily enough, he looked more like a Jon than a Kenneth. Though it had a certain ring to it. Evidently, he was impatient for her response.

"I'm sitting bored in my office. The minions surrounding me are annoying. Longing for some exotic company.

How are you fixed on Tuesday? Meet me at the North Circular Greenwich Hotel at 2:00 p.m."

He was obviously accustomed to communicating with little regard for a reply.

"Hey! Can you meet Wednesday rather than Tuesday?"

She consulted her phone diary to check that she hadn't any prior arrangements. Wednesday was usually a day she kept free for her son's school, as they fervently encouraged parental participation in any events that they were organising. Her phone calendar confirmed that she was free in two weeks' time.
"Are you really doing this?" she questioned herself. "Go on… Take a chance." She heard herself respond in a voice straight out of a Disney Christmas movie.
She replied for the first time knowing that now he would know her real name too.

Cayenne.Richards72@gmail.com

"Either the 14th or the 21st is fine."
Simple and to the point.
His response was instant.

"Wednesday next week or the following Tuesday?
Let's act out role play."
His direct crudeness jolted her from the realms of fantasy that she was temporarily coasting. Suddenly she was uncertain again.
She placed her phone down and busied herself with preparing for the school run. She simply wouldn't think about it any further until she had given it much more thought. After all… no harm done. If she never saw him again, what would it matter?
She glanced at the time, and it was five minutes from the end of school, so she slipped on her trainers so that she could run. Running was always a good way of clearing her head, particularly when there was a steady headwind. Cayenne was immensely proud that in her early 40s, she could potentially outmanoeuvre most of the other mums with ease, even whilst walking. She had always paid attention to taking care of herself, but found that the older she got the more emphasis she placed on becoming her best self. A better mother and

a better role model for her children. As she approached the school gates, she was beginning to tire; but as eyes were on her, she braved the last few strides energetically and tried desperately to disguise her heavy breathing as she waited alongside the hedgerow where year 5 were dispatched at 3:30.

Her thoughts ran as usual, to what they were going to eat for dinner. Her afternoon escapades had prevented her from preparing something earlier. It would probably have to be fast food or some other convenient alternative.

She noticed her daughter's thinly disguised smirk as she appeared at the blue exit door. The same one she always displayed when she came out of school and spotted her mother in the crowd. She knew she stood out. Not particularly because of her attire which was more often than not gym gear, it was the whole aura of confidence. Of knowing who she was. That and the fact that she always took time to look presentable. Every day. Regardless of where she was going, or what she was doing. It was simply who she was now. The reluctant smirk on Sugar's face acknowledged all of this, and the evident pride twitched the corners of her lips every time.

"What do you want to eat? I didn't have time to cook anything."

Her little urchin face screwed up with delight as she displayed the goofy grin she used whenever she wanted something but was uncertain of the answer.

"Pizzzzaaaaa!" she sang hopefully.

Cayenne smiled down at her, secretly thankful that there were never usually complaints on the rare occasion when she hadn't had time to cook. God had blessed her with children who were easily pleased and very accommodating.

Thankfully Papa Johns was literally a stone throw from their apartment, which meant she could place her order, take Sugar home, with just enough time to go and get Ocean from the designated bus stop and pick up the order at the same time.

What seemed like moments later, she was standing at the corner of the main road waiting for his school bus to arrive. As it approached, she always tried to gauge whether Ocean had behaved well or not by the conduct of the staff and assistants that handed him over; and she took every opportunity to flex her discerning ability to read body language, though usually they were far too professional to give much away.

As he stepped off the bus and towered over her, she marvelled at the thought of how tall he would be when he was his brother's current age, in four-and-a-half years' time. She often teased that Ocean would outgrow all of them.

"Hello… How was school?"

He rarely answered. With another few prompts, his usual response was, "Good", before he would fall silent again. He was on the sector of the autistic spectrum that meant his verbal skills were somewhat delayed, and he at best attempted small sentences usually to do with his wants and needs at any given moment. She knew he had the potential to do more. To become more. So she spoke to him as though he could answer whatever question would be thrown at him. *The system may limit him*, she often thought indignantly, *but as for me and my house…*

Ocean was trying to drag her in the direction of the large superstore across the road. Probably with the intention of grabbing some blue soap or the colouring pens and crayons which he was obsessed with.

His strength was exaggerated for a boy of his age. She often wondered, had she not been so strong a disciplinarian and perhaps opted out of showing him an air of authority; whether he would be able to literally pick her up and take her to the store, hitched on his shoulder, against her will by now. As it was, he mostly listened to the tone of her voice and responded. Unfortunately for school, this was not always the case.

"No Oshee… I have to pick up the pizza at Papa Johns. I've ordered you some chicken bites as well…" She added knowing that pizza was really Sugar's preferred choice, whereas chicken in any form was just fine by Ocean.

Later that evening, the younger two were in their shared room whilst Cayenne was enjoying debriefing with her eldest. A tradition that they had both come to appreciate and was one of the reasons why they were so close. They had always discussed everything. She had held nothing back from him. In contrast to growing up in the indomitable Caribbean culture, where very little of importance was discussed, she had determined early on that there would be no carpet to hide anything under when it came to her own style of parenting. Everything would be out in the open. She often felt that Diego was perhaps the only person on the planet that fully understood her and her idiosyncrasies and could appreciate why she often operated in a way that others considered uncommon. He didn't judge her on her estranged relationship with her own mother as most did. Her own mother had abandoned her at the most vulnerable time in her life. But she had survived—scarred and a little wounded but as fierce as a lioness. It had made her who she was. She could now look back and be thankful for those experiences, as she had emerged as someone who wasn't desperate for approval or validation, having lived through her adolescence starved of those very virtues.

"Oh guess what happened today?" she cooed excitedly, suddenly remembering the events of her uncustomary afternoon.

Diego rolled his eyes with mock exasperation.

She threw her head back and laughed, appreciating the fact that she had her very own sounding board of advisors and well-wishers right here at home.

"Well…" she gulped, dramatically, as though she was about to expound on a Shakespearean sonnet.

"After going to Ocean's assembly…"

"Oh, was that today? How did it go?" Diego often accompanied her to see Ocean at school whenever he had free time from college, though more for moral support than out of enthusiasm to see his younger brother reluctantly perform.

Cayenne paused for a moment, thrown from her train of thought and tilted her head as she tried to recollect the events prior to her lunchtime encounter.

"Erm… Yeah, it was okay. You know Ocean. You could tell that he wasn't particularly enjoying it. I could just imagine that he had left a half-finished activity on his desk in the classroom that they would have literally had to drag him away from, and that he was desperate to get back to. It was as though he was looking for the first opportunity to run off the stage…"

Diego nodded knowingly. He was most familiar with his younger brother's antics, and the mischievous nature he enlisted to test the versatility of outside boundaries.

"Anyway," Cayenne flicked her hand in a dismissive gesture to emphasise the point that he had interrupted what she had been saying. "Soooo, I was heading back home, but made a stop in Canary Wharf 'cause I remembered Sugar wanted that new book she's been going on about…"

"Oh, the David Williams one?"

"Walliams," she corrected. "Yeah, there's a new one out…"
Diego was smirking, "And she just happened to mention it, right?"

"Yeah…"

"She asked me to buy it for her this morning…"
Cayenne shot him an accusing glance. Had she known this, she would have insisted that he buy it for her. Insisted being the operative word, as it was household legend that Diego was extremely frugal with the money that he earned from his part-time job, at Five Guys Burger Restaurant, on the days that he wasn't studying performing arts at college. He certainly hadn't adopted her spendthrift tendencies and delighted in not having to spend his own money.

"So I get to Waterstones."

"Oh yeah? What d'you buy me?"

"And I'm in there for about ten minutes trying to find this book, so the lady helps me find it, and I leave the store, and I was walking out of Cabot Square; d'you know where you come down the steps towards the D8 bus stop?"
As usual, Diego was staring intently at his phone; a fact which annoyed his mother, as she considered it rude and disrespectful. He glanced up when he realised that there was a prolonged pause as she waited for his full attention.

"I'm listening," he insisted before quickly typing something into his iPhone and throwing it down on the sofa beside him in submission. He rested his head back into interlinked hands, stretched out his long legs and crossed them comfortably onto the rectangular-patterned rug in front of the sofa. His expression resigned to the fact that this was not going to be a quick recap of the events of his mother's day, but that he was required to be in for the long haul. He knew that she needed to offload. He had come to realise that as a result of feeling unheard when she was growing up, she was often reluctant to share her thoughts with others and consequently held back as if not wanting to burden them; and she likely would have continued on that way well into her golden years, had she not had an obliging son who was more than happy to fill in that role. After all, she was his hero as far as he was concerned, and he made a point of telling her almost daily that he adored her.

The stern expression she had adopted whilst waiting to regain his attention disappeared the moment his iPhone hit the sofa. "Then I was waiting for the bus, and this guy approached me."

"Oh yeah? Look at you," his tone of voice rose dramatically.

"He was a white guy," Diego's eyebrows raised towards his hairline, more out of interest than judgement.

"Reasonably good-looking, I suppose. Business type…"

"Okay, okay." Diego was sitting up now, leaning forwards slightly and pondering her words.

Unlike a lot of children who often become possessive of their primary carers, having gotten used to having their full attention, she felt fortunate that her children unselfishly would rather their mother be fulfilled. Having said that, she was also mindful that her teenage son would not necessarily want to hear the gory details of any dalliances that she may encounter and made a point to keep any intricate details to a minimum.

"He asked me where such and such a place was," she waved her hands flippantly, trying to remember the location that Kenneth had referred to. "I was just about to say 'No!'; you know I don't usually answer those questions anyway, but before I could answer, he said that he had actually seen me in Waterstones and followed me out to the bus stop…" She laughed incredulously at the recollection.

"Really?" Diego, like his little sister, was proud of the way she took care of herself and nodded with interest. "So what did he say?"

"Well… he asked if I would join him for a glass of wine…" She knew that Diego would often scold her for not responding well to advances and grimaced painfully when she recounted her frosty dismissals.

"Oh no. So what did you say?" he braced himself for one of his mother's customary putdowns, which he found to be cutting but funny at the same time.

"Well, I thought about it for a minute. First I said no, but he kinda said, 'Oh go on, I've had a bad day at work. Just one glass of wine'… So …"

"Sooooo?" Diego was circling his hand impatiently, willing her to get to the conclusion of the story so that he could resume his phone activities.

"So I agreed. And do you know something? It was rather pleasant. He's an accountant, and he didn't get the promotion that he was going for. We had a good chat, and he says he'd like to see me again. Nothing serious. But… it would be good to get out once in a while…"

"Yeah. Okay, okay…" He had his phone in hand again now and was clearly over this conversation; his mentoring duties concluded, but was nodding approvingly.
It was only then that she remembered that she hadn't checked her phone for several hours. Unlike Diego, her phone was only really useful to her for necessities. Her children were often stupefied at the fact that she could quite happily go for months without using her phone. In fact, as long as her children were around her, she could go for months without speaking to another soul. Possibly as a result of spending a lot of solitary time as a child, she relished her own company. To engage with other people often felt like a challenge to her. She really had to apply herself when facing social situations. Then again, her father had been a loner and individualist, so perhaps it was hereditary.
There were four emails backed up on her phone when she finally got around to looking at it.
It was clear that the stranger was determined to remain in character.

"Jon is enjoying a strong hard on right now… want to see? :)"

Embracing the sudden daring mood she found herself in after enjoying a solitary glass of wine, she decided to be a little cheeky not knowing whether the offer still stood several hours later.

"Oh, go on then…"

"Bad girl :) Does Jon get something back – although he's aware Bethany has no requirement to respond…"

"I'm quite sure Bethany will oblige at some point. Unfortunately, she has an evening yoga class to attend."

The next morning, it seemed Kenneth was sensing her hesitation. "Hey, shall we just catch up for a glass of wine and see how Bethany feels?"
She inwardly sighed with relief, as she had almost talked herself out of this crazy idea of a hotel meet-up with a virtual stranger.

"Yes, let's."

"Actually Tuesday afternoon may now work instead. How are you fixed?"

She was beginning to find the constant changes rather irksome, and again he appeared to be able to read her mind.

"Apologies… work diary keeps changing."

"Tuesday is fine; 10:00–3:00."

"Great! Let's meet for lunch at North Greenwich Tube Station—12:00 p.m."

"Okay. It will have to be brief though. Almost forgot I have a 2:15 p.m. appointment."

"Do you have a 2:15 p.m. appointment on Wednesday too?"

"No. Free Wednesday till 3:00…"

"Okay, let's do Wednesday… I do hope Bethany still wants a toy to tease. I want to be your toy…"

"Bethany is most certainly intrigued at the thought of playing with Jon…" Perhaps the appeal for her at this point was that it was just empty words. She could quite easily delete his details at any point. It seemed to be a fun, harmless game.

"Good girl. Jon promises she will get what she needs out of him…"

"Oooh. I love the confidence, Jon…"

"Jon wants Bethany to be naughty…"

"How naughty?"
"As completely far as she wants to go. Whatever she has ever wanted to try… he wants to be her toy for all of it.
As I write this, Jon's white cock is getting hard…"
How far did he intend to go with this, she pondered.

"There are levels of naughtiness. Even meeting in secret at all is a little naughty." She glanced at the full-length mirror opposite her bed and stifled a laugh at her own expense at how prudish she sounded.

"What did you envisage when you spotted Bethany in Waterstones? Had you thought much beyond the glass of wine. Honestly?"

"Ideas were forming… Jon is looking forward to meeting Bethany in secret…"

"Bethany must admit… she is a little excited…"

"So midday Wednesday, North Greenwich… further details to follow."…

Wow. How thoroughly intoxicating. He clearly had specific plans in mind and had given this all some thought. The fact that he seemed to have all the plans in hand, and that all she had to do was wait for further instruction made her feel as though she had become embroiled in some kind of real-life mission impossible escapade.

"Jon wonders… is it bad that his cock stiffens the more he considers what Bethany might want from him?"

"The difficulty is, Bethany is also considering."

"Do tell Bethany. Anyway seriously, Wednesday will just be a good chance to catch up…"

"It will be an extraordinary catch-up considering neither Bethany nor Jon are willing to reveal too much…"

"Hopefully, there's nothing more to be revealed… Hopefully, Bethany wants to play, and Jon can be her toy…"
She decided to leave the conversation there. She would meet him on the designated Wednesday and see how she felt then.

On Wednesday morning, she was considering what to wear when her phone signalled several notifications one after another. She had considered that she might not hear anything from the stranger after all. She almost expected that he would cancel at some point. Perhaps the wounds from her own past ran deeper than she cared to admit.

"Morning, Bethany.
Meet me at Gaucho at the 02 at 12:00 p.m. Looking forward to seeing you…"
The bolt of exhilaration that pursed through her body was undeniable. She decided to discard the black-flared trousers and crew-neck jumper that she had planned to wear in exchange for a figure-hugging black jersey dress. It clung to her every curve and accentuated her pert, rounded bottom. It also tended to ride up as she walked to reveal a generous glimpse of gym-honed thigh. She would wear her knee-high boots with it which were comfortable but sexy. What on earth was happening? Why did she want to be sexy?

Hours later, she glided across Peninsula Square towards the main entrance of the 02. She had never been to Gaucho before. She had passed through the 02 many times with the children, to see a movie in the upstairs cinema or to eat out at one of the friendly eateries. Usually, they ended up visiting two or three different places, as Diego always favoured Five Guys flame-grilled burgers as he knew exactly what went into them. Sugar's favourite was Nando's. Ocean's only requirement was that he could have a second helping of whatever protein they decided upon.

Gaucho was situated on the corner near the 02 main entrance. She must have passed it several times before and not noticed the discreet exterior and certainly didn't expect to find an elegant restaurant amidst all the family-friendly burger bars and American-style joints that they usually frequented.

Once inside, she was very impressed with what she found. The foyer boasted an unapologetic vision of monochrome which was echoed throughout the entire restaurant. The carpets were black, and the black walls were offset by several floor-to-ceiling mirrors and white leather furniture. It was decadent and old-fashioned glam.

"Hello. Table for one?" the receptionist approached her with an unusual accent and a curious expression on her face, as though she was unaccustomed to seeing unfamiliar faces.

"Is a Mr Halpern-Smith here?" she asked forthrightly in an effort to dispel whatever dubious thoughts that appeared to be forming in the receptionist's mind.

"Halpern-Smith?" she adopted a blank expression and retreated behind her desk to check the large book that lay open on the high counter. She shook her head and came back around the desk.

"No, no, we don't have a reservation for that name. You are welcome to wait in the bar?"

"Yes, thank you. That would be lovely."

"Would you like me to take your coat?"

"No, thank you. I'll keep it on for the time being." She wasn't quite ready to expose her figure in the black-fitted jumper dress that she had selected.

She followed the tall slim lady, who was dressed smartly in an off-white crisp shirt and pin-striped pencil skirt, into a large circular open-plan seating area with groups of white leather-tub chairs nestled together. The effect of the lighting on the black and white interior was dazzling. She felt like she was walking onto a glamorous 1940s film set rather than a restaurant bar.

She opted for a table at the far end of the room so that she could take a good look at the stranger when he arrived. She could just about remember what he had looked like.

"Would you like something to drink?" the lady asked.

"Yes, please, can I have a glass of red wine?"

"Yes, of course. Would you prefer a Malbec or perhaps a Shiraz?"

"I'll take a Shiraz please…"

"Shiraz. Certainly Madame…"

Just as she had tasted the wine and confirmed that it was acceptable to allow the waitress to fill up her glass, the stranger suddenly appeared.

"Hi, how are you?" He bent down to kiss her cheek and eyed her approvingly.

"Hi. I'm good thanks," she nodded immediately feeling a little flustered.

"How's the wine?"

"It's lovely…"

"What can I get you to drink, sir?" the waitress had been standing silently watching the exchange.

"Oh, I'll have the same please…"

"Of course. I'll be with you in a moment, sir…"

"It's great to see you again. Thanks for coming…" He turned his attention toward her and positioned himself directly opposite—his eyes scanning her. Positive appreciation was emanating from him which flooded her senses. She immediately gave herself permission to relax. This was a new thing, and she liked it.

His long, floppy fringe was hovering over his brow; and even though his glasses reflected flickers of light from the art deco light fixtures, she could tell that there was genuine sparkle in his eyes. He had a long thin nose and thin lips. Not too thin though, not typically white thin like two thin strips of ham, she observed. He was just about kissable. His teeth were discoloured, which was forgivable given that her own had long since lost their brilliance, and the bottom row of incisors looked overcrowded and uneven. She wondered why someone of his obvious means wouldn't have addressed this matter. He was wearing a pink pin-striped shirt and dark pin-striped trousers. She noted how he had perfected a confident walk as though certain of his perception of having some kind of allure. He seemed to like striding around without the jacket to his suit and with his shirt tightly belted into his trousers, which indicated to her an esteemed level of body confidence. Just as the first time they met, he maintained a strong bond with his hair. She could tell that he loved the feel of it, and the confidence it gave him. She dreaded to think how he would cope if the barely visible thin patch at the top of his forehead, turned out to be the onset of recession.

"Are you hungry? Shall we have a meal? The food is good here…" She liked the way in which his eyes glazed over with a nurturing concern, whenever he directed a question at her.

"I'm not really hungry, to be honest…"

"I haven't been able to stop thinking about our… 'Rules of Engagement',"
She sipped her wine and stared confidently at him. She felt powerful knowing that her very gaze caused him to be slightly unnerved. "Have you thought any more about what… Bethany might want to happen. What she's looking for?"

"To be honest, this isn't exactly something that I'm used to"

"Yes… I can see that. You're a strikingly beautiful woman. You deserve some high-end treatment. Frankly, I find it rather hard to believe that you don't have men queueing at the door."

"I'm not exactly what you would call… a social butterfly. Believe it or not, even though I am supremely confident in general, I can be socially awkward. Sometimes I think that I would like to develop more of a social circle, but over the years I haven't found it easy making friends; but I think I have high standards for friendship, and I won't compromise." She giggled at his expression. He looked dazzled by her words. "I'm not entirely sure I would make a good friend either. I like my own space, I value my time. Outside of children and the gym, I don't really have time for much else."

"That's extraordinary. You must have family or some close friends though, right?" There was that antipodean lilt again.

"I'm from Torquay originally, so the family are mostly there. We aren't a particularly close family. Even when we lived there, we didn't see them very much. I don't really have friends. I have a few acquaintances I suppose, from the gym or my children's school, but I wouldn't necessarily class them as friends. I suppose I'm something of a loner. What about you? Do you have a lot of friends?"

"Yeah… University will do that for you. I've got a group of around four or five guys that I would say are good friends. One of them I go running with every week, although he's far more agile than I am. He's into cardio and weights, and that kind of thing. I don't have the coordination for all that." He laughed self-deprecatingly and soothed himself running his hands through his thick hair. "What kind of exercise are you into?"

"I've always kept relatively fit, and I used to go running every morning, and I've always relied on DVDs, but I've recently become a member of my local gym. I never really considered myself a gym person before. In fact, I remember distinctly running past the gym every morning and stifling a laugh at the people staring out from the treadmills and looking at them as if to say: 'I'm doing the exact same thing but for free'. But I found myself going in there one day and enquiring about the facilities, and they showed me around; and before I knew it, I was booked in for a trial and complimentary personal training session, and here I am," she raised both hands in acquiescence.

He was listening intently. "How often do you go?" She couldn't quite decipher whether his expression was of appreciation or intimidation.

"Every day."

"What kind of things do you do? Are you into the cross-fit thing?" He stopped short of rolling his eyes.

"Kind of. I do cardio and strength training which I think are pretty similar, well… in that they are fast-paced and extremely difficult at least, but I like to do a bit of everything. I also do boxing classes and yoga, and occasionally I'll do pilatés."

"Wow! So listen, I'm thinking it would be great to meet up again. My company has a contract with the North Greenwich Hotel, and I'm there for meetings sometimes. It would be nice if you could meet me there next week. Let me get to know Bethany some more."

She nodded, still contemplating whether or not to branch out of her comfort zone or retreat hastily back into her current reclusive existence.

"I guess it couldn't hurt to see how well Bethany and Jon get on," she giggled into her glass suddenly, unable to make eye contact.

"Great. I'll update you of the time over the next few days, but it'll be around midday. How does that sound?"

Chapter 5

At the last minute, Cayenne had decided to get a taxicab to North Greenwich. This would give her much needed moments to steel herself for what she was about to embark on. What on earth was she doing; going to a hotel to meet a virtual stranger, knowing full well what he had in mind. She tried to tell herself that this is what the vast majority of people did. For some women, this was a normal weekly occurrence. Perhaps it was about time she got with the program. It was only harmless fun, wasn't it? He didn't appear to be an ogre, so that she couldn't retreat if she felt any discomfort. "Just go with it. Open your mind Cay," she scolded herself.

When she eventually strode into the hotel after the doorman had kindly escorted her from the taxi, the nerves were becoming more and more prominent. Or was it excitement. She couldn't decide. At least taking the cab was the right decision, as the long walk to the hotel from the train station would have made her feet sore. Stepping into the reception area, she tried to dominate the sudden onset of self-consciousness, as though the doorman and the lady behind the large opulent reception desk could immediately tell that she was up to no good. Just as well she couldn't visibly blush.

"Excuse me, which way is the lift?"

The receptionist, a short lady with a blonde bobbed haircut resting just above her broad shoulders, on any other given day would have passed as a relatively normal friendly person; however, today it was plainly obvious that she was the very emblem of guile and subterfuge, eyeing Cayenne curiously; her gaze lingering on the gold-tip burgundy boots. She pointed to the corridor to her left, "Just at the end of the corridor on the right, madam."

"Thank you."
Cayenne could feel the woman's eyes boring into her back, much of which was exposed through her backless top, as she strode

in the direction that had been pointed out to her, making an effort to squeeze her glutes with every step knowing that the tight black leggings she was sporting were providing generous insight.

Moments later, she stepped out onto the fourth floor, as directed in the series of emails she had received earlier. Room 425, she discovered, was at the very end of the corridor immediately to the left. Pausing for a moment to collect herself, she knocked twice, slightly harder than she would normally but stopping short of an abrupt bang. She stood back straightening her spine and pinning her shoulders in place. She was uncertain quite what or in fact who would be greeting her. Would it be Kenneth or would it be Jon? Would she be able to tell the difference? Was this question even relevant?, bearing in mind she didn't know Bethany any more than he did. "Well… this is your chance to explore," she chided herself just as the door swung open, and there stood… It was definitely Jon, standing proudly with one hand on the door, and a glass of something that looked distinctly champagne like in his other hand. He had a cocky smirk on his face, and she couldn't ignore the disconcerting fact that his right foot was poised in a dance-like pose resting on the ball of his foot in some kind of plié, which immediately gave her stomach the strong urge to reconnect her with her breakfast. Jon was clearly in theatrical mode; although to her, he resembled more of a seedy B-movie candidate.

"Hi," he drawled in a tone that he perhaps perceived Tom Cruise would use in an effort to seduce a femme fatale. He would be wrong. It turned her off immediately. She could feel herself getting colder by the second. Any notion of titillating enjoyment drained from her body.

Luckily for him, he didn't appear to notice this.

Just as she was beginning to wonder whether his newly acquired Texan drawl would continue for the whole afternoon…

"You look fantastic." His eyes scanned her. "Can I get you a drink?"

"Yes please." He picked up the bottle of what turned out to be white wine from the mini-bar that was resting already opened on the table and poured some into a waiting glass and handed it to her. She wasn't accustomed to drinking white wine, a fact he might have observed from their previous two encounters. The deep freeze was rising steadily, and she was certain he would soon see the frost in her eyes. He had disrobed himself of his trousers, the same pin-striped ones he had worn the last time they met, which were now slung over the back of a nearby chair. His favourites, she surmised, and was wearing only a light blue shirt which he had unbuttoned to his lower, slightly hairy chest. Whatever underwear he had on were thankfully hidden. There was no hint of affluence in his attire. Simple practical uniformity, as though he had been directed to an accountant's uniform website and ordered the standard package. Nothing to indicate flare or individuality. No evidence of haute couture or any obvious signs of quality in the fabric or lining. Probably designed to draw minimal attention to himself, but she suspected more than likely driven by a need to fit in.

"You look great," he repeated. She walked over to the bed and perched on the edge, placing her black leather jacket and her burgundy leather bag with gold clasps, perfectly matching her boots, on the floor beside her. He was striding towards her now; and without warning, he took the as yet untouched glass from her hand in one suave swipe, moving as though there was music playing in his head; in a failed attempt at debonair and in a manner that he appeared to have practised several times before with no regard for improvement, placed it down on the table with one hand and cupped the back of her head with the other before pulling her to her feet. His mouth was open, and his eyes were flitting over her as though contemplating where best to lick an ice cream cone at the imminent melting point.

Suddenly his tongue was in her mouth and then out again. He was practically licking her with dramatic juvenile strokes, much like a child licking an ice-lolly, as though she was a thing. A thing that he was proud to have captured and couldn't wait to tell his friends about. He was abrupt and full of himself which indicated that the women in his past or current life had mistakenly communicated that he was executing with expertise. Had no one ever told him that this was a far cry from a lesson in seduction? Even she knew that and her experience would look minimal to most socially active teenagers.

She began to feel nauseous as she responded in kind to his tongue's command.

His hands were on her behind but with uncertainty at first, as though the firmness and structure caught him by surprise, though any qualms rapidly transforming to the fierce enthusiasm of an ancient explorer overcome with mesmerising gratitude in finding that the earth was in fact round and not flat.

He eventually pulled back from his tongue excursion and looked at her dreamily and appeared pleased with himself. His face had adopted a dramatic snarl as though trying to convey sexual hunger, similar to a wild cat about to devour its prey.

To her relief, he picked up her glass again, barely taking his eyes from her and in a final choreographed swoop, handed her the wine. While she drained the contents hastily, he sauntered around the large bed and dived onto the covers turning to look at her as if expecting Olympic applause. He reached out his arm to invite her to join him.

She considered whether to bolt now? In seconds, she could grab her belongings and be back in reception faster than Florence Griffiths-Joyner. Within the hour, she could be at home with a glass of her preferred red, pretending that this afternoon was simply a figment of her imaginary thoughts. Before she could deliberate any longer, she decided to go with it. Don't be too hasty, she counselled inwardly. Things may yet improve.

He quickly removed his shirt, throwing it casually over a nearby baroque style red-and-green-striped antique chair exposing shapeless, ill-fitting black boxer shorts, much like the ones she would grab in Primark for her sons during a tight budget month. He lay back onto the pillows gallantly, with his legs wide apart, adopting a pose that had previously been met with approval or enthusiasm; though she debated on which planet this could have occurred.

She removed her sleeveless top as though in some kind of trance, the dramatic slash at the back rose all the way up to her shoulder blades revealing the delicate curvature of her lower back and offering a deliberate glimpse at her genetically lifted derriere.

She pulled off her knee-high, deep-red boots with the gold toe-tip that coordinated with her shoulder bag and lipstick and blush cream and eye shadow and slipped out of her glittery leggings.

He took off his glasses that had developed a film of condensation and gaped at her bare body with the longing of an orphan on visiting day. Like a man whose wildest fantasy was coming true. He was literally dribbling with glee.

She stifled the recurring nausea and climbed onto the bed beside him. He made another attempt to obliterate her mouth with mechanical strokes of his tongue revealing his misplaced arrogance. He was clearly enjoying himself with absolutely no notion of her own enjoyment.

Suddenly he got up and sauntered confidently towards the table where his phone lay. Whilst he was checking his phone, he popped his hip in a dramatic and highly unattractive manner for anyone other than a female catwalk model at the end of a runway at fashion week and glanced at her as if willing her to be patient and wishing to assure her that the seduction will continue shortly. She attempted to reassure him non-verbally that he could take all the time in the world on the other side of the room. She swallowed hard. Something on his phone caused him to screw up his face and run tracks through his hair.

"I may have to get back to the office a little sooner than I thought," he sighed with frustration.

Cayenne sighed too. Inwardly thanking the gods for their powers of perception.

He flung his phone down and climbed predatorily across the bed towards her, like a panther stealthily crawling through long strands of African grass. He was slobbering over her again, presumably trying to imitate a passionate kiss.

He lifted her up until she was straddling him. His hand was gripping his cock and wielding it, as though it were deadly weaponry, clearly very proud of his instrument. Admittedly it was impressive in size compared to her Caucasian expectations. Slightly larger than average thickness, long and straight with a perfect dome at the top. He replaced his hand with hers, and she dutifully massaged his penis trying desperately to muster some enthusiasm for his pale soft body, with its numerous liver spots like some kind of overgrown Dalmatian.

"Come on, show me what I've been missing. Show me what a black woman can do that a white woman can't," he hissed.

She began to gyrate above his hips but instantly regretted it as the nausea turned to motion sickness. Her knickers were still on—floral thongs with black lace on the fringes. To her surprise, the sexual simulation was at least beginning to provide a little enjoyment. All she had to do now was close her eyes and summon the essence of Chris Hemsworth. He gripped a firm round glute in each hand, squeezing and guiding the circular movement of her hips. She ascertained that he did not want sex from her. At least not yet. Probably motivated by fear rather than a moral judgement. Whilst her eyes were closed, she felt the lobes of her pussy being stroked.

A flow of gushing cream escaped and saturated his fingers. He groaned excitedly and elevated her bottom up toward his face until she was virtually poised on the bridge of his pointed nose. He inserted his tongue rapidly between her legs, protruding through the crotch less thongs; and the sound of him supping hungrily made her arch her back in ecstasy. His lips squeezed and cajoled her labia, seeking more of her delicious honey. The sucking motion tingled the core of her being, willing her to produce more. A deep satisfying convulsion overtook her as she thrust herself back and forth across his face, leaving trails, like the sun across a glacial plain, until the rapture subsided. She looked down at his face which was a picture of spent euphoria, mouth wide open, eyes glazed and glistening. She rolled off of him, and they lay looking up at the ceiling. Just for a moment, for the first time since she arrived, she was exceedingly glad that she came.

The hours that followed were curious and strange. He had quickly showered, inviting her to watch.

She had just managed not to reproduce the white wine that she had consumed earlier as he asked in his best old Hollywood voice, "Wanna watch me show'r?"

She couldn't help but ponder, quite what events had developed his exceptional body confidence which seemed genuine despite the distinct sense of inadequacy that he carried with him. She had declined his offer; but once in the bathroom, she found herself bending over the sink whilst he spanked her. She may even have encouraged him to swing harder enjoying the full impact of his hand on her buttocks. The speed with which she had consumed the wine clearly taking effect. The excitement for him was almost overwhelming. His eyes widened, like an exuberant child, as she bent lower and encouraged him to spank harder.

Soon he had returned to the office or whatever appointment beckoned. He had encouraged her not to rush but to enjoy the room that he or his company had paid for; and the wine that he had bought, which was conflictual with the subsequent doubts he expressed at the prospect of leaving her there alone, as though worried, that she may take advantage. Run up the phone bill perhaps or order endlessly from the menu.

His reaction left a bad taste in her mouth, although she had outwardly reassured him that he had nothing to fear, inwardly she was full of reproach.

He had said there was a possibility that he may be able to return later in the afternoon if she would like, and if he could find the time.

As she was preparing to leave, she was suddenly overcome with dizziness and fatigue. Perhaps it had been the sudden indulgence of white wine when she was accustomed to red. Come to think of it, she hadn't had lunch.

She tidied up her makeup without having to reapply, so that the hotel staff wouldn't be further alerted to her sordid antics. By the time she closed the door behind her, she couldn't help but question her judgement afresh.

Chapter 6

You would almost think that the whole Canary stranger episode hadn't happened. Cayenne threw herself into her new gym routine and resumed the pattern of normal life. Whenever the stranger came to mind, for instance, his exaggerated swagger, his open invitation to join him in the 'show'r' or his cocky demeanour, she would swallow the nauseous sensation that emerged or placate it with a strong mint and turn her attention to something else.

It was a harmless experience, she told herself; and she supposed that people usually regretted far more the things that they didn't do, right?

For someone who had never considered herself a gym person, she was amazed at how quickly she had taken to this new life. She was soon organising her life around the online class booking system via the gym app on her phone, where she could book up to three days in advance. She was booking at least two classes a day, ranging from yoga to boxing. High intensity classes became her favourite. The really challenging classes with minimum recovery time which made it resemble abstract torture, but she was convinced that before long she would see the much-desired results. She knew she looked good, particularly for her age and having had three children; however, it just wasn't enough anymore. Was it too much to ask to be ripped? Why couldn't she have protruding abs and defined arms, toned legs and the kind of crafted back that inspired envy as she walked through the gym in the tiniest of gym bras? Just because she was older, with children, who's to say she couldn't achieve maximum fitness. She was determined to see how much she could achieve, and how far she could go when she put her mind to it.

The first few classes had been difficult and not just physically. Almost every class she entered was like walking into a wall of hostility. She knew she didn't particularly come across as the most engaging personality herself, but she hadn't expected such a frosty reception. No one had welcomed her or even said hello. Not that that mattered, she was more than proficient at adapting to new situations and growing up in a Jamaican household had more than prepared her for living with hostility and judgement. It made her all the more determined to knuckle down and push herself in class. After all, she wasn't there to make friends. She was on a mission. She was even able to push through the fact that most of the women were clad in amazing modern gym gear combinations and elaborate gym sets with matching-coloured trainers and accessories. Whereas she rocked up in an old cheap pair of luminous training shoes that she had bought on the internet, and a couple of bits that barely resembled work out gear that she had been quite content to use in the privacy of her bedroom, where she had been working out for the past year, utilising YouTube exercise videos and the occasional DVD. She ignored the curious glances that she got, or the sniggers—real or imagined—that hung in the air and focussed solely on the instructor at the helm and on putting in 100% effort.

Over the coming weeks whilst attending the early-morning sessions, she developed a rapport with Eddie Carter, the aerobic trainer, who it had to be said, didn't resemble the image of a personal trainer by any stretch of the imagination. He was rather short, around five foot seven, and it would be polite to call him stocky—very well built with a mass combination of fat and muscle in equal measures. He had a shock of almost white hair due to his inherent albinism—a condition that caused his hair and skin to lack pigmentation. There was something about Eddie that obviously appealed to women as they appeared to flock in droves to his classes first thing in the morning, and many often loitered after class and sat around casually, post workout, listening to his tales of extra-curricular wrestling contests and weight-lifting achievements.

Cayenne particularly liked the way in which he explained each exercise well and the point of the exercise, even though he didn't appear to have any intention of taking part himself once the demonstrations were over. After one particularly gruelling body-conditioning session, she decided to take him up on his regular offer of delivering any feedback, whether good or bad, about the session and approached him to thank him for a challenging class and for introducing what she considered, unusual exercises that she hadn't come across before. He had looked nervous upon her approach, as people often did until she smiled, but softened considerably on receipt of her compliment. She also enquired about some strength sessions he was offering at an extra cost; and before she knew it, she had booked a personal training session for the following week. She could scarcely afford it, she knew, but decided to take the plunge, electing to see it as a personal investment.

Eddie was waiting for her in the open-plan reception when the day arrived. He was folding numerous white towels and placing them in a huge pile at the end of the desk, ready for arriving patrons. After completing some paperwork, he had escorted her around the gym, pointing out which areas were good for warming up. They climbed down to the lower level of the mostly underground building. The general colour scheme was metallic grey to match the iron monuments dotted around. The vast expanse of flooring was a similar industrial grey with designated areas for specific activities identified by shocks of yellow linoleum. Parts of the ceiling were painted with the same canary yellow, and Cayenne spotted at least two walls with spray-painted murals reminding her of graffiti-clad walls she had seen in the underground of New York City.

"So what would you say your fitness goals were? What in particular do you want to work on?" He asked as they strode down the metal steps which formed the spine of the building.

"I don't know really, I just want to improve my overall fitness, but I always want to be a little bit thinner. Doesn't every woman?"

"So you seem quite competent in class, what forms of exercise have you done before?"

"Well, I was never a gym person to be honest; so for the past year or so, I've been working out at home using YouTube videos and DVDs…"

"Oh okay." He hadn't quite managed to hide his disdain when she mentioned her enjoyment of Taebo, the total body fitness system founded by Billy Blanks which incorporated martial art techniques popularised in the 1990s.

"Let's go down to the basement and get you warmed up, and then we'll have a go at some weights. How does that sound?"

"Yep, sounds good…"

After a few rounds of sit-ups, press-ups, crunches and the dreaded burpees, Eddie walked her through some kettlebell lunges up and down the far side of the basement, in full view of, and to the inescapable primal sounds of several big grunting bears lifting heavy iron. She found this disconcerting at first and felt terribly exposed, but decided to use the extra attention to will her on to try to save face and not quit when the pain and discomfort got too much.

Eddie proved to be very chatty. A little too much for her liking, although his friendliness was endearing. By the end of the hour, she was certain that they had talked more than they had worked out, and she certainly wasn't dripping in sweat, but she had learned that he was the eldest of a large family, that he had been severely bullied at school and had had a dream to go into the military in his native Morocco which he had achieved, only to discover that an illness had rendered him medically unfit for duty which had sent him spiralling into deep depression, sending a formally mild character on a treacherous angry rampage. She had learnt quite a bit about his hometown, his best friends, his wrestling mates and some girl called Calmari who was just a friend, even though her name seemed to crop into every sentence he spoke. Something about his energy made her think that he was suppressing his anger as opposed to having come to terms with and moved on from it.

The entire cool down period of the workout consisted of lying in the stretch area chatting, with several more references to Calmari. However, she was impressed with the weights that she had lifted and was pleased that she appeared to have natural strength, which Eddie had fine-tuned with corrections to her posture and technique.

As they ascended the metal stairs towards reception, he was asking her about a follow-up session. Uncharacteristically not wanting to disappoint, and she suspected, against her better judgement, she had agreed to book another session for the following week. No doubt she would discover whatever there was left to learn about Marrakesh and perhaps come to know all about Calmari's life story too.

Meanwhile, at home, the current state of the apartment, with its dire décor that she had inherited from the previous occupants, was beginning to feel untenable. She had tried to postpone the renovation, reasoning that the larger jobs such as the kitchen and bathroom should be attended to first. But as Christmas was approaching, she suddenly felt it was time to address the elephants in every bloody room. Namely huge floral atrocities on supposed feature walls and unsightly off-white carpets.

The previous tenants had totally whitewashed the apartment, apparently due to the belief that dark colours caused migraines. Cayenne rather thought that the migraines could easily have been attributed to the fact that at four foot nine, the former tenant was currently carrying her eighth child. Her older children, who were eight and ten, were already of similar height to their mother. Cayenne could tell that beneath the yards of black material that Hiyjinda was draped in, there was very little mass to her diminutive body. She appeared malnourished, and it was hardly surprising that she found time to eat at all with so many young children to attend to. Her husband was some kind of out-of-town taxi driver, which meant that she was shouldering most of the responsibility herself.

The apartment had been painted white from floor to ceiling, including doors and skirting boards. The carpet had been cream-coloured, once upon a time, but had clearly seen better days and was suffering from the daily assault of seven small children. She had explored the option of hiring professional help but had quickly ruled it out as financially unfeasible. She had managed to renovate the hallway so far, quite successfully in her opinion. She would tackle the rest of the apartment one room at a time, starting with Sugar's room. Her daughter's favourite colour was purple, so she began googling various shades of purple wallpaper, particularly on the lookout for something unusual. Sugar was also fascinated with astronomy and even had a favourite planet. Cayenne was very excited to come across a company that produced prints of various planets. The printed strips of wallpaper had already been sized to measure which would make the execution fool proof. She was relieved to find that it was excellent value with good quality durable sheets. When she had cut the wallpaper according to the height of the wall, using the perforated guidelines, the second strip automatically aligned with the first strip; and before long, a huge portrait of Saturn emerged amidst rock formations and stars on a blanket of black sky. She stood back and admired her work. For a first attempt, this bode very well for the rest of the room. Days later, the purple wallpaper she had ordered arrived. The quality was less impressive, but the colour was a vibrant indigo. The window and radiator areas proved tricky, which exposed the poor quality of the paper. She found that this wallpapering lark appeared to be a matter of timing. If she pasted the walls and the strip too soon, it was almost dry by the time she came to hang it; and if she left it too late, the paste was too gloopy and damp. Working two evenings in a row, the small room was soon finished. It was totally transformed from the box room with its former blue floral feature wall, that had remained unused by the previous family, perhaps because they assumed it was too small to utilise as a fully functioning bedroom; or perhaps they much preferred to squash nine people into two bedrooms. Now it appeared bigger somehow, and she mentally visualised where the bunkbed, which Sugar and Ocean would share, would be positioned, and how much space was left over for a wardrobe and a good-sized desk.

The stark white doors seemed whiter still against the backdrop of purple. Suddenly she felt a sense of daring. "Yes!" she exclaimed aloud. She would paint the doors black. To replace them would not be an option yet. Over the coming months, she completed the other two bedrooms in quick succession, and before long, the living room was complete too. She had chosen a bespoke, striped brown and bronze wallpaper for the main living areas; and just as expected, it gave the home a rather regal feel, creating the ambience of a smart boutique hotel.

She loved the finished result, but something was still bothering her. She recalled looking through Pinterest images and coming across painted ceilings and marvelling at the effect that it had on a room. It wasn't long before she found herself in the Stratford branch of Wilko comparing various shades of chocolate brown wall paint, finally deciding on a nutmeg shade and ordering several containers, trying to gauge how many would be required for the large living area, factoring in a potential second coat.

She knew she wanted to create an atmosphere; and to ensure a complete contrast to the dazzling blandness of the communal hallway, completely eliminating the colour white from the apartment. She pictured herself arriving home and turning the key of her apartment, pushing the door open and immediately being submerged into a cavernous, dimly lit ambience. When all the painting was complete, her vision had been accomplished. She worried that it was a little too dark but reasoned that her original brief and been to create something shady and mysterious. There was no turning back. She would perhaps need to be creative with the lighting, utilising an elaborate installation or an additional perfectly placed picture light.

She was most proud of the fact that she had paid particular attention to the accessories and finer details. The touches that many gave little thought to. The majority of homes she had come across seemed to consider the wall accessories or lighting fixtures as rather an afterthought. She had seen far too many bare bulbs and casually placed mirrors. She was not ashamed to admit that she had acquired the accessories long before considering the main furniture she would need. Thankfully, the children were very trusting of her process and barely pressured her with expectations. She discovered some bronze and copper ornate mirrors on eBay, and her bronze bust of a romantic couple embracing, and her African inspired wall-feature of a man and woman in hold, seemingly performing some form of creole dance routine and dressed as though they had been plucked from a New Orleans jazz establishment, which all helped create a distinguished atmosphere. She was discovering how fulfilling it was to come across unusual finds for a fraction of high street prices, and she was amazed to discover that she appeared to have a knack of knowing exactly where to position her acquisitions.

Taking pride of place on the far wall of the living room was the large mahogany-framed mirror that was one of only a handful of items that she had insisted on bringing from the previous house in Torquay. In fact, they owed their arrival in London to this mirror. It had provided the vision board for their quest into the universal law of attraction, on which they pinned images of the capital and wrote positive affirmations to help keep them focussed on their plans and desires. They had even resorted to scribbling potential moving dates on there with permanent marker pens, which would be hastily scrubbed away and rewritten as each deadline passed.

Now they were here. Looking at the exact same mirror in their desired city. The same mirror in which she now scrutinised her workout gear before heading to her daily gym classes.

Laura, pronounced Lou'ra, which Cayenne assumed was the authentic Hispanic pronunciation, was the instructor for the abs classes. Cayenne soon learned that Laura had the gift of making the classes seem rather like punishment. Quite often she would bark out orders for them to execute 50 repetitions of star jumps only to command, "More, 50 more," in her clipped accent. Just as they were on their last legs and panting with exhaustion, she would command, "50 more."

The class would look at her incredulously assuming that they must have misheard what she had said, only to be met with,

"Come on, quick quick! Speed up, speed up!"

Even the venomous glances she received when she insisted upon 300 push-ups, failed to deter her enthusiasm. Though she may not have exactly led from the front in her classes, Laura could often be seen putting herself through her own punishing routine around the gymnasium in between classes, which almost always involved heavy weights or kettlebells, as she squatted her way down the length of the gym. Her hard work had certainly paid off as evidenced by her well-developed physique. All 5 feet of her was hardened muscle. What she lacked in personality, she certainly made up for with her drive and focus.

Another trainer that Cayenne failed to establish a rapport with was Adam Feeney. Tall, good-looking, something he clearly didn't doubt; he was of slim-build, not at all muscular, much to his chagrin. He seemed pleasant enough on the surface, but she often felt that whenever she attempted to challenge herself, he didn't appear to like it. She wasn't sure why it should threaten him, but he even exclaimed rather harshly when she selected a heavier ball than he had indicated for a squat throw challenge,

"Let ME challenge you."

He was not averse to making snide comments, usually singling out one of his favourite minions and pointing out their virtues, which were hidden to Cayenne. She considered that he singled them out because of their barely disguised admiration for him, and he in turn bolstered their esteem with his high praise, creating some sort of co-dependent appreciation alliance and to her mind, exposing their insecurities.

Often when he considered that striking potential conquests were present in the form of tall, lithe model-like blondes, he would momentarily lose his military resolve and seem distracted and unable to divert his attention away from the source of his desire, leaving the rest of the class feeling as if he had no interest in their overall progress.

Cayenne came to the decision that she would only participate in the classes that made her feel good. The ones that she considered nourishing and inspiring. To only give her time to the classes that rewarded her commitment in some way.

She hadn't particularly enjoyed her second personal training session with Eddie at the gym either and had rather hoped to avoid him for a while. That was until she was returning from the school run with Sugar one afternoon and happened to bump into him. The local Tesco metro backed onto the square where she lived, and on this particular occasion, he appeared around the corner on his way to the store; and she couldn't help but notice the cigarette stub wedged between his fingers which he quickly discarded of, she suspected rather sooner than he would have liked. She knew she really shouldn't, but couldn't help feeling sorely disappointed at the realisation that many trainers did not pursue a career in personal training out of passion for fitness.

"Free for a PT this week? I'm free on Wednesday afternoon and Friday morning."

Feeling decidedly put on the spot, Cayenne found herself agreeing to the Friday appointment.

As soon as they were out of earshot, Sugar enquired, "Who was that!?"

"The guy from the gym. The one I do the personal training with."

The expression on her daughter's face was comical.

"What?" she enquired already formulating an idea of what was on her daughter's mind.

"He's just not what I expected, that's all."

When Cayenne had asked exactly what she had meant, knowing full well what remark to expect, as Sugar was fast becoming a chip off the old block, Sugar had simply used her hands to emphasise the size of Eddie's stomach.

After the third session, Cayenne still wasn't convinced. Predictably most of it was taken up with chatting, generally about his favourite subject—himself. Before long, she was well-versed in the unfortunate events of his childhood, reliving the severe bullying owing to his being inherently on the large side and nature's failure to balance it out with his height. His descriptions of being beaten repeatedly seemed to run into each other, and it was difficult to follow the chronological order, but he had clearly been shaped by the perpetual nature of these experiences. Whilst on the surface, Eddie had come across as relatively confident and self-assured, he was soon confessing to chronic low self-esteem and bouts of depression, which she presumed he was attempting to bolster with his multiple extra-curricular endeavours. Many in the class had been encouraged to follow his semi-professional journey via Instagram, which showcased his weekly training schedule, and his success or failure in various competitions he participated in. She noted quite quickly that he would caption many of his videos with excuses as to why he may not have been able to complete his attempts at various challenges or by way of excusing poor technique, almost as though he anticipated critical responses. He would seem to pre-empt the potential reprovals that the videos would attract from fellow enthusiasts, by apologising in advance for his substandard form.

It wasn't long before Cayenne began to question just how effective these one-to-one sessions were for her, when she knew she had sufficient motivation to push herself, and she was beginning to suspect that many of the trainers simply used PTs as a way of subsidising their salary. She definitely felt that she was challenging herself more in the classes which seemed to create an accountability and an expectation to give of your best and often left her exhausted in a sweaty heap on the floor. The one-to-one sessions began to feel like a weekly catch up with a mate, rather than a unified, focused voyage toward her fitness goals. Therefore, the sessions soon fell by the wayside. They were still on friendly terms however, often exchanging jokes when passing each other at the gym or sharing stories reflecting un-politically correct humour that they both seemed to enjoy.

That was until one particular night when Cayenne had turned up for boxing class on a Monday evening which was usually undertaken by Frank Garming, the resident boxing expert, though other instructors were qualified to teach the beginners boxing program in his absence. Unbeknownst to Cayenne, this was one of those times. Even though they were on friendly terms, Cayenne would have probably opted out of boxing had she known that Frank was on leave that week, and especially if she had been alerted to the fact that Eddie would be taking this particular session. Moments into the class, had she been paying attention to her instincts, she would have hot-footed it out of the gym forthwith.

As she descended the metal staircase down to the basement and approached the boxing ring, a few other members had begun congregating around the base of the elevated ring waiting for the class to start. Cayenne successfully disguised her disappointment at Frank's absence and quickly made the mental adjustment necessary before Eddie could discern her mood. She nodded a few 'hellos' to a few people that she recognised, mostly regulars of previous classes and introduced herself to a young Japanese couple that she hadn't met before. She noticed one individual who was limbering up inside the ring, away from the others, with the fervour and intensity of a world-class heavyweight champion. He was an older gentleman; she would have guessed that he was around 50 years old, though he was in particularly good shape and looked very strong. She remembered seeing him in another class, and he had seemed pleasant enough.

As the class began, an ever-discerning Cayenne could have sworn she could sense that Eddie was a little unnerved by the pro-boxing energy emanating from the ring. She remembered during their talks, masquerading as personal training sessions, him telling her that he had begun boxing at the age of eight years old, and she had presumed that he had continued some form of participation or other since then.

"Has anyone done any form of boxing before?" The question was directed to the whole class, though Cayenne noticed that Eddie's head appeared to be trained in the direction of the boxing champ who had by now climbed down from the ring and stood towards the back of the assembly—his broad shoulders taking up the width of two people. His hands were clasped slightly defensively in front of him, and his piercing eyes were fixed straight ahead at Eddie.

Most of the class raised their hands in acknowledgement of the question, and a few individuals shook their head to confirm that this was a new endeavour. Cayenne remained silent as she was too busy reading the subliminal signals that were crisscrossing the battleground. The boxing champ, who it transpired, wished to be addressed as Mo, raised his hand too. Cayenne was about to question in her mind whether Mo was short for Mohammed, as in Ali, when she heard Eddie enquire,

"Oh, what kind of boxing 'ave you done then, mate?" Raising his eyebrows expectantly with what Cayenne discerned as a hint of cynicism.

Cayenne wondered why Eddie hadn't directed the question at any number of other possibilities. Or whether the question even needed to be asked. This was a beginner's class after all. Anyone mistakenly looking for a WBA full-contact combat facility would surely soon realise their mistake, and kindly excuse themselves at the first opportunity.

"I've done some kick boxin' and thai boxin'…"

Before Mo the champ could elaborate further, an unrestrained laugh escaped from Eddie's mouth, laced with a decidedly mocking intonation.

"That's not boxin', but they are contact sports," shrugged Eddie seeing the need to state this conclusion in a matter-of-fact manner, simultaneously extinguishing any conjecture and perhaps to reassure himself at the same time.

Cayenne could almost see the testosterone circling around the two men in a cosmic vortex, as their chests puffed out, and their shoulders broadened visibly. She daren't look directly at them and felt a sudden urge to diffuse the rising tension. If only she could think of something to say. Soon they were being paired up. Never in a million years could Cayenne have imagined that she would soon be face-to-face with the indomitable white Ali. An angry Ali, a fucking pissed-off Ali. An Ali with a point to prove.

During Frank's sessions, he generally intermingled with the whole group throughout, giving advice where needed and demonstrating what he expected from them in each individual round, often bringing the group back together as a whole intermittently before dividing them back into their pairs to execute his next instruction. However, Eddie remained in the elevated ring for the entire session making full use of the height advantage.

Whilst boxing wasn't necessarily her favourite class, Cayenne did appreciate the cardio element, and the way in which it developed stamina, as well as the self-defence aspect of it. However, the pairing with the various characters that boxing tended to attract, namely those who considered, at least in their own minds, that they had formerly been one tournament away from turning professional, was by far the hardest and least enjoyable part; and unfortunately, tonight's bout was no different; as by a process of elimination, she had ended up in the Cassius Clay firing line.

Immediately she felt the brunt of Ali's frustration. A vexation that she could only imagine was exacerbated by the competitive energy between himself and Eddie. She could tell that Ali wasn't intending to cause her pain, it was clear by the glazed look in his eye that he was barely aware she was there. All of his focus was directed towards the elevated boxing ring and it's albinistic occupant.

Every forceful punch imploded into her boxing pads with venom as Ali grunted, growled and manoeuvred his way around his hapless opponent, mauling her as though she were a helpless lamb in the mouth of a hungry carnivore; with such ferocity that at one point, the pad flew out of her hand and landed feet away. As she crouched to retrieve it, she could feel the empathy of the iron-pumping congregation nearby. Part of her wanted to petition them to intervene, but instead, she blinked her glistening eyes and reluctantly made her way back to the hostile arena. Ali, however, displayed no such sensitivity. If anything, she could have sworn that she could detect an air of triumph at this vicious display. She clocked his split-second glance in Eddie's direction, as though he was secretly hoping that the trainer had witnessed the leather pad soaring through the air as testament to his supernatural strength. Cayenne would have thought this might prompt the instructor to intercede, but to her disappointment, if he had witnessed anything, he was disguising it with aplomb. The rounds continued apace, and Cayenne, who usually considered herself a relatively strong woman and at the very least a competent beginner in class, was inwardly pleading for a viable escape. At every opportunity, she shot a desperate glance at Eddie, fixing her eyes on him directly now, any prior abashment quickly dissipating. She felt sure he would pick up on her non-verbal pleas, having gotten to know her a little over recent weeks, although truth be told; even a patient passing through on a stretcher, barely conscious, would have had little difficulty in reading her distress signal.

She was convinced that Eddie, whilst obviously registering her plight, was in no mood to come to her rescue. It was plainly obvious that she was beginning to drown amidst the torrent of jabs and uppercuts that she was attempting and failing to bob and weave her way around. The barbaric display only served to diminish Eddie's already fragile ego; and every punch that Ali threw her way seemed to metaphysically affect Eddie, rendering him defenceless against the psychological ropes.

She soon gave up sending him signals, as he was clearly overwhelmed by the situation and determined to further ensconce himself into the devoted mentoring role for the two Japanese girls that were paired up in the ring with him. Even in such difficult circumstances, she could certainly understand why the beginners warranted so much of Eddie's attention, this being their first boxing lesson. Unfortunately, anyone else who may have required Eddie's surveillance that day were to be sorely disappointed, as they would have found themselves vastly out of the vicinity of his comfort zone.

Not soon enough, the ordeal was over. On autopilot, Cayenne packed her boxing gloves into their case and returned the borrowed pads to the large tarpaulin basin tucked away in the space beneath the stairs. Without a backward glance, let alone a thank-you and goodbye, she walked zombie-like towards the yoga studio at the other end of the basement. She usually liked to get there a little early in order to calm her mind and prepare herself for the zen state that yoga required, following the high intensity of the boxing class. However, on this night, she was late to arrive, and the room was almost already full of attendees resting in Savasana in the semi-darkness. Cayenne carried her wounded soul over to one of the two remaining unoccupied mats after discarding her things against the wall as quietly as she could, as there was nothing worse than trying to relax only to have one's sense of tranquil and serenity abruptly interrupted. Bringing her mind into submission for what was usually one of her favourite elements of the practice was proving difficult as she tried desperately to ignore that it was clearly still wrestling and in utter turmoil. It was as though she had subconsciously stifled her feelings about the boxing ordeal whilst it was ongoing; and now that she was in the safety of this eastern sanctuary, all of the subdued emotions suddenly rose to the surface.

She made another attempt to bring her consciousness to yield, but to no avail. Before long, she felt the sting of tears prick her eyes and felt the warmth of its trail running down her cheeks—the droplets sinking into her mat. This was not on. There was no way she was about to lie there and dissolve into a dribbling wreck. With her cheeks burning in competition with her eyes, she rose before the practice could get going and raised her hand to excuse herself. Céleste the French instructor, who was poised at the helm casting a critical eye over the resting mass, nodded in acceptance; and she quickly grabbed her items, pushed her feet into her open trainers and without waiting to fasten them, darted out of the darkness, straight into the noisy brightness of the bustling basement. Somehow, she would have to make her way through without anyone detecting her upset. Racing up the metallic stairs of the underground warren up to the ground level reception, she kept her head down and pulled her hood over her face and raced through the main door into the dark, rainy street.

Chapter 7

Cayenne had always been an early riser, and so as long as she had made the necessary preparations for the children's pre-school routine beforehand, she found she could easily fit in a 30–45 minute run to start the day. Running wasn't her favourite form of exercise, but she had decided to commit to a regular routine in the hope that it would speed up her results. She was toning up without doubt, but what was this insatiable need to be smaller? More defined. Look a little different in her clothes. No matter how much exercise she did, she couldn't seem to see any drastic change in her body. Admittedly she wasn't as disciplined with her food as she could be, and the habit of a glass of wine after her evening meal was difficult to shake off, especially when it demanded the accompaniment of something sweet, complemented by a healthy portion of custard; all of which went down rather well after a little savoury post-dinner snack.

To help push through the elements and the fatigue as she ran, she chose her audio content carefully. She often took to listening to motivational videos on YouTube which helped push her to another level of perseverance with the dramatic music, impassioned speeches and testimonies of successful people.

It was in the midst of one of these speeches one morning that there was an unfamiliar notification alert on her phone which temporarily interrupted the audio which flickered momentarily, then recalibrated and continued.

She reached into the zipped pocket on her gym-leggings which was quite awkward to do whilst running. She glanced at the phone and swiped upwards in order to see what the notification was, being careful to glance up every other second so as not to run into a lamppost or another jogger or down a couple of unseen steps. It was unusual for her to receive messages when it was barely 6:00 a.m.

She almost lost her rhythm and tripped when she saw the email notification as she instantly recognised the sender.

"Hey… All okay?"

Cayenne managed to keep running albeit at a slightly slower pace as she processed what she had seen.

She had to admit that Jon had scarcely entered her mind since the episode at the North Greenwich Hotel several weeks before. She recalled that she may have felt a little disappointed that he hadn't followed up immediately to at least enquire how she was after leaving the hotel, but she was also quite pleased that the incident had soon disappeared from memory. She remembered reflecting on the day immediately afterwards and recalling some of the cringe-worthy elements that almost caused her to regurgitate. The way in which he stood at the door on her arrival was almost worthy of a Golden Raspberry Award.

She had known instantly that he was not being his authentic self, but perhaps that was to be expected given the circumstances; and it really didn't matter for the purpose of their terms of engagement.

Hadn't that been the point, to escape for an afternoon from the perceived humdrum and pretend to be other people? It made perfect sense that they wouldn't expose their true selves to one another. But somehow it still irked her, possibly because she knew that even in her most inauthentic moments, she was too honest a person to detach completely from who she essentially was.

She picked up the notion that Kenneth looked altogether too comfortable parading around in his alter ego. She wondered whether he had gotten so comfortable with it that he had confused the two. How many times had he entertained women, she imagined, in that same hotel.

She was perplexed how someone who clearly had issues with his true self could appear so self-assured to parade around semi-naked. She had to conclude that perhaps it was easier to be expressive as someone else, much like the performers who found it easier to hide behind a character and are able to be more daring than they would usually be.

By far, the most irritating thing about him had been the unmistakable snarl on his face that she supposed was intended to be an exaggerated look of desire, but in actual fact made him look as though paralysis had set in. He had held his phone in his hands almost the entire time, which was annoying as it communicated that he was clearly distracted during a task that would have required him to summon the entirety of his faculties in order to pull it off to her satisfaction; and it was also abundantly clear that he did not have a free afternoon at all, but had carelessly thought to entertain her during a few stolen moments of an obviously busy schedule. It was as though someone was alerting him to how much longer he could get away with.

Although she was pleased that she had applied herself to her 'seize-the-day' mantra, the episode had left her with a bitter taste in her mouth. She hadn't enjoyed much of it; and by the time she had left the hotel, she remembered feeling physically ill, and a tad sleepy which was unusual; and through the haze of her recollections, she was aware of Jon repeatedly looking into her eyes intently and enquiring, "Are you okay? Are you sure?" which she had initially put down to a caring, attentive attitude, on sobering reflection, she dared herself to question whether something untoward had been at play.

But now here he was. Suddenly enquiring if she was okay, out of the blue.

She had no intention of giving this matter any more attention and went about her day mentally and literally relegating the email to her spam list.

Unfortunately, no one had informed the stranger of this, and his diligence showed no signs of abating.

"Is everything okay?"

Re: Rules of Engagement

Hey????

Have I done something to upset you?
The least you could have done was to respond and let me know how you are?"

Chapter 8

"Come on, Mum!" Diego had his guard up, and a determined expression on his face. They were circling each other in the boxing ring, and her son was portraying two roles—opponent and supporter at the same time.

"Come oo-oon, hit me," he punched the side of her head. "Keep your guard up." He barked reminding her that she needed to protect herself as well as prepare her attack.

He had insisted on coming to the gym with her that day. They had discussed her recent defeat at the hands of Ali; and at the time, he had remained calm and said very little. In fact, at first he had appeared to have challenged her response suggesting that she may be overreacting. Cayenne had been a little disappointed by that, though she knew he was simply helping her to process what had happened. As was his custom, he had remained quiet about it for a few days and then suddenly told her that he was taking her for a boxing lesson, even paying the £15 day fee applicable to non-members which was unheard of for her frugal son.

Now it seemed he wanted to test her. Push her. See how much she could take and what she would do if caught in a difficult combat situation.

She saw her opportunity to throw in a jab, followed quickly by an uppercut to his stomach.

He winced, but then his face softened. "Whoah, that's it, Mummy, come on…"

His pain pleased her. "You've got one powerful punch, Mummy. Not so much the jabs to my face; but when you attack my stomach, it's powerful." She smiled knowingly and appreciatively and thanked him with a quick torrent of punches to his head. Most of which he blocked, but she had managed to sneak a few in too, to answer his previous assessment.

He responded with several powerful punches. She felt the weight of them, but strangely they didn't hurt. She was too focused. Too intent. Too poised. She rewarded him with her newly acquired signature shot and then another one. He doubled over and glared at her, half-smiling. They were sparring with such intensity that people around the gym were beginning to notice.

After their final round, Diego had set another challenge for her.

He stood menacingly—tall and proud—his arms and shoulders beginning to form as he entered his adult phase of life. She stood against the ropes, panting but still hungry, looking up at him awaiting her next challenge.

"Okay, you need to get me across to the other side of the ring quickly. No punching now, just with your body weight. I wanna see how strong you are."

Cayenne stood upright and took in some deep intakes of breath, summoning as much strength as she could muster. She glanced behind him at the opposite ring corner, gauging how much distance she would need to cover. She pinned back her shoulders and then geared herself up as she listened to his countdown. "After three. Ready? Three… two… one…"

Cayenne catapulted herself against his body and at first reverberated back a step, but she somehow knew she had more in her. She gripped the floor of the ring with her toes through the soles of her trainers and forced her mind to dominate this blood opponent. She could sense him giving in. she could tell he was surprised at how strong she was. He hadn't anticipated this power; and whilst it pleased him, after all, that had been his objective, his competitive side was not about to accept defeat. He pushed against her, but she kept edging forward. Her body followed her mind and moved the muscle mass in her path; and within seconds, they were at the other side of the ring, with Diego pressed against the padded corner in defeat.

"Nah-nah-nah-nah," he shook his head incredulously. "We are doing that again."

She wandered confidently back to the other side without an ounce of self-doubt. Her new discovery fusing her with new determination. He too looked confident, obviously assuring himself that the outcome must have been some kind of fluke. Perhaps he hadn't been prepared. Lost footing at some point. Whatever it was, he was now determined to alter it.

"After three." Cayenne was silent. Conserving her energy for the challenge. "One… two… thr'."

Cayenne forged forwards again. More determined now than before. She quickly gained momentum. He was losing ground again. He seemed to be amusedly perplexed that his body was letting him down. He was facing his own weaknesses whilst testing hers. He made another attempt to challenge her, but her progress rendered it futile. Once again, they found themselves in her victory corner.

They repeated the exercise another four times with the same result. "Okay, one last time. We are not leaving until I do this." They both laughed. Unfortunately for him, he was beginning to tire, which rendered his defeat certain. They tried it the other way too. Him trying to get her to the other side. He managed it twice out of five attempts which soothed his bruised ego somewhat. By the time they mounted the stairs towards daylight, gleaming with perspiration, they were both smiling inwardly. Cayenne with a new realisation of her strengths, and her son hugely proud that his mum was a badass.

Christmas was fast approaching which brought much excitement to the Richards' household, even though Cayenne didn't necessarily subscribe complete allegiance to all the festive traditions. She had made certain to disabuse the children early on of any notion of St Nicholas and his reindeers being real. "No Santa Claus, no tooth-fairy… no, it was me. The presents came from me, I replaced your milk-teeth under the pillow in the middle of the night with money. ME."

Just days before Christmas, Diego handed her her phone.

"I hope you have a good Christmas, Bethany."

"What is it, Mum?" Diego had clocked the surprised look on her face.

"Remember I told you about that guy that approached me in Canary Wharf?"
Diego nodded, still looking at his own phone.
"Well, we met up a couple of times, but I wasn't really feeling it."

"Why?" Diego was always willing to give people the benefit of the doubt, especially as he was well-aware of his mother's propensity to judge people quickly and perhaps harshly. Cayenne appreciated that her son was always willing to play devil's advocate.

"I'm not sure," she could feel her face screwing up at the memory. "He was just... not being himself, I suppose."

"Maybe it takes some people longer to get to that point." Diego was scratching his head. "So you just wrote him off, just like that. Damn, that's cold."

"He keeps messaging me, even though I don't respond."

"So respond."

Chapter 9

Cayenne was averaging two gym classes a day at this point.
    By now, the old tatty gear was quickly being replaced by new colourful designs. She was aware that people thought she was unusual as she always made sure that she looked her best; as to her mind, she wasn't dressing for the occasion or the venue but for herself. She ignored the sly glances from those that didn't understand. The people that wondered why she would bother applying makeup when she was going to sweat it off anyway. As she began to see results in her body, she paid even more attention to herself. The leggings were more fitted, the tops more revealing to show off the definition that was beginning to show in her abdominals. When the shaping began to develop in her back, she sought out gym bras and backless leotards that emphasised her progress. She knew that this would not make her popular, but she was used to that. She decided that she was going to push through the hostility, the pain, tiredness and fatigue and get it done until she was collapsed in the corner, dripping with sweat. Often, she would look up to see bewildered faces looking at her, as though they had never seen anyone work out so hard. Cayenne questioned why they even showed up, but she always showed up to win. To be prepared to face failure. To improve on yesterday, to push past her limits and compete against herself and challenge herself mentally as well as physically. She knew that if she worked on herself every day, that she was becoming stronger as a person.

    Cayenne loved walking into the Yoga studio which today formed the venue for Body Balance, which was a new class she had decided to try. She learned that it had been around for a number of years, and it intrigued her because it was a combination of Yoga, Pilatés and Tai Chi.
    The usual instructor was absent that day, so when she stepped into the room, she was met with someone she hadn't seen before. A short black lady was limbering up on her mat at the front of the class.

She walked with a slight bend in her back; and Cayenne was certain she could detect a grimace, as though she was masking an injury.

"'ello, my name is Claudine, and I will be teaching Body Bal-ance today. Joanne 'as been called to an urgent meeting."

Claudine, it turned out was French, and her thick French dialect flowed poetically out of her mouth and hung thickly in the air. Cayenne warmed to her almost immediately; as when she smiled, it was coming from an honest place. Selecting a mat from the corner shelf, Cayenne lay down and waited for more members of the class to arrive and listened to Claudine having to repeat her welcoming message over and over again.
The class began to fill up as the calming hums of music filled the room. Claudine faced the waiting group and introduced herself yet again to those that had come in late.

"Is z'ere anyone who 'as not done Body Bal-ance before?"

Two of the ladies present raised their hands nervously.

"Okay, welcome to di class. Body Bal-ance is a combination of Yoga, Pilatés and Tai Chi. If you 'ave done zese practices before, you will definitely recognise some of the moves. I will be giving you two or three different options throughout, and just take the option that is better for you.
Before we start, does anyone 'ave any injuries that I should know about, or is anybody pregnant?"

This time there were no raised hands, and so the sequence of Body Balance began. The combination of the three disciplines, put together into one choreographed dance to music, combining strength, agility, core and balance.
Although Cayenne found some of the movement challenging, most of it was familiar as she had practised yoga and pilatés on and off over the years and by far her most favourite part of the routine was when Claudine instructed the class to turn to the right and face the mirrored wall, which was always handy for monitoring technique and the accuracy of the postures.
"Come into a deep lunge, reach up and into a small backward bend. Clasp your 'ands behind your back, palms togezer if you can.

Come onto your front leg and lift your left leg up. Balance if you can. Hips square to duh floor…"

Cayenne knew that balance was one of her strengths, unlike the flexibility aspect of the practice. It was at this time that she felt the attention of many behind her watching most acutely, as though they were waiting to see if she would maintain her balance throughout where many were struggling to maintain the pose.

Claudine's next command was totally inspiring as it was expressed in a way that transformed what was usually a common yoga pose into something magical and mystical.

"Raise your clasped 'ands behind you away from your bodee, raise your right leg and dip down as far as you can. Go on, see if you can dip fur'zer."

Cayenne managed to do just that and pressed her weight down into her toes and held her core firmly.

"Now turn to de uzer side. Deep lunge, raise your 'ands to ze sky into backbend, now come onto your left leg, clasp your 'ands behind your back and raise your 'ands away from your bodee."

Just then the music softened to a whimsical melody. "Come forward and lift your left leg, lift your 'ands higher above your head. Come oo-oon, spread your wings, let's flyy-yy-yy-yy-yy-yy-yy-yyy."

Wow. Cayenne glanced cautiously around the room; the light from the stairwell above illuminated the dimness in the far corner at that moment, just as they dipped with their arms outstretched behind them like birds. It suddenly felt like they were ascending up above the clouds, towards the sun.

Chapter 10

"I sincerely hope you have a happy Christmas, Bethany, and that you and the children have a great day."

It was going to be a quiet festive season. No Christmas parties or glittering nights out. Not that she minded too much. She was more than happy to cuddle up on the sofa with the children and watch the New Year celebrations on the television as fireworks disappeared into the sky above London, Sydney, New York and Toronto.

"Happy New Year, Bethany.
Did I do something to upset you?"

The advertisement in the gym window, and the similar one on the website, was asking for someone who was looking for a challenge. Someone committed, determined and with a passion to inspire others.
BECOME A PERSONAL TRAINER, it beckoned from the page. Cayenne had been giving serious thought to what was next. What was her next challenge going to be? What was going to be different about the New Year? She now wondered whether she may just have her answer.
There was little cost involved, but a real commitment of time would be required. Could she manage it around the school timetable? On the plus side, she spent most of her time in the gym anyway. Why not take it to another level and eventually make a career out of it.

Cayenne was well-aware that she was of an age that she would have to put real effort in to maintaining her own well-being. So she made sure that after each training session, particularly if it had been a challenging one, to go to the cool down area, where she could stretch properly, do her own abs routine and then use the foam roller over as much of her body as possible. She wasn't satisfied with the token minute cooldown that had been added to the classes, so she put in the extra time knowing that it would aid her recovery and keep her body strong. She felt irked whilst witnessing a trainer putting their client through a supposed cool down, whilst chatting away about their own business, not really focusing. Then within minutes, they would be saying their goodbyes and slotting the next session into the diary.

She would watch them disappear towards reception whilst she was still in the first phase of her own cooldown. She could just imagine Diego's eyes rolling in his head if he could hear her thoughts right now. He would surely throw her a knowing look as if to say, "Have you heard yourself? Who do you think you are?"

As soon as Cayenne emerged from the lower depths of the gym, and her phone regained its signal, she was alerted to a reminder from Sugar's school that a meeting had been scheduled the following morning. There were others seeking her attention.

"Please come back.

Are you at the bus stop?"

The following day, there were more.

"Any chance of a rescue from the January blues and dull Canary Wharf normality?
Jon has to stop messaging as it is messing with his head!
Hope I didn't upset you at any point. ☹"

Cayenne was looking forward to trying Yin Yoga that evening, as it was another discipline that she hadn't come across before. She wasn't disappointed. As its name suggested, it was almost the opposite of traditional Yoga; in that, it wasn't so much about the dynamic poses, as it was a more internal focus on breathing and its positive effects. It was an interior scan of the body, locating tension or discomfort and recognising it without dwelling on it and then using the breath to let it go.

When she arrived, others were already preparing themselves by lying quietly in the dimly lit yoga room in various positions. She noticed that they had a pile of props beside them and so made sure that she selected a block, a curious looking strap and a blanket.

Just as she lay down on her back and rested her arms by her sides and closed her eyes, a small voice called out, "Hi guys."

Charlotte the instructor was as warm and delicate as her voice—tall and slim with shoulder-length blonde hair, and a figure that told the story of her disciplined life. She gingerly stepped through the room being careful to avoid stepping on the many bodies dotted around the floor on purple mats.

After putting on some soothing music, Charlotte gathered her own mat and props and settled at the front, ready to begin the class.

"Okay, guys, thank you for coming. If this is your first time here, and for those that are new to Yin, it is a practice that focusses more on our internal selves.

I'm sure many of you know, our minds are constantly bombarded with stimuli, and so it is easy to end up with a busy mind that is constantly processing all of the information that's thrown at it. What can happen is the mind gets so used to that amount of information that it starts to crave the stimuli in quiet moments as well, so it ends up looking for stuff to fill the gaps when we really would benefit from training our minds to stay empty for some downtime. To allow the mind to just be…

Any kind of dynamic form of yoga caters to this aspect of keeping ourselves busy. Although the mind may calm down as a result of the active exercise, we are still essentially feeding the part of us that craves intensity and wants to be stimulated. We just happen to have found a healthier stimulus.

Now the purpose of our practice is not to rule out the dynamic yoga but rather to balance all the on-the-go aspects of life, and Yin Yoga is a great way to do that.

The first part of our practice that I'm going to lead you into is a dynamic breathing exercise that you might find useful to just settle the mind for today's session, and the great thing about it is it's something that you can adopt at any time when you leave here, whenever your mind is feeling overwhelmed; or you feel you need an instant burst of energy, this will be a good one to try."

She nodded encouragingly around the class.

"So I want you to find a comfortable sitting position. You might find it useful to sit on one of your blocks; this will help you to sit up straight. Cross your legs in front of you, or have them straight out along the mat if that feels more comfortable. Place your hands on your thighs, palms facing upwards. Gently close or soften your eyes, and we are going to breathe in for the count of five; hold the breath in, sitting as tall as you can for five, and then we are going to breathe out for five."

The class listened obediently, and Cayenne could hear the soothing sounds of inward and outward breaths all around her. It was a challenge holding the breath in for that length of time, but she found that it served to intensify the outward breath, and the feeling of release that came with it.

"Okay, nice guys! Now if you would just place your palms together at your chest, raise your thumbs to your third eye, the spot between your brows and I want you to set an intention for this practice. Whether it be to cultivate more energy in your day-to-day lives, or it could be to work on your flexibility, but it could also be something that is more personal to you in your life that you want to focus on specifically during this practice. So let's close our eyes, and we'll set our intention. We can seal this by taking in a full intake of breath and breathing out, and then we can begin…"

Cayenne was appreciative of how the intonation of Charlotte's voice seemed to dance high and low which had an immediate soothing effect on the class.

She closed her eyes, and for the first time in an extraordinarily long time, she set her intention to open herself up for some love in her life in whatever shape or form it materialised.

It perhaps wasn't the best idea to go from the tranquillity of Yin Yoga straight upstairs to the strength studio, but alas that was the timetable, and she was determined to experience the wide range of classes that were available and identify which ones suited her.

Strength was an intense 30-minute frenzy involving weights and fast-paced movements that were timed and then repeated with very little recovery time. It was certainly a shock to the system, and many times she found herself heaped in a corner gasping for breath.

As she was still relatively new to the gym, she was always surprised that her classmates weren't friendlier and more welcoming. She didn't need them to be, but she did find it a tad disconcerting when she walked into a class and was met with a frosty silence. She decided to ignore it and concentrate on herself as she reasoned that her own intense energy probably unnerved people too.

By the time she had finished the class and ran through her cool-down routine, it was past nine o' clock. She practically hopped and skipped the two-minute journey from the gym to her apartment, buzzing with energy. The children were still up when she walked in. They had helped themselves to the dinner she had prepared earlier but had failed to clear away after themselves.

"Dieeeeeego!" she screeched at the top of her voice.
"Yes, Mum."
"Get in here right now."

Later whilst listening to music as she dozed off to sleep, the sound was interrupted by a message signal.

"SHOULD I STOP?"

When she awoke, there were more.

"Is Bethany coming out to play?
Aaaaaaaarrrrrgh☺
What happened to Bethany? Can I tell Bethany a story?"

Chapter 11

Cayenne sat in the reception area of Sugar's junior school waiting for her turn to meet with the class teacher. Thankfully Sugar was doing very well with her studies, and the only area of concern that the teacher highlighted had been her reluctance to involve herself in class discussions and her general reticence to speak up. Admittedly, she was a very sensitive child and at a very self-conscious age. If only Cayenne could somehow relay to the school that they needn't worry. She herself had been a very quiet and somewhat withdrawn child; and that she was almost certain that in time, Sugar too would find her voice and eventually be able to assert herself. For Cayenne, that process hadn't happened at school. Finding herself alone in the capital aged 20 and falling into toxic relationships had accelerated her worldliness; and as a result, eventually, her confidence had begun to develop too.

Later her phone vibrated in her hand; she had forgotten to take it off silent after the meeting earlier.

"Had any naughty fun yet this year?... I need a taste.

Hey! Did I upset you????"

She paused for a moment. Imagining the stranger in absolute turmoil, needing to know whether there was anything he had done to upset her. She suddenly found his concern endearing. He had started messaging her almost three months before, just prior to Christmas; and yet, it was nearing the end of February, and his persistence was showing no end. She didn't quite know what to make of it. She had been convinced that after a few days of not hearing anything that he would give up, and she would never have to think about him again.
Perhaps it was time to put him out of his misery.

"No. It just wasn't particularly enjoyable, that's all. Wow. You are the very definition of persistence."

His response was immediate.

"☺ Hey! Apologies on both accounts – persistency and failing to give you a good experience…
On persistency, this was due to the complete cut-off. Negative honest feedback would have been better than the full silent treatment (Jon could have taken it!).
On good experience, any pointers? Care to share?
Irritated that I failed on this (I thought you wanted the spanking ☺… please let me know if I can make proper amends with a nice bottle of red wine.
Anyway, good to hear from you."

"As I recall, it was a bit of a non-starter.
I remember leaving the hotel thinking… I've just spent £35.00 on taxi fares to sit in a hotel room, following an exceedingly jittery fumble.
You spent most of the time on your phone looking increasingly nervous…
I mean… just not in a hurry to repeat.
Sorry.
That's honest."

"Everything you said was completely valid. You're fucking gorgeous and deserved full attention with proper non-jittery treatment… I should have booked time off to treat you properly rather than try and satisfy you in my lunch hour!!
It's annoying me that I was so immature.
Let me make it up to you… I will even pay taxi costs. ☺"

She decided not to respond. A couple of days later, he sent her a picture that she had sent him from their encounter in the hotel. For reasons that now escaped her, she had decided to send him a seductive picture of herself just prior to leaving.

He was now expressing his appreciation.

"Bad girl.
The memory is making me hard.

Gorgeous sight for sore eyes. In fact, gorgeous sight for any type of eyes."

At some point, she must have mentioned that she hadn't been feeling too well after the wine they had consumed and perhaps inferred that it had been a deliberate act to pacify her.

"Okay, this one gets long…wanted to make a couple of points FULLY clear regarding the mini-bar bottles – we opened them together, and we both had glasses from them!

In fairness, they were very strong, and I don't think either of us had eaten – they cost me nearly double the taxi fare you mentioned, so I remember wishing I had brought really nice champagne in for you instead of raiding the mini-bar!!

I should have mailed you back that night to check how you were (I did mean to), but I got stuck at work until very late.

BUT WHY would I behave in the way you mention? I had not forced you in any way to come there.

This next bit is slightly corny… stupidly, I really enjoyed our fantasy chats (had withdrawal symptoms) and thought we did actually have a connection around the honesty, no hassle rules and what you wanted.

I was simply looking to give you a break from the norms of the tough job you do and family stresses. I wanted to treat you and, as you know, simply be your toy!!

I admit I was a little nervous (I don't see that as anything but complimentary – you are beautiful), but I also thought at times on that afternoon it really was rather intense between us?

I genuinely don't like the opinions you've been left with—can we not discuss face-to-face over dinner?"

Chapter 12

She waited outside Bar One—the bar where they had gone for that first fateful drink. She always liked to arrive early. She was about to reach for her phone to message the stranger when she saw him waddling towards her from the other side of the pedestrian bridge. He was dressed in his usual office attire accompanied by a thick, knitted cream sweater. He had clearly gained weight over Christmas. She could see the additional mass around his chin area as he walked towards her. Her heart sank just a little. Soon he was upon her and embraced her warmly and kissed both cheeks.

"Hi. It's so good to see you. I've been desperate to see you…" He steered her inside, and soon they were sitting opposite each other again.

He stared at her shyly unable to keep the smile from his face.

"Are you okay?"

"Yes, I'm good, thanks."

"How are the kids?"

She appreciated his interest. "They're fine, thank you…"

"Look, I've gotta admit, I was pretty perturbed by your insinuation that I gave you too much to drink."

"I'm still not entirely certain that that didn't happen." Cayenne was partially goading him.

"Are you serious?"
They looked at one another and simultaneously burst into uproarious laughter.

She was slightly taken aback at how comfortable she felt around him. She had expected to feel more guarded.

He updated her on what was happening at work. The changes taking place, the new bosses pulling strings and the uncertainty in his industry. He maintained the melancholy that he had expressed before and a deep sense of unfulfillment.

"Have you had any nights out yet?"

"No. My social life pretty much revolves around the gym really."

He was looking at her with that look of bewilderment again.

"Don't you go out with your friends?"

Cayenne was sure they had covered this topic the first time, but as it was several months ago, he must have forgotten. "Mmmm. Friends. I've always had trouble acquiring those."

"What do you mean? You have friends though, right? Surely?"

"Erm, not really. I mean…. How can I explain? I think I may have developed some trust issues early on, so it seems even when I have had opportunities to develop friendships, I seem to shy away from them. Well actually less shy away, and more accurately, sprint in the opposite direction; but then again to be completely honest, I love my own company. There isn't anyone's company that I enjoy more than my own." They both dissolved into laughter again. Though his laugh emoted a twinge of scepticism. She liked that they laughed easily together.

"I think friendship can often be a tad overrated. How about you? Do you have a lot of friends?" She recalled his previous answer, but decided to go with the 'covering-old-ground' theme.

He sat back in his chair, stretched his arms and linked them behind his head as he contemplated the answer.

"Yeah, I have a group of core friends that I communicate with regularly. I regard those as my real friends. I have a lot of associates as well. University will do that for you, as I've said before."

They paused as they sipped their drinks. During the pause, he looked directly at her, taking her in; so she sipped some more, thankful that her dark skin belied the burning red sensation emanating from her cheeks. She was suddenly aware of how hot she felt and shifted in her seat.

He clenched his jaw and narrowed his eyes and fixed them on her. "You are unbelievably brutal. All the messages I sent you. I mean did you get them, or did you just ignore them?"

She hid her smirk with the half-filled glass of wine in her hand.

"To be honest… I had no intention of responding. After we met at the hotel, I started to feel a little unwell just before I left."

"Yes, I seem to recall you messaging that you weren't feeling well. I should have followed up to see if you were okay. I meant to, but I just got caught up with work."

"It was a couple of days before you messaged after that."

"No, I messaged you the same day, later on, didn't I?"

She shook her head. She remembered scrolling through the emails and noticing the two-day gap before the onslaught began.

"Oh, I'm so sorry."

"Why are you apologising? It doesn't matter."

"Well, it does. I mean. I wish I had now. I'm sorry I made you feel uncomfortable. I actually had a really good time."

They laughed again. She noticed that their laughs seemed to mirror each other. They both tended to fall forwards with their mouths ajar, fully engaging in their humour.

"There's a memory that I cannot erase from my mind." He covered his mouth with his hand, as though what he was about to reveal was classified information. "I remember you standing naked in the bathroom and me slapping your arse—you're gorgeous, firm, round, tight arse." He looked bashful and gleeful all at once, cherishing the nostalgia.

"Was none of it enjoyable for you?" He was clearly having difficulty comprehending the juxtaposition.

She dipped her head slightly and shrugged as if to concede. "Well… I suppose now that you mention it, there were moments."

He smiled appreciatively. She sensed that this meant something to him. That he really cared that he had managed to provide some enjoyment for her too.

"Let me…," he paused examining her body language closely, as though he daren't set himself up for rejection again or risk offending her, pre-empting another lengthy cut off.

She gave away no apprehension and looked up into his eyes. His gaze softened too, and his shoulders dropped as though released from incarcerating tension. There was a pleading in his eyes.

"Can I…? I'd like to try again. It really doesn't sit well with me that you were left with the impression that you have. Give me a chance to put that right."

As convincing as his argument was, Cayenne simply wasn't sure. The whole thing had weirded her out, which is why she was able to ignore his emails for so long. The memory actually gave her chills. He seemed upset when he heard this but reasoned, she could have blocked the emails, and for whatever reason had chosen not to. Perhaps there was a margin, a very slight margin…

"Look. If you don't want to, I'll understand. I'd be happy to have a glass of wine with you every once in a while. Just sitting opposite you makes me feel good. Perhaps I can treat you to a meal."

She blinked hard, wanting to say no, but she heard herself say, "I don't want to go back to that hotel. I found it a little creepy for some reason."

"Why don't you choose?"

"I'm assuming the high-end terms of the agreement still stand?" More laughter.

"Of course. Only the best for the Queen."

Chapter 13

Cayenne and the stranger were now communicating regularly by email. She wasn't quite sure why they hadn't exchanged numbers. She recalled that she had been the one to stipulate that they enter into the agreement casually, and that there was really no need to give too many details about each other. He clearly relished this idea too.

She suspected that he may have some complication in his life, but then he could suspect the same of her, and that most certainly wasn't true. She decided not to jump to conclusions. He had confirmed that he was unmarried and had no children. She gauged that he must be around the same age as her. An age where most men would have at least attempted starting a family by now. She was beginning to get the impression that he was one of those men that always thought things through and procrastinated every one of life's milestones. He had probably talked himself out of getting married and having children for years, telling himself that he was waiting for the right moment and assessing the pros and cons.

Cayenne was enjoying the excitement he gave her. Whenever she received an email, she would beam even before she had read it; and for some inexplicable reason, she began to really explore her sexual imagination like never before. She was able to express herself completely, and this opened up areas that had thus far remained dormant.

She had made her preferences for venues clear, having decided that Greenwich was too close to home. He had offered escapism, therefore, to select somewhere further afield would allow her to feel as though she was really escaping into another world. For convenience, it had to be Central London; furthermore, he had offered luxury, so surely no less than a four-star hotel would suffice.

She had forwarded some suggestions, but in the end wanted him to decide and take charge in order to add to the thrill and sense of subterfuge.

He had said to leave it with him, and that he would sort out the finer details. She would receive instructions as to the location and times and dates. In the meantime, they wasted no time in speculating as to what the proceedings might entail.

"MMMM… I want you to open your legs and let me crawl over to you… and taste."

"I'm not particularly flexible, so when I open my legs, you may need to apply pressure …
Pressure to my inner thighs… and I find that if you elevate my buttocks from beneath, this can aid flexibility."

She soon became daring enough to post him pictures of her bare bottom or posing in backless tops exposing a panty-less tush.

"Naughty girl. I think you need a spanking… you look utterly delicious. I need to taste it."

"I've decided that I have to be very particular about the tasting. I have to be very specific here." She was recalling his unpleasant, juvenile licking technique.
"I want a specific balance of sensitive, tentative, exploration and passionate hungry aggression. It is imperative that the taster is so engrossed in his chosen delicacy that he barely comes up for air…
Any insecure looks seeking approval MUST be avoided. Single-minded focus towards climatic euphoria is essential."

Later that night, the conversation continued.

"Still awake to discuss? I wouldn't stop … your pleasure is my only priority."

"Mmm, I was just lying here fantasising. I need to be satisfied."

"You do have such a gorgeous ass…
I will definitely supply the combination you require. You know how hungry I am… how desperate… feed me… I'm thinking about you and hardening… I can't wait to dress you in sexy lingerie, something that shows off that long, gorgeous black body."
She closed her eyes and allowed her hands to follow the yearning between her legs.

She required no saliva lubrication tonight. Her imagination had obliged plentifully until the bed beneath her was damp. He was delighted to hear this.

"I wish I could see. I want you to feed me."

"I want marathon tongue teasing first… feeding must be earned."

"It is only right that you get what you want. Did you come hard?"

"The climax was devilishly and deliciously intense. An absolutely necessary release.
Of course, I must get what I want, or what would be the point. It seems I have been lured out of my solitude… now you must fulfil every tantalising promise for fear … into seclusion I return."

"I am hungry for you and utterly desperate to please…
I want my face straddled by your wet chocolate pussy. I want to smell and taste your juice."

"I pictured you watching just now. Taken aback by the ferocity of my orgasm, you were gripping my body in a bid to connect."

"Wish I'd watched… like a voyeur … not allowed to touch as punishment."

"I will accept nothing less than desperate hunger, for only then will my pussy respond."

"You like the brutal power and control you have over me, my desperate need to win you back."

"I must enforce punishment… your sanction… you may only watch from afar as I indulge myself."

"I'm secretly quietly stroking with my left hand and writing to you with my right hand, whilst the rest of the house sleeps totally unaware of my desperate need for what you offer."

This was the first real indication of the possible complications that she suspected were lurking. What household was he referring to? If not a wife then a live-in partner perhaps. His description alluded to more than one person. So if they weren't his children, were they hers? Or could he simply be referring to extended family?

She decided not to ponder any further.

"What wretched torture is now upon you?"

"So bad, brutal punishment. I always try to catch your eyes, but your knowledge that I am so desperate and hungry only serves to heighten your own indulgence. So where can I indulge you further?"

"Mayfair."

"I want to disappear into your warm mouth again.
Sleep well, bad girl… I've been tortured enough tonight. Invite me 'round to discuss plans."

Cayenne suddenly felt cold. Aha! Had he no real intention of taking her on the high-end voyage that he had described. Why was he inviting himself 'round to her home? The distasteful essence returned to her mouth.
Her tone grew immediately hostile. "Would you invite ME 'round to discuss plans? I fear and suspect that alas this is simply yet another disappointing goose chase. Enjoyable though it was …into oblivion I once again scurry, never to be tempted out again by juvenile folly."

"No, no!!! Not at all. I'm getting ahead of myself in wanting a taste… Bad boy. Let me take my punishment. Let's meet at Agent Provocateur and take it from there."

Cayenne had switched off her phone in annoyance. It was only the next morning that she was aware of his pleading.

"Hey!!! I am SERIOUS about Mayfair.
Are you there???
Oh God, no. Not a brutal cut off again.
Hey, when can we meet to discuss the shopping spree I promised?

YOU ARE SIMPLY A NIGHTMARE—I will do whatever you need.

DO NOT SCUTTLE AWAY.

Do you not think you torture me enough? Don't throw me away again because of one bad line.

This is nightmarish for someone so fucking desperate to taste and please you and be your toy.

HEY!"

Chapter 14

"AGENT P AND MAYFAIR HOTEL.
 Meet me at the Mayfair Hotel at 1:00 p.m.
 DO NOT TORTURE ME WITH NON-ATTENDANCE.

 AAAAAARGGGGGGGHHH!!!!
 I am in a void, deranged and tortured …
 You visited me in my dreams to enhance my insanity…
 You tied my hands and pleasured yourself incessantly in front of me, first with your fingers, then toys, then with another man's cock…
 I am hungry and fucking desperate to please you.
 My mouth is arid and dry and can only be satiated with your juice; your wet, black pussy juice …
 I need my chance to please you, to entertain you as desired…
 The lingerie, the dinner, the champagne, the seduction…
 GIVE IT TO ME OR THE BARRAGE OF PERSEVERANCE WILL BE LIKE NOTHING YOU HAVE SEEN."

"How could I resist such a masterful command?"

"You made your point. I will deliver"

"It was fortunate that I hadn't put on my crotchless ensemble this morning. Your command may have caused an inconvenience."

"Did I soak your thong instead?"

"Let's just say, thank goodness I was close to home."

"Where will you be at one-ish. Can we meet?"

"Clearly the anticipation is proving too much for you. Where would you like me to be at 1:00?"

"Chiquito, North Greenwich. 12:15 to 12:30 would be helpful…

Fine fare, fine wine, discreet bar, DO NOT WEAR PANTIES!"

By the time Cayenne walked into the colourful Mexican restaurant, she wasn't quite sure what was causing her upper thighs to moisten. Was it the moisturising cocoa butter oil that she had used after showering, or was it perspiration from the mad lunchtime rush, or was it something else?

Kenneth or Jon looked casually handsome as he waited in the half-empty rustic bar downstairs. She needn't have worn a garment as she decided to keep her overcoat fastened the entire time. A flush of self-consciousness no doubt. But that didn't prevent the stranger from getting better acquainted with the fabric of her outfit, paying particular attention to what lay beneath.

They followed the Portuguese waiter up a small flight of wooden stairs to a discreet dining area surrounded with dark, wood-panelled walls and a brown leather booth which curved angularly to form an intimate cocoon. Shortly afterwards, the waiter presented them with the menu, and they quickly decided on a shared starter of fully loaded nachos.

She thoroughly enjoyed her spicy chicken with cranberry salsa, whilst her companion amorously sampled the caramel condiments now lining her skirt. At times she was chewing seductively in complete synchronicity with the stroking of her clit. They continued their coordinated dance—hers above sea level, his entirely beneath—until both were satisfied. Cayenne could scarcely recall a time when she had been fed simultaneously to being emptied. What a marvellous correlation it was too.

Chapter 15

The black lady behind the counter had a long, bright blonde Beyoncé-esque wig on and impeccable makeup. After eyeing up Cayenne from across the floor, she approached bearing a friendly smile.

"Y'alright, luv? Lookin' for any'in in particular?"

She had a thick Liverpool accent which didn't quite fit with her image.

Cayenne loved imitating accents which had caused her to develop a particular skill for it. She had to bite her lip not to launch into her best Liverpudlian drawl.

"Erm, yeah. Kind of. I'm going out to a fancy restaurant. I love your accent by the way."

"Oh, thanks. No guessing where I'm from, eh? Were you thinkin' of sutten full-length or shorte'?"

"Not full-length. Preferably something fitted, yet forgiving. And I've decided to go for black."

"Right. Let me show you this one we've got over 'ere. You can feel the quality from how heavy it is. It is bodycon, buuuu', it's not ultra-tight, d'you know what I mean?"

Cayenne observed the dress which at first didn't appear particularly striking or impressive. Upon further inspection, she could see that it was simple but with a classical edge. It was ribbed, and the sleeves flared out slightly. It was short but not too short, and it had a v-neck which she wasn't altogether sure would complement her small bosom.

"Can I try it on?"

"Of course you can, let me show you to the changing rooms."

Cayenne followed Scouse Beyoncé towards the back of the store, which was as glamorous as the shop floor with its dark brown walls and carpet and gold drapes and mirrors. Cayenne stepped into the dress without removing the gym gear that she was clad in. She was pleased to see that it accentuated her waist whilst leaving a little room to spare. The length was just right, and the v-neck more flattering than she had imagined. The unusual sleeves gave the outfit an extra elegant touch. Perfect and reasonably priced to boot, she decided. Sasha Fierce proceeded to gift wrap the dress, as though it was being prepared for royalty, carefully folding it with the security strap intact, to be removed by the new owner at their leisure, then placing the package delicately into a peach-coloured gift box which was then adorned with a strip of mint coloured ribbon. It looked so beautiful it would have made a perfect gift. And it was... Only to herself.

A few days before the scheduled appointment with the stranger, the bubbles of excitement couldn't be contained. She even made a quick trip to Stratford to her favourite hair shop to see if she could improve upon her current wig. Pity, she hadn't asked Sasha where she'd purchased hers.
She made sure to book some extra classes at the gym so that she would feel extra confident on the day.
She was enjoying using weights and finding out how strong she was. She had managed to deadlift 115kg in the strongman class and found she was able to shoulder press more weight than most of the women there. The result was the sharp definition beginning to form in her arms and back. She loved going home and showing off her newly honed muscles to her children who considered her boasts amusingly distasteful.

When the all-important email arrived to inform her of the details of their meeting, Cayenne felt like a child at Christmas. That was until she read it fully. The excitement soon turned to bafflement when she looked at the destination that he had booked.

"Hilton Canary Wharf.
The suite is booked for the 9th.

Just make sure you are available to indulge yourself."

Her eyes narrowed with contempt. What had happened to Mayfair and Agent Provocateur, the Champagne and shopping spree? And hadn't she stipulated that the venue was to be away from her immediate vicinity. Canary Wharf Hilton was but a stone throw from her home. That would hardly feel like escapism.

She knew that he had written the message in a deliberately forthright manner, perhaps in the hope that she might be dissuaded from challenging it. He was either the type of personality that was used to being in control, making decisions and expecting people to fall in line, or he was hoping that she wasn't. He was subtly exercising his perceived authority. She interpreted his dismissal of her request as failure to comprehend her value.

"Dear Mr Disingenuous,
You CANNOT unilaterally alter the terms of our verbal contract.
Please refer to previous correspondence.
Terms.

1. Escapism from usual environment (hotel on the doorstep does not serve this purpose).
2. Shopping, dinner, Champagne and seduction (provided your skills have improved somewhat). In that order.
3. My pleasure and happiness MUST be paramount.
4. Exciting new experiences as respite from the humdrum.

It is clear to me that your sincerity with regard to these points is in question.

I find your casual disregard for my plans, at such short notice, abhorrent. It is unfortunate that you did not place sufficient value upon our chance meeting as it first appeared.
I have no doubt that you will experience absolutely no hardship in securing alternative chocolate fancies to enjoy at the Hilton. Indulge and good Luck! (They'll need it.)"

"Oh, Fuck!
Completely ignore the Hilton plan... I thought it suited you!!! I've cancelled.

I was simply trying to be masterful.

Okay, points made. I will amend the itinerary with a more appropriate plan aligned to you and a venue of your choice.

Please disregard previous plan.

Please make your way to Knightsbridge.

Agent Provocateur will be followed by cocktails."

"I am seething at your obvious tendency to devalue me.

Your audacity deeply astounds me.

I refuse to be dismissed as a mere distraction from the pressure of work that can only be utilised between the convenient hours of 12:00 through 2:00 p.m., as though I am somehow underqualified to receive qualitative attention.

Might I suggest that should you continue to lurk lewdly beneath the underbelly of the wharf, eventually you will solicit just the kind of simpleton you so obviously desire…who will fall for your disingenuous offers which come disguised as wanting to 'please' whilst you are fully intending to concentrate purely on your own personal greed.

Perhaps you should station yourself near some sort of immigration service where undoubtedly, queues of unsuspecting ethnics emerge who would prove ideal candidates with which to fulfil your every chocolate fantasy.

They would surely fall for your counterfeit 'high-end' promises and be so duly flattered by the prospect of fine-dining and escapism.

I am clearly of higher calibre than the prey you were hoping to snare, as I remain completely unbeguiled by your below par attempts to impress.

I wish you every success in your continued endeavours to indulge your fetishism for the seduction of minorities.

As for me, I shall continue my pursuit of an earnest Caucasian that longs for a Nubian Queen, whom he sincerely holds in the highest regard.

Perhaps I'll try Mayfair."

Cayenne laughed at herself when she re-read the message. Yes, she had been a little offended by his oversight, but where had all this vitriol come from. Was she simply humouring herself and taking advantage of his willing nature?

She put her phone down to recharge the battery and resolved to think no more of Mayfair for the rest of the weekend.

Chapter 16

"Wow, happy weekend to you too…
This is a brutal thesis and requires a proper response, and there will be one.
Devaluation of your character was never the intent, and I'm hurt you think this is so.
I am drafting a full refute.
Leaving that to one side, are you being entertained by an appropriate squeeze?"

Cayenne was touched by his response. She could sense his sincerity, and she was most impressed that he considered her message worthy of a 'proper response'. Her hardened heart softened just a little.

"No, for some inexplicable reason… you are consuming my thoughts. I'll put a stop to that."

"Good.
I still want a taste. You tormented me again last night. This time I was tied up watching you writhe in absolute pleasure as a woman tasted you.
I was dry. Desperate for your juice.
Are you okay? I am sorry that I am not the complete solution for you.
I think you are very impressive."

"Typically, you consider five lines a 'full refute'. Is it a coincidence that this is not the only occasion that your perceived delivery far outweighs your initial promise?"

"Cheeky bitch!

No, the full refute hasn't come yet."

"Where have I heard that before. You were never meant to be a full solution.
We shared a glass of wine in the Wharf, you were having a particularly bad time at work, supposedly.
Perhaps we should have left it there. Often in life, the very thought of something is better than the reality."

"I do like you though and your damning indictment of me has a number of scary truths."

"I wondered whether you would recognise yourself in any of it. There are plenty more tropical fish in the sea."

"Nah not bothered, as the three month estrangement showed.
You have a skill with words, you wrote very well.
I still think that we could explore our sexual desires in tandem."

"Anything is possible."

"We both have a side to us that you don't find often."

"Affirmative."

"We need to do something with that.
You were very wet at lunch. That can't be denied."

"What can I say. I was turned on."

"What colour were the panties that I told you not to wear?"

"Red with black lacing."

"Perfect. I wanted to get inside them."

"I know. Such promise."

"We are NOT done… let's explore."

"What makes you so confident?"

"Because I am more than happy to be your toy."

"I did consider experimenting with toys, though I had the artificial kind in mind."

"Experiment and use ME."

"If you insist. That's an awfully kind gesture allowing me to take out all of my pent-up frustration on you."

"Fuck me! Use me, indulge yourself. Exploit whatever dark desires you have."

"As you wish."

"I'm desperate for it… I want to see you cum. I want to make you cum. I want to be your dirty little secret that engages in all your dubious fantasies. You will know mine."

"I'm soaking wet right now. Have been most of the day. I'd probably cum in an instant."

"Do it…"

"Do you promise to lick my pussy incessantly? If I promise to open really wide, would you solemnly swear to bury your head between my legs and endlessly nuzzle?
Would you???"

"Yes-yes-yes. I want it. I want to taste it. Open wide and wet. I want my tongue to tease you first before diving in. I will be so desperate to please. I need my fix."

"I shan't be responsible for how drenched you may get. I trust that is okay?"

"I will not stop until you release.
Until you fucking orgasm on my face.
Until I taste your black juice.
Until you are satisfied.
I'm your bitch. I want to be covered."

"I'm not sure you're ready for the deluge of richness."

"I need my second blacking… do it… drench me. I want your black pussy juice on my hard white cock."

At first, Cayenne was a little taken aback by his choice of words. Blacking? It sounded strange to her ears.

"I want to shower in it, I want the smell of it."

"You will be utterly saturated."

"Feed me your wet black, juicy pussy."

"I can hardly wait to relish your hot tongue teasing my clit."

"Do you like having such an available slut?"

"I will feed you."

"Heavenly. You won't have witnessed such desperate hunger… all about YOU… all about giving you a release.
I'm a dog on heat in your company.
A dirty whore.
I need your black pussy juice."

"I only hope that you don't tire before I am satisfied. Desperate hunger from you will only serve to create more juice. I've never had my pussy licked until my heart's content. Be my first."

"You know exactly what I am, what I get off on. What I go out looking for…
You know how I am desperate to please you, so I get fed…
I harden at the idea of having my face straddled and suffocated by your wet moist black cunt that I have to lick out for as long as you desire and need.
My white cock is so hard."

Cayenne suddenly felt a twinge of something that she didn't like at his comment; it jolted her back to reality again. Here was a man that regularly went out looking for something. Was this something she should be concerned about? Was he inferring that his search would continue? Why did that bother her? Whatever it was she was feeling, clearly fuelled her next statement…

"Perhaps I'll go out looking for the same. Maybe we can go out looking together."
He must have picked up on her sudden burst of terseness.

"I was referring to your damning thesis. Now that you mention it, does it spark interest?"

"What?"

"An orgy… a threesome?"

She wondered whether this was a serious question, or was he exhibiting a little fear of his own.

"No. Though perhaps I can be persuaded to scale Knightsbridge seeking adventure."

"Horrible image cheeky. I couldn't behave like this or reveal such depravity with just anyone you know."

"You do seem to have a knack of putting your foot in it and pissing me off at the most inopportune moments. I think I may have to gag you just as I'm about to climax, as you're bound to say something that will make me go cold."

"Goodnight gorgeous. I'm going to dream that I got fed your juices. Don't worry, nothing will get said to stop you. You need to climax!!!"

"I shall be incandescent with rage should you interrupt my release."

"Wouldn't expect anything less gorgeous. Sleep well."

Chapter 17

The email had requested her to meet him at Green Park Tube Station at 2:00 p.m. on Wednesday.

"I want you wet with anticipation."

"That's a given, which makes it all the more risky that I won't be wearing panties."

"How evil and delicious will it be when you push my face and mouth into your wetness for my next taste of your black chocolate pussy juice."

"Now now. First, you must wait whilst I initiate as you watch. Only meander towards me when you can take no more. I insist on slow and controlled licks, both exploratory and for my pleasure. Finally… after I burst with unrestrained passion… bury yourself… disappear until you become molten in my chocolate furnace."

"Don't worry, I want to be a voyeur first to heighten my need."

"Absolutely. Don't forget I am accustomed to pleasuring myself. Introduce this new dimension to me slowly"

"I am hard with anticipation at what the next meeting will bring."

"I too am tingling with excitement. Wait until you see my dress."

"May I ask what colour it is?"

"Black, fitted and sexy."

"Naturally. Mmmm, remembering how good it felt putting my hands on your legs at the Gaucho lunch, knowing what was nearby, desperate to inch closer. Such dirty reckless behaviour."

"Yeah. I liked it too as I am sure you could tell."

"I will have to find a discreet setting."

"Yes, our intimacy must be closely guarded."

"Are you aware of how corrupt and bad you have made me?"

"No. I am only aware that you are going to drool all over me tomorrow."

"That's all you need to know."

Wednesday 9th

"Good morning"

"Good morning."

"Getting ready?"

Later when Cayenne arrived at Green Park Underground Station, she realised that there were at least three exits. She messaged the stranger.
"Any particular exit? I seem to have intuitively gravitated towards the Palace."

"I'll be there in a few minutes."

"Heading back to the main street. Too many pigeons at this end. One must ensure my courtiers do something about this."
Cayenne stood outside the station at the opposite exit, where a coach was boarding as a small crowd congregated. She wasn't yet

familiar with the inner city and savoured the life energy all around, seeing inspiration in all the activity around her. She caught sight of the stranger, who was predictably straddling the balance of office attire and smart casual tones. She presumed that he must have unloaded the rest of his attire and baggage at the hotel already.

"Good afternoon, my Queen."

He leaned in and kissed both cheeks. His facial expression let her know that the effort she had gone to was much appreciated.

He offered to carry her bag. She declined but noted that he was a kind of gentleman. He took her arm and guided her across the busy main road, in the direction, she was to discover, of the Mayfair hotel. He had mentioned earlier that he had already booked a table for lunch.

The reception area was buzzing with crowds of people coming in and out. The restaurant too was busy, although it was close to closing time for the afternoon, so gradually most of the tables became vacant. Unfortunately, this also meant that there wasn't a great deal of variety available in the kitchen.

"I've ordered some tapas. Do you like tapas?"

"Erm... not really. I think I tried it once during my travels around Europe. If I'm not mistaken, it's not really a cuisine that appeals to black people. But it's okay. I'm happy to try it again."

His face dropped, forlorn infiltrating his features. "Oh no."

"No, really it's okay."

"Are you sure? We can go somewhere else."

"Not at all, it's fine." She couldn't deny she was enjoying his focused intention to keep her happy.

When the tapas arrived, it did nothing to change her first impression, and even the chips had clearly not been prepared fresh. The squid looked unappetising and overdone. The hotel had attempted to be economical and quartered the scallops. To add insult to injury, they had saturated the scallops in some sort of acidic vinaigrette laced with an undefinable herb which, if intended to enhance the flavour, was failing miserably. The mini burgers were perfectly average and unexceptional. Cayenne would never profess to be an expert on authentic Spanish cuisine; however, she was quite certain that this was not it.

She got the distinct impression that their late arrival had conveniently provided the near-closing kitchen an opportunity to discard of whatever leftovers that the lunch period had produced.

She had built up in her mind that the Mayfair Hotel would be an extravagant experience from start to finish.

She glanced over at the stranger who was devouring his meal as though it had been prepared by Michel Roux Jr himself. Not a hint of distaste was visible on his face, and Cayenne almost choked when he asked expectantly… "Try the scallops? What do you think?"

This clearly wasn't a good start.

"The burgers are okay," he commented, chewing avidly, absent-mindedly, unconsciously.

"Erm, a little tasteless I thought. I can't seem to detect any seasoning."

His face dropped again. He seemed very sensitive to her response to things.

She wondered whether he usually ate without really expecting flavour. It must be a white thing, she reasoned. She considered whether his acceptance of what was offered, as though to receive anything at all is all one can expect, was an attitude that he applied to his life. Why expect more?

She drained the wine from her glass. He had ordered white again. She couldn't help but feel sorely disappointed with the Mayfair offerings.

They rose from the table, and she walked towards the reception area whilst he took care of the bill. Once he had joined her, they headed up to their suite which turned out to be rather small and basic.

Had he really wanted to impress her, he could have chosen better.

She questioned whether it could even be legitimately described as a suite. The curtains, which were beige with deep burgundy swirls, were tightly shut which made the space feel even smaller. The walls were beige too as was the velvet throw that covered the queen-sized bed. There was a large desk that ran alongside one wall which had a small safe built into it. A kettle and a selection of cups, saucers and spoons were nestled on a tray alongside a dish containing packets of tea, coffee, sugar and milk. A smaller desk by the window was adorned with the usual array of hotel stationery, with a smaller selection on each of the bedside tables.

Before she could put her bag and coat down on the chair, he appeared behind her and clamped her head in his hands, turned her towards him and stuck his tongue into her mouth mercilessly. Each stroke was clearly not meant for her pleasure.

She felt uncomfortable and cold. Erotically cold. Completely turned off. His approach was abrupt and unsensual. How did he get away with this in his real life? She would expect this kind of behaviour if she were a mature cougar in the company of a teenager or some kind of opportunistic gigolo. After his masterful embrace, he disappeared into the bathroom looking decidedly pleased with himself. He turned to throw her a glance before the bathroom door closed behind him as if to assure her 'don't worry, there's more to come'. She hoped her face offered him a 'I-can-hardly-wait' expression and hoped even more that it appeared believable.

Before long, they were lounging on the bed in their courtesy white robes.

"So what is it about your job that you're not enjoying anymore?"

He sighed a heavy-weighted sigh, "I don't know. I stopped enjoying it a long time ago. I think I may just need a change. A new challenge. In fact, I was speaking to an old colleague today about a possible transfer to New York. Would you come and see me out there?"

"New York? Is that a real possibility?"

"Well, my old boss has a company out there, and I did send him a discreet email some months ago. It's something I could possibly follow-up. But then again, I'm not sure that's the answer. I've got…"

He paused a lengthy pause as though contemplating how much to share.

"I've got responsibilities. You know family stuff."

She recalled some of the details of their earlier conversations and remembered how concerned he had appeared about being solely responsible for his elderly parents.

He dipped his head and soothed himself by fingering his hair.

"Does the family tend to rely on you a lot then?"

His deep sigh provided the answer. She guessed he would probably feel disloyal saying anymore. She wondered whether he was so accustomed to letting life happen to him and not standing up for himself, that this had contributed to his discontentment. Rather, he had allowed it to be of other people's making. Whilst on the surface, he appeared to be a high flying executive, to a lesser degree, she could see that he was the kind of soft soul that would allow people to bulldoze their ideas and then privately grimace and stress about it later. A trait that he clearly hadn't grown out of in his formative years. She couldn't help but wonder how this played out in his working life. Hadn't he claimed to have some sort of managerial role, making mention of his 'team'. Perhaps in the working environment, he was able to assert himself whereas it was still a challenge in private. She could just imagine him getting home at the end of the day and breathing a sigh of relief that he had managed to pull it off one more time.

She decided to lighten the mood. The last thing she wanted to do was add to his stresses.

"So, I have a magic wand." She bolted upright and pointed an imaginary magical instrument in the air. "I can wave it, and you can become anything you want. What would it be?"

"I don't know; a movie star?" There was little hesitation, and Cayenne was impressed that he had been brave enough to share that with her, as she was sure it wasn't something he would usually reveal. And why didn't his choice of career surprise her?—judging by his theatrical performance in North Greenwich. The poised plié, the constant tossing of the hair, the hideously feminine popping of the hip, the counterfeit swagger and the Hollywood drawl—come to think of it, he was acting every day of his life.
"But I've also always harboured a desire to enter the political arena."

"Really?"

"Yeah. It's always interested me."

Somehow, judging by the look in his eye, she wasn't buying it. It was most likely something he had heard out of the mouth of someone that he held in high regard.

"So would you consider it… I mean seriously?"

"I'd love to." He began to frown, and she could almost hear his inner demons stripping away at his confidence. "But then I think, you know I've got a good job, earning good money that affords me to do things like this." He stroked her arm, tugging her towards him.

As she melted into the nook of his torso, she felt a calmness that she had managed a slight glimpse of the real him.

After much kissing and touching, she could finally begin to feel the stirrings of sexual desire returning. The warmth of expectation slowly thawing the core of her erogenous zone. He stood and slipped out of his robe and pulled off his boxer shorts, which she noted were fairly nondescript for a wealthy city accountant. They looked rather like the ones that she sourced as new cleaning cloths when her son's boxer shorts were beginning to look worse for wear, and the current cleaning material was in short supply. Bland and shapeless, much like the owner.

"I'm creaming my pants. This is so embarrassing." His glasses were steaming up, so he took them off and placed them on the bedside table. He was clearly bemused by the intoxicating rush of her presence but confused by the juxtaposing effect on his libido.

But even though there were parts of him that evoked acute nausea, she was sufficiently enticed by now to want a closer inspection of his cock. He was generously endowed, a fact he was immensely proud of which clearly fuelled his shameless strut around the room trying to sustain his firmness which was threatening to soften with delirium.

He clambered over her again cursing himself as he tried to stem the leakage from his penis. "I can't stop it… I don't understand, this doesn't usually happen."

She reassured him that it was okay and pulled his head down to the opening of her robe. The warmth of his tongue on her pussy made her arch her back with delight. She opened her legs wide to allow him further access. Her eyes were rolling back in her head as she relaxed into his rhythm. When he pulled away, she was sure it was to position himself to heighten her pleasure.

"Oh God. I'm so sorry. I've come."

He reached for his robe and used it to soak up the flow of arousal that was pouring out from him.

He was embarrassed and frustrated, but Cayenne could clearly see puzzlement in his expression as though he wasn't accustomed to this level of sexual intensity. She found herself wondering if his response would be similar if he happened to encounter a properly prepared, seasoned and well-executed scallop, oozing with its unique natural flavours as opposed to customarily accepting wholly inadequate replicas. Whether an authentic platter of tapas would derail him. Whether his eyes would pop out of his head with wonder at the realisation that life had more to offer. There were other levels.

He continued to compensate her with his tongue, taking her on a journey into the depths of her abdominals until she released her own juices as her body soared towards an orgasmic crescendo. There was barely a trace remaining after he had feasted at the mouth of her cunt.

Afterwards, they lay in each other's arms as she listened to him berating himself for his inability to delay his ejaculation, which only served to feed her sense of betrayal. Cheated of a fine-dining experience. Cheated of authentic haute cuisine tapas. Cheated of an executive suite. Cheated of penetration. Cheated of the ultimate orgasm.

"You're welcome to stay overnight. I can try and come back tomorrow and finish what I started.

She paused considering that the children would be expecting her back that evening. He mistook her delay for discontent.

"I'm so sorry."

"I won't stay over because the children will be expecting me, but I may come back tomorrow."

"I will make it up to you."

All throughout the journey home, whirling around her mind as she greeted the children, etching into her memory as she showered and changed into her own comfortable bathrobe, all throughout the meal the children had left for her; and whilst she set the apartment straight in preparation for the next hectic morning, she pondered exactly what she would say, and how to let him down gently without permeating his ego further. His ego which was both delicate and exalted all at once.

"I honestly believe that you are a great guy…
Very sweet and sincere, and I am impressed with your resilience when not many people can withstand the force of nature that is Cayenne Richards. You even laugh at my humour at your own expense. Believe me, that is rare. I'll actually miss that a little and your daily emails. But I feel, at this early stage, it would be prudent to finish on a high (of sorts) while we still like each other. Whilst we can still sift good memories from the fray.

How's that for honesty? Farewell my friend."

A good night's sleep did nothing to pacify her sexual frustration.
After the school run, she marched directly to the DLR Station and began her single-minded trek with a forthright demeanour that parted the crowds in her wake. Destination?… Mayfair.

Chapter 18

He had left his electronic door key behind when he left the hotel. It was still on the bedside table where he had placed it alongside some screwed up receipts and an unused packet of condoms. The discarded towels and soiled robes lay where they left them, and the bed remained a dishevelled vision of unfulfilled desire.

As it was still early, and she hadn't had breakfast, she decided to order some from room service hoping that the hotel kitchen fared better than the Spanish restaurant downstairs.

Thirty minutes later, she opened the door and stepped aside as the waitress, dressed in a black full-length garment with a white apron tied around her waist with an embroidered white cap covering her hair, wheeled a large food trolley past her and proceeded to dismantle it to reveal a hidden table.

Cayenne cast an approving eye over the delicacies before her. Slices of wholemeal toast stood upright alongside a small dish of an assortment of butter, honey, jams and marmalade.

A small pot of hot chocolate awaited its creamy component. The waitress lifted the steel dome which was covering a large porcelain plate to reveal a generously portioned omelette, which only hinted at the creamy cheese and wilting spinach that lay within its fold. The aroma reached her nostrils and assured her stomach that a treat was in store. She wasn't disappointed. The perfectly cooked protein melted in her mouth.

She spent the rest of the morning watching an interview on the sports channel, where a former boxing champ was reliving his momentous career and reflecting on the challenges that he had overcome, but she deliberately avoided wasting time on mindless viewing. As she was flicking through the luxury magazines that were piled at the end of the desk, she began to feel peckish again.

It didn't take much deliberation for her to decide upon beef Carpaccio and Caesar salad, followed by an Angus beef steak with a side of creamy mash with chives and a large glass of Baron de 'L' Pouilly-Fume, Ladoucette. Perhaps she could learn to appreciate white wine after all.

She was feeling so fully recompensed for the previous night's disappointment that by the time she heard a faint knock on the door, she had little need for any executive contribution.

She kept him waiting long enough to require a second knock and sauntered at her leisure to let him in. His eyes lit up when he saw her, and she knew instantly that he had come fully prepared to reimburse any previous failure. She deliberately flexed her glutes as she strode back to the upright chair next to the desk and she could feel his goggling eyes from behind, checking out her tight black trousers and embroidered vest top. She sat down seductively, draping one leg over the arm of the chair, both for comfort and his torture. He complimented her on the maroon choker around her neck, and how it enhanced the burgundy stain of her lips, which he seemed unable to draw his gaze away from.

She fixed her face firmly as he began to walk towards her, confirming to him non-verbally that matters were not about to proceed as expected, and that sanctions had been put in place in light of his doomed attempt towards her fulfilment.

The look of shock remained on his face for the rest of his time there. The two-hour slot that he had managed to secure away from the office in order to rush into Central London from Canary Wharf, and attempt the seemingly unattainable task of satisfying her mounting need, was now rendered grossly insufficient.

She remained resolute right up until he slipped reluctantly out of the door to return back to work. His eyes lingering in the hope that she would relent and allow him one last caress. One last kiss, a sympathy hug.

Her parting gaze was as cold as her unspent libido. Facing the closed mahogany door for only a second, she considered how best to spend the final hour before she was due to vacate the room.

Pulling back the heavy curtains, she put the kettle on to boil and helped herself to a cup of Mayfair coffee and a packet of shortbread from the minibar, savouring the buttery crumble as she watched the Mayfair citizens bustling through the streets below.

The stranger would have been long gone by now, but yet still, her eyes were cast intently, just in case they happened upon a luckless soul, with downcast mien, floppy hair hanging hopelessly over a furrowed brow, disconsolate eyes hidden behind clouded glasses. Shoulders hunched in despair. The doormen must surely have blinked a double take from their sight as an inward bounding Man of Steel, full of vigour and heroic enthusiasm would have re-emerged from the rotating doors shortly thereafter, the tail of his Clark Kent frock coat wedged firmly between his legs.

Chapter 19

Several days passed without her checking her emails.

"Okay. I'm not liking this deja vu sensation—the threat of that brutal cut off.
I am your bitch, I am your white slut. Can you not see what you achieved the other day? I was on the brink of giving it all to you. The thinking was done, I was seduced and utterly corrupted.
THE ONLY THING THAT STOPPED ME WAS THAT AFTER THREE HOURS OF PLAY... I COULDN'T HOLD.
I am fucking annoyed I didn't fuck you. Especially when I had you wide open in front of me...
I don't now need further torture!!

I'm now sadly back to reality... no Mayfair pad to run to today!"

"I know. Cast your mind back and enjoy the memory. Contrary to your opinion, I wasn't cutting you off. Rather, I have managed to carve out a life that I don't have a desperate need to escape from, and I was enjoying it."

"I'm still reeling from the harsh non-touch policy you inflicted on me."

"Was it harsh? Surely it's a human reaction to protect oneself from further disappointment."

"Ha-ha, yes, I suppose it makes complete sense...
Having you there... Available like that...aaaarrrrrggghhh!"

"I know. My very essence will haunt you forevermore."

"Claridges next?"

"I love a man who pulls out the big guns."

"So there is a way of tempting you back into bed…
This addiction is not easy!!!"

"Changing the subject, I've just got an email that I may have managed to secure some work for the Easter and summer holidays.
Finding work in the limited school hours is difficult, so that's good news.
To answer your question… with a man of your stealth and resilience, I'd imagine it would be an absolute breeze."

"Hey, well done—is it local?"

"Yes. It's to co-ordinate school holiday play/activities at St Peter's Catholic School. Very convenient too."

"Good stuff—seriously well done."

"Aah, thank you."

Cayenne was touched by how pleased he seemed for her; she sensed genuine care.

She had been sent a random email advertising the school holiday vacancy and had decided there would be no harm in trying, even though working with children was hardly a passion for her. The demands of her own children were more than enough to fulfil any such desire.
Later that night, Cayenne took the initiative to message the stranger.
Her body's hunger prompting her to share her thoughts.

"Just had a vision flash before my eyes.
I'm sitting in a chair by the window in a hotel. I'm wearing a shirt tied in a knot at the waist with a wide florescent leather belt and '50s-style skater skirt. My legs are bare except for a sheen of cocoa butter. I'm wearing black kitten heels which is most appropriate, as they perfectly compliment the throbbing pussy

between my legs. I cross my thighs seductively as you approach looking crestfallen and riddled with anxiety.

I press my thighs together, determined not to let your drooping shoulders soften my resolve; but the moment you drop to your knees, something takes over me. The next thing I know, my legs are akimbo over the arms of the chair, and I'm pressing down with my legs so as to elevate my derriere.

My legs move up and down in a flapping motion causing my pussy to rise and fall in complete synergy with your tongue, which is showering my clit.

The flared skater skirt is willowing around with the sensation of my quivering body. I can't seem to lift my ass high enough to satisfy my desperation to bring myself closer to your mouth. I let out a deep groan as a warm pleasure engulfs me."

To her disappointment, there was no response. Perhaps he was attempting to punish her.

The following morning, her phone was still silent.

It was two days later before she realised she had been holding her breath…

"Hey! Been away for the weekend without good internet connection—just back. Will catch up first thing and try to restore lines of comms!!"

A twinge of jealousy stabbed at her ego, and she could feel herself beginning to seethe. Her juvenile instinct reacted before she could engage her brain.

"Don't bother.
I'll be away with my new internet fuck… getting a good screwing FINALLY!"

It was the following morning before he replied…

"Okay, great news. Enjoy."

"The hunger for black pussy has clearly waned already." She could have cursed herself for not having the strength to disengage.

"Cheeky…
I really do need to give it to you hard.

You've turned me on as I walk in the office. Severe hardening in my pants. Excitement pulsing. Bad bad girl.

So no, the need for your tight wet black pussy has not waned. Home alone?"

"I'm in the Wharf with a wet pussy."

"Really? … no wonder I'm on heat … where are you?
Let's do tea at the Hilton."

Cayenne arrived first and headed towards the bar at the rear where she ordered a pot of tea for two. She advised the bar staff that the gentleman arriving shortly would add the order to his bill as instructed.

As she waited, she checked her appearance in the mirrored wall behind her and noticed an Arab-looking gentleman seated at the other end of the restaurant. He was dining alone and was unashamedly staring in her direction.

She was wearing her gym gear in preparation for the classes booked for later. She wondered how the stranger would react to seeing her in gym clothes. Doubtless he would appreciate how they clung to her curves.

The stranger arrived moments later looking his usual flustered self. Shirt open with the top few buttons undone, and his signature office trousers. He kissed her cheeks and sat down opposite casting an approving eye over her attire. For someone who had just enjoyed a weekend away, he didn't appear to be well-rested and tanned as she expected. When she told him as much, he simply replied…

"No… it wasn't like that." There was a hint of something in his eyes. Was it sadness? She couldn't yet tell.

What was blatantly obvious was how happy he was to see her. He could scarcely hide his bashful smile and made several failed attempts to speak.

"So how is my little weekend errant toy?"

Chapter 20

"How did I stop myself from crawling under the table… unzipping you and sugar-coating your hard cock?" They had now returned to their respective endeavours.

"How did you know I was hard? Hard as a rock…"

"Mmmm, I should have sat on your lap."

"I'm now back at my desk, purely innocent."

"Imagine I'm there. At your feet, pawing at you and playing with myself.
Juicing while you take the occasional peek."

"You bad dirty beast…
Just imagining you wet, open and dripping—you need white cock."

"Yes. This black succulent pussy needs desperate white cock. Rampant and plunging, legs are akimbo. Clit pulsating. Repeatedly.
I'm remembering the delicious sensation of cradling your cock. Sensuous cupping. Feeling it harden in my very hands. Would love to see your face in desperate concentration during a board meeting as I suck underneath the desk. I bend over, head to my knees as I straddle your erection and dance to my own rhythm whilst you hold court. Only the very astute in the room would notice a black curvaceous bottom spiralling in your lap."

"They'd all want a go… I need practice holding… more rubbing definitely required."

"Yes. I believe in you. With practice, you will be able to maintain your rigidity and eventually give me a good solid pounding."

"I need my teacher. Strict discipline…"

"Meanwhile… I suppose I will have to make do with being eaten. Mmmm, no real hardship. I'm sure I can suffer your tongue teasing my vacant pussy. I'll even open extra wide… see if you can bury your entire mouth in it.

Oooh, I bet your cock is throbbing.

Wish I could see the rise and fall in your trousers from across the board room and see your brow glisten as my fingers disappear inside my panties."

"Fuck this torment.

Throbbing hard. Trying to express what a dirty toy I want to be whilst looking innocent to all around me…

I need drenching by your black cunt juice."

"Open your mouth, my minion, and let me drool my erotic caramel onto your palate. Let me quench your parched soul."

"Going somewhere discreet so I can express my filth properly."

"Ooooh, I'm a fly on the wall… tongue hanging out in anticipation of your bulging crotch. If only I could kneel looking up at the volcanic eruption. Massaging your balls to encourage the flow and offering my arse as a catchment bed for your cum."

"I'm on absolute heat now… can't concentrate. I need my black mistress to calm me down.

Only black cunt will calm me. I need a feeding.

I need to taste it, smell it and be in it.

I need my hands on your chocolate tits as you fuck my face hard and unabated.

I'm tempted to wank my white cock in the men's room as I think about how you seduced me to the dark side… I'm a toy for a nasty bad black bitch, and it makes me hard."

"Write your initials on my glutes with your white sauce. I will writhe all over your face fast, then slow to allow your tongue free reign in every nook of my fanny."

"I'm caressing my cock at fucking work. You're so bad!
I so need to release my juice over your delicious chocolate."

"Oooh, the thought of you selfishly caressing your cock is making me jealous. I must see this furtive gallop. I must be there for the gorgeous finale.
I want to sit on it with no finesse whatsoever… so fucking hungry."

"I want my hands on your black ass… I'm tempted to taste it too. I need to stop touching myself, but my cock feels really good right now—it should be in your black chocolate hands, mouth and then … cunt…
This white cock has a black bitch owner now…
Torment achieved."

"Hands, mouth, cunt… in that order. Ooooh yeah.
Squeeze yourself into my cavernous ecstasy. Don't be afraid of the narrowness of my feminine corridor. My juice will aid the accommodation of your white hard cock."

"Mmmm, just thinking about your ass now… That really would be the final corruption
Black chocolate hands, mouth, cunt… ass."

"My cunt will be so intoxicating… you will be desperate to explore further and deeper… hands on my black buttocks as you forage ever deeper into my fallow heath.
I can almost hear the squelch of abundant juice as your cock dips tentatively inside before being drowned out by my yearning screams."

"Naughty, delicious, evil black mistress… you've got me hardening again…
Must go and actually do what I am paid for now…
Still can't believe I was actually getting off at work reading your filth whilst stroking a nicely hardening boner… what am I becoming? The thrill was intense."

"You certainly bring out my inner bondage side. I love tormenting you."

"I can't keep this up. Could lead to filthy underbelly ruin! If I keep on like this (actually wanking at work), the underbelly will be where I'll end up."

"I can see that the prospect of tight black pussy gripping your white cock, like a vice, with juice spurting from the seams is becoming too much for you. I don't wish to put you in jeopardy. I will retreat. Your work is important…"

"DON'T YOU DARE. I may stalk the Wharf. Where are you?"

Cayenne had received an urgent call from Ocean's school stating that he had been unwell with a suspected tummy bug and could she come and get him.

"Hope all okay."

"Yes. We are back home now, and he seems fine. Either his discomfort has passed, or his talent to deceive is exemplary."

"Anything like his mum; we may be looking at the latter."

"I knew you'd say that."

"Meant in the nicest possible way."

"As I was passing through the underbelly and cast my eyes asunder, I suddenly thought… if I happen to see you stalking for alternative ethnic skirt… I shan't be responsible for my actions."

"There's nothing in your class out there. Be assured I have already trawled incessantly during abandonment V1."

"Such lewd behaviour. You are absolutely right. I am a uniquely intoxicating potent mix."

"I can't deny it… other options bored me."

"You would be prudent to keep me in the manner to which I have become accustomed… lest a more earnest stalker entrap me."

Chapter 21

The stranger had taken to sending her videos that he liked the look of.
    http://pornhub.com/view_video 456445ke4

    Cayenne waited until the children were tucked up in bed before dimming the lights and settling down to watch.
    It was a good one admittedly. During the years of having to satisfy herself, she had developed a particular penchant for the ones that got straight to the point, no hanging around with banal chit-chat. He clearly felt the same way.
    Immediately she was thrust into the throes of an interracial fuck fest. A sultry black woman in a lace, crotch-less, all-in-one outfit being pummelled from behind by an eager to satisfy Caucasian. She was getting it good too. Cayenne felt immediately aroused. Inspired by the erotic visuals, she pleasured herself into a satisfying slumber.
    The next thing she knew she awoke the following morning having had a decidedly thorough rest.

    Later she messaged the sender with gratitude and found him knee-deep in furtive research.

    "In the Marriot, working on my CV for 45 minutes… just got a secret peep at this one…

video s0sk3
I think I can find better
Trying to view the others without the female business centre supervisor thinking I'm a dirty boy."

    "When you find better… show me in person. Be the dirty boy who dreams incessantly of my cocoa cunt."

    "I need it…

I so love the taste of your cocoa cunt."

"I have a similar outfit as the recipient in the video with an appropriate face-shaped hole."

"Dirty, bad yummy mummy getting off on racially corrupting a nice, innocent white boy.
His white cock only answers to black dripping cunt now."

"I'll not stop until you are utterly corrupt. You'll have an intolerance for bland Caucasians by the time I'm finished with you."

"Although he does often wonder what it would be like to disappear up the sensational black chocolate ass of his secret deliciously evil mistress.
Oh don't worry, I am already so intolerant to whites now, it would make me soft... I can only rise to wet tasty black chocolate pussy."

"Wonder no more, my milky minion... how utterly pointless would it be for your jungle excursion to end without thorough exploration."

"I'm hard at my terminal... so much for time out to work on my CV.
I can't escape my need to be your whore."

"Your white cock must now only stand to attention in the presence of Nubian royalty."

"I need to watch a clip of your last video, but I'm being watched like a hawk now."

"Don't worry, your time has not been wasted as you have indeed spent this time researching cunt verification.
Who is watching my minion?...Does she not know he is accounted for? Let me at the bitch."

"I'm a fucking white slave to black cunt...I need a feed of my black pussy juice."

"Who dares to impede investigative cunt verification?"

"She's a white bitch... so it's not like you have to worry... perhaps I need to show her what I'm into.
Hilarious. I like the cunt verification... may need to make this a daily task."

"I need you to show me what all those white bitches are missing.
Demonstrate your allegiance to the blackberry and confirm the hidden truth... the blacker the berry, the sweeter the juice."

"So tempted to stroke... This is now a no-go area for white bitches."

"Ooooh, what I would give to be under that terminal table... gnawing at my white tool. We must reinstate segregation. No whites allowed. I will lynch any white trash I see in the vicinity of my cock slave."

"Yes, I will make them realise I'm a black pussy whore."

"Any venturing on enemy lines will lead to annihilation. Your species will become as endangered as the ivory tusk. I will show them that you are now totally at the mercy of your slave owner."

"You get off on this, don't you?"

"Thoroughly enjoying presiding over my milk plantation. Nurturing strong white cock...
One simply won't suffice. I will need to breed a herd of them."

"Don't you dare!
White master now enslaved to be used as a toy. Tied up and fucked and aggressively used as his black bitch mistress sees fit. I'm on heat again as I walk around—shame you can't show yourself to tease me."

"Where are you?"

"Trawling the mall... ignoring anything white."

"Yes, my minion... your Negro devotion will be duly rewarded."

"Funny as I wrote that I noticed one of my colleagues behind me… do you like what I have become?"

"Be careful on your Negro trawl… they may look like me, but most are far less refined than they appear to the untrained eye."

"My cock needs YOUR juice. Not just any negro."

"I love what you are becoming. I want your addiction to black pussy to be drug-like. You will need intense rehab to rid you of the hunger for berry juice. I want total domination. Slavery to my pussy precedence. You will become a black pussy cannibal. May you suffer extreme withdrawal symptoms when away from my cinnamon cunt."

"I think I'd only ever be subservient to your black queen pussy… I'd surely suffocate without the smell of your queenly black cunt and ass."

"May every white pussy now distinctly lack equatorial spice—shouldn't be difficult."

"Cheeky bitch.
My cock is leading me to South Quay. It must detect cinnamon."

"Yes… the tightness and juice and sheer blackness is insatiable. I want you begging for berry juice. Follow the pussy trail. Sniff like a coke addict desperate for the high of Caribbean cunt."

"I'm wandering South Quay warped, hard, waiting on every line you send, dry and desperately in need of a feed … There's black pussy on the street that can't hope to divert me from my cock's direct line…
I suppose I will end up in the Chanel Café tortured, addicted… obsessed. No one here knows what a slave to your black cunt juice I've become."

"I'm thrilled that pussy-eating devotion is literally on my doorstep.

Your melanoid internship was brief. You quickly excelled to advanced black onyx pussy devotion."

"Time to head back and regain my composure… know that your white fuck toy was lured by his cock seeking your caramel from his safe bland office."

"I want it again but slower. Want to savour your tongue and feel it advancing my feminine corridor.
The Caribbean cunt juice will be more potent tomorrow, as it will aerate like a fine wine. I must entice you until you are helpless to my ebony aroma."

"Let me into your landing… Make me grovel at your door. I won't come into your home if you disapprove… white boy knows he's not allowed on the black queen's territory. Give me a taste tomorrow before the need for a fix gets too much. I'm a fucking corrupt whore."
This was the cue to Cayenne snapping out of her stupor. Something about him wanting to encroach upon her life irritated her.

The stranger must have sensed this and did not ask again.
They exchanged videos, both making mental notes to share what they had learned with each other.

"I'm looking forward to sitting on your face as you tongue fuck every orifice, while I reach back and stroke your cock."

"Do you remember what you were telling me as you fucked my face in Mayfair?… As you relieved yourself in my mouth."

"I don't. Please remind me."

"Bad racial slurs that I daren't repeat. Although I distinctly recall you grabbing a fistful of my hair, forcing my face between your legs, and your accent adopting a sudden Jamaican lilt as you commanded something that sounded like 'fuckin' nyam it'…
I need to walk off this newly generated hard-on. Perhaps your former colonial master needs to give your chocolate ass a spanking. Meet me in Chanel at 4:00."

The Canary Wharf Chanel Café was a family run eatery conveniently situated halfway between the stranger's office and Cayenne's apartment.

Their meeting had been brief. A quick catch-up over a cup of tea. Seeing each other for even a short time seemed to enhance their day. Especially the semi-public grope and fondle as they explored each other's mouths on their departure.

She thoroughly enjoyed the fact that before he even reached the office after their meetings, he would feedback how she had made him feel.

"You looked fucking hot."

"Had you reached inside my skirt...you would have made a soaking discovery."

"Communal stairs for a desperately hungry tongue fuck?"

Cayenne ignored the suggestion.

"Send me some dirty interracial filth..."

Cayenne duly found an appropriate hot session and forwarded it to his email whilst pointing out the highlights.

"Look at that white cock in that fucking black cunt... I'm so jealous."

"I can't right now. But don't worry, I will be enjoying it later."

"My pussy is literally drooling in anticipation."

"Wish I had put my hand up your skirt."

"I was positively dripping walking home."

"I could have had my taste of delicious black pussy juice."

Cayenne laid her unlaid self on her newly laid bed and began to imagine their next meeting.

"Imagining the plunging. Ferocious and rampant. Perhaps we shouldn't. What if it evokes an insatiable need and desire that cannot be recapped. Preferable to remain in control of my urges surely. Even thinking about your cock… pummelling my nether regions in wild abandon makes me wet. I'm horny as hell."

"After the real thing, after we take the plunge… it may unleash a beast…"

"Even I don't know the intensity of this new monster simmering within. If I were in the same room as you now… fuck!… your brains would be like splintered shrapnel… I'd fuck you into oblivion. For fuck's sake… somebody relieve me."

"I will relieve you. You will get it. I will be the rampant white beast fuck that your cunt needs. More to come tomorrow."

She rewarded him with a sexy video. His appreciation was amorous.

"Bad dirty bitch. I liked the woman in the video… liked seeing her oiled ass.
Send me another one."

"I too will be oiled to the hilt. Going to bed now dreaming of your hard white cock. Going to finger myself discreetly beneath the covers… my fingers imitating your cock delving into my already saturated pussy."

The next morning, she awoke to a video of his choice.
She sent him an urgent response.

"Check out the finger and simultaneous pussy lick. I wonder how it feels in the ass… they enjoy it so much… it must feel fucking amazing."

"Mmmm, nice morning viewing… I like how she slaps her clit while masturbating."

"Slap my clit too. Execute your every whim and desire on this tight black juicy pussy in this once-in-a-lifetime opportunity."

"Think I might have sent you repeated viewing. Apologies for the error—don't want to upset the black Queen. The copied link from previous viewing was still there… must remember to remove such evidence of my dirty secrets."

"No apology necessary. Your generous contributions are revitalising a prematurely retired pussy."

"I've got a three hour onsite today… how the fuck will I survive such boredom."

"You will survive safe in the knowledge that a black pussy fuck fest awaits."

"Oh yes… only white bitches on this onsite, nothing to get my cock hard."

"Give no more thought to such pale plebs with their dry, worn pussies. Pussies that require artificial lubricants. At every juncture, direct your mind to my dripping, aromatic, black-truffle fragranced, succulently seasoned cunt."

Cayenne dressed carefully as she knew that Diego would want her to make an impression. It would be the first time that she would be witnessing her son's professional performance since he began his performing arts course a year ago. She knew that he had been working hard with his classmates on Shakespeare's *A Midsummer Night's Dream.*
She had always known that he had a natural talent. Not that he exhibited a particularly showbizzy energy. He wasn't one of those children that sought out opportunities to perform, or that put on plays for the neighbours and at family gatherings, but it was something they talked about a lot; and during long summer holidays with his cousins when they were younger, they would record their own home-produced movies, complete with soundtrack and special effects. Occasionally she would challenge him to rehearse a particular scene from a classic movie. She knew he had something, and to his credit, he hadn't deviated from his chosen path, even when it must have been difficult, such as when his peers didn't consider his choice fashionable.
Now they were here in the capital, and she was going to see him on stage for the first time.

She prepared a meal for Sugar and Ocean and left them instructions to prepare for bed at 7:00 p.m. Sugar had already learned to use this scenario to her advantage.

"Can I have as much Oreo ice cream as I want if I eat all my dinner?" She gave her mum a thumbs up and squinted her eyes into a cheeky irresistible grin.

She insisted on accompanying her to the elevator where they had developed the habit of replicating scenes from classic movies, and the elevator scene from one of their favourite films *Kramer Vs Kramer* was more difficult than it looked.

Cayenne as Joanna Kramer would wipe away a tear and smooth down her hair to regain her composure following an emotional exchange with her ex-husband Ted regarding custody of their only son. As she entered the elevator on her way to explain to the waiting child that he would be staying in his father's primary custody after all, following a harrowing court battle; and after adjusting her hair and coat, she looked up tentatively for reassurance.

"How do I look?" Cayenne was trying desperately to emulate Meryl Streep's emotional portrayal.

Whichever of her children that happened to be standing on the opposite side of the elevator as it was about to close would do their best impression of Dustin Hoffman's Ted Kramer as he smiled affectionately having decided to forgo any previous angst…

"Terrific."…

"Terrific," smiled Sugar. Looking more like Jackie Chan than Dustin Hoffman as she squinted her eyes again and threw her an impromptu thumbs up just as the doors glided to a close.

Chapter 22

"Just thinking, I want the first ass I ever try to be yours…"

"Mmmm, possible exciting analysis experiences ahead. The videos certainly make it look pleasurable.

Sorry for the typo – I meant anal, not analysis.
Mind you… Analysis of anal… That could work."

"I want to see your black ass."

"You will see my black ass from every possible angle. Study it. Poke it. Prod it. Penetrate it. Lick it. Taste it. Squeeze it. Slap it. Cream it, massage it with intense scrutiny. You will be able to expound knowledgeably on the inner workings and mechanisms, not to mention delights of the black cunt. Consider how fortunate you are to be embarking on this Nubian adventure with such a tight, almost virginal vaginal maze. Its intricate nooks and crannies … Endless. Its mystery… intoxicating. The hidden sources of its lubricants… highly addictive."

"Our thought paths must have crossed.
How lucky am I to have such an evilly delicious secret chocolate delight who wants me solely as a toy for her pleasure, which fully reconciles with my deep, dark corrupt fantasies."

His constant reiterations and insistence that her only requirement of him be as a secret toy was not lost on her. It was as though he was trying to ensure she didn't get carried away and lose sight of the fact that clandestine adventures were all that were on offer.

"Deep dark fantasies? What thrilling promise."

"Secret black pussy tasting, fucking, corruption. I am a white whore to the power of the black Queen's intoxicating chocolate cinnamon caramel pussy juice mix. I want my white cock drenched in it.

The next time you stroke me, I want the lube on your hands to be your own dripping juices."

"Oh, dip your cock into the Black Sea… with its myth-like folklore and hidden depths. Wade in step by step and let the waves of the dark tide engulf you."

"What do you think of these?
https:// www.redtube.com/234 (milfs)
https://www.redtube.com/4578 (oil)
https://www.redtube.com/5209 (black/white)"

"The black 'n' white one is hard to beat. Perfect start… cradling her in his arms while patting and fingering the black pussy. Coconut mix is my favourite."

"Of course. What you up to?"

"Putting dinner on amongst other domestic humdrum chores."

"Are you wearing panties?"

"No. I avoid such annoying restraints unless necessary.
My divine puss puss likes to feel the cool afternoon breeze."

"I like the image… domestic but also dirty and available."

"Yes… bending over to reach the nooks and crannies… Exposing my black ass to the elements. Later, I'll shower, caressing the pussy that nobody sees… putting on my mummy persona… little do they know… a black hungry minx is in their midst. I may have to dose myself with a feminine scent to disguise the intoxicating incense of my wreaking pussy."

"I will be thinking about this when I go in for my afternoon of annoyance at 2:00."

"Think about it you must…as I cruise through Canary Wharf…potent black pussy scent will weave amongst the unsuspecting crowd and waft through your open board-room window, like a heat-seeking missile… ignoring every other white cock under the table… until it finds yours. Keep a straight face, won't you… whilst your cock detonates in your trousers."

"The torment you indulge in… so bad, so deplorable… makes me even more desperate, hungry and hard for black juice."

"The harvest is plentiful."

"No one knows what you've turned me into."

"I prefer to think that what you have become was already an innate part of you… waiting to be uncovered, lest you forget, it was I who was accosted in the wharf underbelly.
You merely had seeds desperately seeking the right climate in which to germinate. May the bulbs flourish and thrive until the autumn season heralds their demise."

"https//www.redtube.com/44637
I want to recreate this speed."
It's clear he wanted her to observe his dedication to improving his technique.

"Yeeeees I wanna be fucked from every angle just like that. Look how fast he is fucking her. So fucking jealous."

"Tea in Chanel?… no panties… torment me even worse than normal. Second thoughts…
Can we make it later this afternoon. It seems I have a moody boss, and a few things are kicking off."

Cayenne decided to make an extra effort for their routine tea date.
She selected a bodycon, lycra figure-clinging black number with strategic transparent panels just above the bust, giving a slight glimpse for titillation. She teamed this with her black ankle boots. The only undergarment was the lashings of cocoa butter causing her legs to glisten in the afternoon sun.

She arrived at Chanel Café first as usual. She ordered a pot of tea and two individual Victoria Sponge cakes and strolled toward the back of the establishment where there were more booths and seating areas overlooking the harbour.

She opted for a booth for more privacy.

Soon after, he arrived with his signature flustered demeanour. One hand stroking his hair, eyes wide with anticipation. Once he had spotted her, he strutted in her direction, stopping briefly to glance under the table. Her shiny legs remained close for the moment.

"Hi, gorgeous." He kissed her cheeks and sat down opposite her. "You okay? Thanks for coming."

"Yes, I'm fine."

"You bought tea and cakes. Thank you so much." He seemed genuinely thankful as though it was the kindest gesture he had seen in a while and he was unaccustomed to not having to pay. "Good to see you. Loving the dress. Are you going somewhere else, or do you always dress like that for afternoon tea?" He was amusing himself at her efforts.

"Are you wearing knickers?"

Cayenne took a bite of Victoria Sponge and licked the cream from her lips seductively whilst shaking her head in response.

The stranger looked visibly perturbed. Hot and bothered, the colour of his face deepening like a gradual tan.

She loved to watch him squirm and smiled, thoroughly enjoying the power it gave her.

He glanced furtively around before taking another sneaky peek under the table. This time she gladly obliged and stretched her legs asunder to the opposing corners of the table, allowing him the optimum view of chocolate fancy.

She knew that he would gladly forsake the traditional Victoria Sponge that remained untouched on the table for a single lick of the exotic delicacy she offered given the chance.

His face fell in frustration. "This isn't enough. I need to touch you."

After they had finished their tea, they slipped out of the rear door and edged around the back of the building in front of the vacant space next door. They still had to be discreet as there were people milling about nearby and who knew what eyes were upon them from the countless vast erect buildings surrounding them.

He kissed her hungrily; and when he thought it safe, plunged his fingers into the silky outpouring between her legs. She could feel the arousal straining to unfold under his belt. Their breathing became heavy and laboured as they looked at each other longingly.

"What have you done to me?"

Cayenne wondered the same thing as she glanced back to watch him walk away after they parted. His hands were stuffed stiffly into his pockets, and his head hung down over drooping shoulders.

Chapter 23

The next few days went by without so much as a word from the stranger.

Cayenne found herself getting wound up almost to the point of resentment. Her mind began to wonder about his personal situation which he kept so closely guarded.

He had told her that he wasn't married and had no children. *So what was the situation?* She pondered afresh.

She knew she had no right to ask. They had been clear about that. In fact, hadn't she been the one to stipulate that they needn't know everything there was to know about each other. She could hardly start lamenting the consequences now. She suspected he must have gone away for the weekend. This was the first weekend of many that she hadn't heard anything from him. She didn't at all like the withdrawal sensation that she was experiencing, which all but resembled a distinct bout of jealousy. She had always prided herself that she wasn't the jealous type, so why then was she sitting up late at night constructing a horrendously mean email in retaliation.

Eventually, he responded.

"Hey! I'm sorry. I'm crazed not being able to message you all weekend."

"I'll bet you are absolutely tight, black juicy pussy starved and deprived of sufficient sensation. However bad you may be feeling, just consider that it could be worse. You could remain as UNFUCKED as the day you were picked up in the girth of the underbelly.

I'm almost tempted to crawl over to your place and share your Caucasian vaginal prolapse existence."

"It is clearly time to smarten my act up so that the black Queen increases her pity."

She decided to give him some of his own treatment.

"Any communal areas where you live? I promise I will attempt to stretch my pussy out, making sure to irrevocably damage the elasticity and dry up the excess berry juice in order to provide familiarity. Is there any other way that I can help?" She knew she was being a complete bitch, sounding like a spoiled child.

"Fuck it, I'm going for a quick walk. You free?"

They must have looked like any other couple meandering around the quays and enjoying the afternoon sun.

"It's so not enough. Not being able to touch you properly."

They linked arms as South Quay came into view signalling imminent severance, knowing that their only solace was to continue in writing later.

"I agree. Less talking. More pussy titillation. I want to be waiting for you in my crotch-less outfit. You walk in…my legs are open wide…you bury your face deep into my pussy hole. Make me scream. I'll be playing with myself as you walk in… watch for a while as your cock hardens. Watch me pleasure myself… until coconut juice is seeping onto the bed.
In the middle of my self-induced orgasm … I'll call out… 'suck it! you white fuck'.
That's your cue to come to the table and feast. 69 me so I can suck on your dick while you lick my cunt and fondle my clit."

"Oh fuck, that's much better. Not the demure housewife but the dirty, hot black goddess whom I hunger for." He planted a hand on the nearest butt cheek, cupping and squeezing unashamedly. "We really didn't get off enough at our meeting earlier, did we? Too nice, too polite, too innocent, too gentlemanly. Racially abuse and use me, my black Queen."

"Yeah…fuck that… that puts us in the same humdrum category as everyone else.
Let's fuck."

"Exactly, we're better than that shit."

"Let's have some good fucking... make hay while it lasts. We're not gonna remember fucking Victoria Sponge and cappuccinos. I want to remember... being bent over the balcony at night getting a good roasting while other boring hotel guests are at dinner. Fuck me on the hotel desk, fuck me in the wardrobe. Against the door. Pour cocktails over my pussy and lick them off. Place the cherries in my pussy and suck them out. I want to suck Ciroc off your dick hundreds of feet above London." She let out a frustrated sigh.

"God, that sounds delightful."

"I need my pussy to be sucked dry and then restocked. Practice your tongue action... make sure I feel thoroughly penetrated. Fucking give this pussy what it needs for fuck's sake. Don't even come up for air. I want to walk out feeling like you've left a gaping hole. Unable to walk straight in the aftermath of your territorial pillage. You'd better be fucking hungry. Eat this fucking pussy mutha fucka. I want to bend over. Black ass in the air. Get in there. I'm going to cock one leg up and press your head into my cunt. Oooh yeah. Lick that clit until I can't take anymore. I'm going to lie back and luxuriate in every single stroke... don't rush me to climax... I want to enjoy it. Lick me like I was a delicate chocolate ice cream. Unlike your average vanilla, think viennetta with its intricate sauce laced throughout. Think of nut sprinkles and speckles of cinnamon. Elevate your pussy palate for the rum-and-raisin delicacy of my vag.

Use your tongue to write on my pussy... engrave your name in calligraphy... 'white slave was here' on my clit.

I want a fucking long eating session... five courses... until cocoa juice explodes... then IT'S YOUR TURN.

Oh bugger, I'm fucking horny and frustrated now."

"You naughty girl... perhaps the tea visit was worth it considering the filth you've just released.

My cock needs a black sucking.

It needs to feel your hot mouth around it.

It needs your chocolate hands stroking it, massaging it, teasing it.

But what I really utterly hunger for right now is your black cunt.

I want to be on it until you cream.

I want to be immersed in your dripping juice.

I then want to smell your black chocolate ass.

I will then need to spank you for making me such a corrupt white whore toy."

"Oh good, I love a good spanking. The harder the better. This rump can take it.
Must I now wait for my white fuck? Bull shit… I should have availability for pussy licking whenever the need arises.
You're cruising for a sacking… if I don't get my fix."

"Slap your black cunt and show me.
Pretend your white fuck toy is watching but can't touch."

"I'm a frustrated black fucking hungry bitch, and you want me to slap my pussy?
Not gonna cut it… I need a white tongue to feed off my cunt like a refugee. Got it?!
I'm on all fours. You get your head up my ass and tongue-fuck me like a rabbit on heat."

"That's better—I need the fear of sacking from my black bitch mistress…
Teas are over… the next meeting is either your communal stairs if you can't wait or a hotel suite."

"Deeper… I want your tongue deeper into the hidden crevices of my cunt. Uncover unexplored territory.
What is the point of you? … slave. What is the fucking point if my hunger levels (once manageable) are now nearing starvation mode."

"Appealing to my underbelly ways…refugee exploitation… cheeky bitch."

"Communal stairs would only be suitable for superficial below-par tonguing with some kind of temporary-resident street urchin.
I'm sure you can find other ethnic minions for that… your trail of the underbelly is a well worn path… I challenge you, revisit it… see what you can find.
Relinquish me to the Canary Wharf executives that place value on a tight black juicy pussy. Clearly, you do not."

"When you're home alone, have me 'round like a whore. I will do whatever you demand... Taste, lick and fuck every hole... I will be completely your toy and only be desperate to please... alternatively, you will have to wait on my diary.

What afternoon next week?? I'm trawling options now whilst hard."

"Perhaps your boardroom colleagues would be only too pleased to get this precious blackberry juice behind closed penthouse doors.

I'm sure they would happily pour champagne on my crystal cunt and fuck me on Egyptian cotton sheets. It appears your underbelly DNA exposes you. I can picture it now... You with a short-term visa immigrant at the Holiday Inn... eating cheap scallops and imitation tapas. And the ignorant coon...stupidly grateful for a free meal and your half-baked signature fuck...

What sayest thou?

I should be subject to my slave's diary? I think not."

"Getting really bad and nasty now, my black Queen, aren't you? I like it.

We will do Champagne. I know your worth. I'm so grateful you pulled me up from the dirt.

You're such a bad, bad dirty girl.

How did I get so lucky?"

"Yes. One must never forget that I rescued you from the wharf gutter.

I'm not sure you're quite worthy of me.

Though I wonder whether our intentions are entirely savage... how can I take you to the dark side, forever leaving you yearning for something you will never have again.

Surely a full session with me would render every white fuck laying wait in your future, useless and unable to muster arousal.

I could permit you to fuck me... absolutely.

But I demand couture fucking for a couture cunt."

"Got my white bitch global CFO meeting now...
Torment me please."

"Just picture her dry decrepit pussy adorned with menopausal granny pants...

And assure yourself that you are on the cusp of attaining a seat at the Queen's table with its rich tapestry, and Michelin-starred cuisine served on the most exquisite black diamond platter.

Tread carefully and you can have a front seat. No cutlery necessary…

All you can eat, hands tied… mouth only.

To think that you would relegate my couture cunt to impersonal communal stairs…

I may have to rethink our association.

Communal stairs???

You deserve white trash.

If I were you. I'd put up, shut up and live forever in suburban, mediocre pussy land. That is what you deserve. God knows it's all you can handle."

"Hey!!! Completely understood. This suggestion will stop.
Still talking to crusty white CFO bitch.
Don't worry, your white toy won't mess up again."

"Crusty white bitch may yet have her uses.
Does she like tapas?
Does she strike you as a quartered scallop dosed in lemon vinaigrette to disguise unpalatable flavour type of person?
Does she appear that she'd be satisfied with only the unfulfilled promise of a decent fuck?
If so… slip her your number. You need never trawl again."

"You nasty bitch. Stop making me want you."

"Take her to Mayfair… preferably before 2:00 p.m.
Don't forget to provide extra lubricant obviously. And don't forget the blindfold. Not for her… For YOU so that you don't have to suffer the sight of overstretched bubblegum pussy and its Caucasian flaps."

"Bad, racist nasty girl.
Open your black pussy wide, so I can make you come."

"Meanwhile, I shall be across town at the Savoy… in the penthouse, slurping Bollinger from your Global CEO's boner.

He'll be feasting on authentic scallops, foie gras, oysters and caviar from the lobes of my black, self-moisturising vag, complete with berry juice marinade. Bon appetit."

"Sorry, baby, my CEO is well-known for his liking of 20-something blondes."

"They all do… pre-tight, juicy black pussy.
Then once they've tasted the exquisite rarity of the most exclusive black truffle cunt, they never go back… Except at weekends… obvs."

"Don't we know it… what afternoon suits you?"

"Then again, 20-something blondes have their advantages of course.
No intellectual conversation necessary to ensure total escapism from corporate stress. Not to mention their culinary tastes are likely unrefined… tapas is one of their known favourites."

"I wouldn't mind watching one getting to taste you and becoming intoxicated on your dripping berry juice.
What afternoon can your fucking white slave toy make it up to his gorgeous black Queen?"

"Oh dear… would you really want me to be subjected to the immersion into the abyss that is the average-white, overused, inelastic pussy?
I cannot abide… I honestly don't know how you stand it."

"I bet you're enjoying my descent into black pussy madness."

"The stealth and virtue of the white man has been hugely underestimated, for they have endured long years of unfulfilling cavernous pussy experiences. Baby ravaged clits and over-stretched vaginal walls, and you all are slaves to it.
Your powers of endurance should be better recognised. We really ought to campaign for a national day of recognition. Like a kind of Remembrance Day, only it will be to commemorate the minute window in which a white pussy remains tight. Is it any wonder society has forced you to disguise your longing for black pussy behind aspersions of contempt."

"I want a dirty black cunt fuck."

"One doesn't always get what one wants… as I learned from our previous excursion. Should the white man ever be renowned for unsatisfactory black pussy plunging… you would surely be in the running for an accolade.
Perhaps it's my fault…
Too fucking tight and juicy.
How to transform oneself into a Caucasian airhead with bicycle pussy or a mature vintage dilapidated affair.
How to dry up this juice and create a parched desolate war-torn existence with unsightly wrinkled pink flaps? I must google it."

"You enjoy wounding your toy, don't you?

There'll be no more devaluation… never my intention. I'm saddened."

Chapter 24

"Undeserved I know… but I want a glimpse."

"Totally deserved… I want a fuck.
When you can satisfactorily fuck me and eat my pussy, like a fat Bengali at iftar… only then will I consider demands."

"You know there was promise when I had my first blacking.
I was rampant couldn't get enough…remember the volume of your moans."

"Queens require more than promise."

"Your volume levels and your juicing told a story in themselves."

"I'll grant you that. Pity you haven't been able to back it up."

"You are DIVINE… I want to make you moan… I want you hungry as I am."

"I am positively close to starvation.
All I need now is to find persons of equal hunger levels.
Distinguished persons that think less, talk less and act more.
Someone who doesn't have to spreadsheet hot juicy pussy."

"Okay. Plan of action is being formulated…
Good luck for tomorrow… Not that you'll need it."

Cayenne was touched that he had remembered that she had been invited to a final interview for the position of holiday scheme coordinator. She had told him about it days before, and he had obviously remembered that it was the following day.

It was strange that he managed to take her from one extreme emotion to another. One minute he would fill her with the anticipation of a newly touched virgin, and the next manage to say something that would make her seethe with resentment, and then he would show levels of thoughtfulness and caring that she couldn't remember anyone else showing.

"On such a cold windy night… being inside your warm, moist dark pussy would be most enjoyable."

"My hot pussy would totally welcome the intrusion.
If entry proves challenging… persevere… for hot caramel molten awaits."

"Let's not have any reminders of my previous failure… Sleep well.
Goodnight my Queen."

Chapter 25

The induction day, which was scheduled for Saturday morning in High Wycombe, went relatively well. Around 60 eager hopefuls attended, although the E-Quip company were expecting twice as many.

The first half of the presentation was an introduction to the organisation. Their history, their progress, their mission statement and goals; and then a speech by some of the head coordinators who the candidates would be answerable to should they progress further.

After lunch, a series of exercises had been devised which were designed to replicate the kind of activities that they were expected to supervise during the holiday camps.

Things like making glue from scratch and then adding some metallic splints to make it more exciting. Cayenne could think of nothing worse than concocting this extra strong glue and distributing it between a hoard of bored children.

She passively spectated as they were shown some of the other activities that they would need to be familiar with. The more time passed, the more Cayenne questioned what she was doing there. Everyone else, for the most part, seemed totally enthralled. She certainly had some thinking to do when she got home.

Fortunately, she had been supplied with plenty of video clips to enhance her journey.
"http://www.redtube.com/3232"

"Mmmmm, thank you."

"More where that came from—I'm educating myself… http://www.redtube.com/76767"

"I can hardly wait to be reacquainted with your newly schooled tongue. Eat me alive."

"I will be so hungry by Wednesday. A ravenous wolf.
You will moan loudly."

"I hope you're not opposed to my moans and screams… after all, you will be watering parched territory."

"No, not at all, I want the housekeeping staff to know exactly what chocolate I'm getting…
Random one below for you… fun between a queenly black woman and one of those crusty white bitches that irritate us both.
http://www.redtube.com/10987."

"Mmmm, yes, I'm going to ride your face just like the video. Then I want to lie back and savour the sensation of your tongue journeying through its own nutmeg expedition. Take your sweet time… I will be waiting back at the entry point."

"https://www.redtube.com/32343
I'm hardening in expectation of my full blacking by you.
https://www.redtube.com/11109
She's a dirty black bitch in this one…
Remind you of anyone?"

"Not sure that I like the look of that dildo.
I want a hard cock to fuck me."

"Very true, seemed a bit too bendy.
Want more???"

"Do Jamaicans like weed?"

"I like this shit far too much.
https://www.redtube.com/5476
Watch how the white slut pushes that black ass down harder on his cock 13:10 minutes in…"

"Mmm… don't think we will need exterior pushing. Between my hunger and your thirst…
See how the white cock disappears into the black hole. So jealous right now."

"Mmmmm, all good as an opening tease.

More to come later."
"Yaaaaaaaaassss."

Later… he didn't disappoint.

"What would you like to watch this evening, gorgeous? Someone's first time getting chocolate?
https://www.redtube.com/202029"

"Whoa… full works.
Finger fuck and simultaneous ass tap.
Pussy takes a roasting and an ass assault to finish off.
Fuuuuuuuck!. Lucky black bitch."

"https://www.redtube.com/4353
Face sitters.com!!!
I can't believe they have such websites!
I'm gonna need to run off my hard on."

She tried to picture him jogging around his local Hyde Park with his running mate which was his weekend custom.
"Late night session later?"

"Absolutely. I'm gonna imagine your cock flapping as you run."

Chapter 26

"Dreaded Monday rat race. How are you?"
He had often shared the near trauma he experienced every Sunday night as a new week was looming.

"Hello,
Hope the Sunday night blues were bearable. I'm good, thank you."

"I watched too much porn yesterday."

"Too much??? What is this absurdity of which you speak?"

"White slaves for black girls was getting a bit too heavy."

"Nonsense! Sounds to me that all is right with the world. All is as it should be."

"Go on Redtube and search for black mistress… I think you will enjoy."

"Oooooh okay. Let me have a look. Be afraid, be very afraid."
Cayenne searched through the offerings his title suggested.
He followed up once she had had some time to peruse.
"Oh dear… did you like it a lot?"

"Exhilarating. We may find it works or it may not, but I'm certainly up for the exploration.
http://www.google.com/gmail/
Is this what you meant? It's a little slow.
If we venture down this road… be prepared to get a pummelling yourself."
She sent him the link for the first one that caught her interest involving a black dominatrix dressed in black PVC, whipping the

two white men in her charge with a dangerous-looking leather contraption.

"I meant go on Redtube website; and in the search area there, type in black mistress.
I get more out of spanking you and telling you what a naughty girl you have been."
She could tell that her selection was not to his liking. He seemed unnerved.

"Not finding anything particularly exciting on red tube… the black dominance videos seemed much more interesting.
Try Black Tube and type in 'make the best out of hapless white limp dicks'. Sound familiar?"

"Oh okay… did I sound patronising?"

"http://www.hd-easyporn.com/pretty-black-gets-white-boner
Is this what you meant? It's okay I guess."

"Err probably not – will find it later. Clicking on these links with the work Wi-Fi—probably not advisable."

"My excitement is waning with these tame examples."

"Nasty bitch…
Annoying I can't watch your selection – your toy will try to do better with his choices…
For fuck's sake! he's having to provide a certain calibre of hotel too… you are so demanding."

"UNFUCKED nasty bitch… if you please.
Demanding?
Sir, if the mission is beyond your capabilities… pray tell now and avoid a repeat of disappointment (on my part, not yours).
I would rather we dispose of our agreement immediately and see you happier in situations tailored to your taste… a quick fuck in a shantytown alleyway perhaps. Oh, I forgot, you don't really do fucking, let me rephrase, that. A quick jittery fumble and blow job in a seedy hostel."

"You do make me smile."

Cayenne was secretly impressed by the fact that whatever she threw at this guy, he kept coming back for more. She didn't even have to filter what she wanted to say. She felt that she could do or say almost anything, and he insisted on seeing the virtue in it.

"I'd be happy to update you via email as to the delight or rather the sheer euphoria of your successors. The white Financiers and presidential fucks I advance to."

"I like the way you ASCEND whilst I DESCEND—cheeky bad girl… I want to have you first… I want my white cock blacked by a Queen first."

"Queens rarely entertain minions that find fault with their master's commands.
Servants who question the pedigree of their black Queen's grandeur… often find themselves relegated to lesser, somewhat paler monarchs."

"You get off on this, don't you?
Whilst taking full advantage of my need for your juice."

"You are consistently causing me to question your credentials and eligibility for cunt supremacy.
May I remind you that YOUR need is of little consequence."

"I can see you saying that with a leather whip in your hand…
You are making me smile."

"I am not amused by your feeble attempts to lower my thinking and consider your position.
I must refrain from consorting with conquests with flawed regal comprehension."

"Your needs are my only concern."

"Your verbal assertions bore me.
I remain a Black Nubian Superior UNFUCKED Queen."

"New thread…
Let's just fuck
See you Wednesday afternoon. Details to follow…"

"Ooooh yeah… Panties wet.
Pardon me… I meant, the Queen is sufficiently lubricated."

"Good. I like the connection… my white cock hardened on telling you, you will get it."

"All being well, the Queen will grant access to her inner sanctum."

"The black Queen will be worshipped well."

Cayenne knew exactly what dress she would be wearing on Wednesday. She had dug into the recesses of her closet and fished out a dress that she had bought for a Christmas party that never happened; so it had not had its first outing yet, which she felt was particularly apt as thus far, the white knight had failed to deliver. She smiled as she twirled holding the dress and watching the minx staring back at her from her full-length mirror. She wondered whether she should consider toning it down in case the dress caused him to not perform well again.
She could scarcely blame him. The dress was designed to raise a man's heart rate. The deep red velvet fabric was smooth to touch. It was short and figure-hugging, and there was a bare strip on either side that was held together by a selection of large gold pins. Unless she could find a deep red velvet thong, this dress required no undergarment whatsoever.

She sent him a video to inspire his resolve.
"Just sent you a video titled *Black Pussy Squirts* for white cock. Check out the pussy finger rub before he fucks her hard.
Fucking bitch got laid.
I want that pussy rub, and I want your hard cock foraging for fucking berry juice.
Dig deep for that volcanic black molten. Ensure your cock plunges into the depths of my coconut cavity.
GIVE IT TO ME."

"Just back from a meeting. Luckily I didn't have my phone with me… my hardening would have been fucking obvious.
I can almost smell that wet black cunt of yours."

"Salivate in anticipation of the taste of condensed milk and honey."

"I can't wait to slap your black cunt."

"Ooooh, tease it with your finger. Scoop out the succulence."

"That is going to be so fun—a full session on black clit warfare, fingers, tongue, full palm, open hand and, of course, hard white penetrating cock. I'm dribbling already.

Hard as a rock in anticipation of finally being blacked… last day before I finally lose my chocolate virginity and see the world for how it should be.

Blacken me good and proper tomorrow."

"You will be genetically recalibrated the moment your white cock disappears inside my black Tourmaline cunt."

"How are you this morning, foxy?
I'm pumped…
Finally fully embracing the dirty whore you've made me into."

"That's excellent. Credit me for your refinement and elevation by all means. I will settle for no less than a hungry forage…an unstoppable pursuit of caramel delights."

"I'm your slut."

"In that case…I'll keep my kinky boots on."

"http://redtube.com/3554
Intercontinental Park Lane Hotel or Waldorf Hilton? Any preference?

One addition – the Trafalgar Hilton has a fabulous rooftop."

"Oooh… a nocturnal, al fresco pussy scavenge…sounds delightful."

Unfortunately, moments later, this option had been ruled out.

"Annoyingly, the 'iconic' rooftop terrace is closed—glad I checked before booking."

"Yes. There is only so much disappointment one can take in one night."

"Could the Queen possibly muster some faith in her toy's ability to deliver?
Final question, Bond Street or Park Lane?"

When she fell silent, he decided for her.

"Intercontinental Park Lane—see you in the lounge lobby at 2:00 p.m."

"I'll be the black fox in the kinky boots."

"Mmmm, fuckable. What are you going to do with your white toy?"

"Your face will be my rollercoaster to ecstasy."

"I need my fix… I feel like an addict and haven't even been fully blacked yet…"

"I suggest you make the most of this golden/black opportunity."

"You should do the same…
Two London premium hotels in a fortnight… treatment worthy of a Nubian Queen… I doubt any other suitors could offer such distinguished calibre."

"It behoves you to ensure that this esteemed sovereign never has cause to find out…
Don't forget in my air hostess days, I was quite accustomed to premium hotels (albeit in far-flung and exotic continents).
I suppose overlooking Hyde Park will suffice."

"There is a Park Plaza overlooking Big Ben, but it's not a luxury 5-star…
I am fully aware of your worth.
It will be relaxed and fun…I promise."

Later Cayenne was busy browsing in Westfield Shopping Centre when her phone buzzed in her inside pocket.

"Find anything shopping?"

"It's come to something when a Queen has to shop for herself.
But as it happens, I found some beautiful undergarments to complement the kinky boots."

"Bet you look stunning—I would have been quite happy to have been in the fitting room."

"I rarely try anything on – after all, I was without my ladies in waiting…
The first time I'll see it on is barely an hour before you see it."

"Remind me how good your chocolate ass looks.
I have to spray tomorrow… if allowed."

"What does spray mean?"

"Release cum, like a water gun or hose."

"Oooooh would like to see that.
So tell me… does one get hard again after the spray, or does the spray signal the finale?"

"I suspect once won't be enough… once you go black, right?"

"My nigga!"

Chapter 27
Intercontinental Hotel
Park Lane

Cayenne rushed home from taking Ocean to his pick-up point and taking Sugar to school. Usually, she always wore makeup and presented her best self to the world even first thing, but today she wanted to take her time when preparing to go into Central London and so had just pulled on a tracksuit and a baseball cap which she pulled down low over her eyes. She had accepted gracefully, that she wasn't one of those people that always looked fresh-faced and youthful without makeup.

Once home, she quickly prepared dinner for later, tidied up the apartment and then took a long luxurious shower, taking time to shave her private area first and then aiming the faucet directly between her legs on full power. The very thought of what she was preparing for was causing some arousal. She carefully chose the scented shower gel and washed and conditioned her hair. Her real hair which was barely shoulder length was usually combed up on top of her head and wrapped in a cap in preparation for her wig of choice. She had been wearing strawberry blonde wigs for some time. The colour complemented her skin, and she knew her natural hair would struggle with regular colouring as well as the routine hair texturisers that she frequently subjected it to.

She was certain that the stranger was aware by now that the hair he loved to compliment, was not actually growing out of her scalp. Thankfully he hadn't commented when he attempted to run his hands through it during their previous trysts, and she hadn't noticed a reaction to his touch being met with rows of hair strips and fastenings. She had to admit it caused her a little concern, but she would cross that bridge when she came to it. She was quite certain that the stranger wasn't ready for her to fling her carefully styled hair across the room in the throes of passion. Even a black man would need preparation for that.

She applied her makeup carefully, selecting the colours—hues of purples and deep reds—that complemented the figure-hugging dress.

She would definitely need to wear a long coat with this outfit in order to protect her modesty. She stepped into her kinky thigh-length boots and admired herself in the full-length mirror. She approved herself with honours.

She decided to take a taxi to Park Lane as the kinky boots were far from comfortable, and she really wanted the stranger to see them. They were a remarkable creation. Suede on the outside with detailed embroidery weaving its way up the sides. Inside was lined with leopard-print faux fur which she knew would excite him.

The doorman approached the taxi as they pulled up in rank outside the hotel. His crisp attire and gold-rimmed hat glistening and polished. He opened the door and welcomed her with a smile. Cayenne felt herself filling up with pride at her reflection as she strode toward the gleaming doors beneath the black marble intercontinental sign. The huge doors were opened by a second doorman who escorted her inside where she found herself standing in the middle of a vast white-marbled forecourt with a long reception desk at the far end, which was simple and elegant in design. The ceiling was dominated by a beautiful chandelier set in an illuminated background. It was oval-shaped and made up of dozens of diamond droplets. Numerous staff were milling around, all looking pleased to be in their environment which heightened Cayenne's expectancy even more.

She approached the desk and leaned over the counter at the smiling red-haired lady.

"Hello, I'm here to meet with Mr Halpern-Smith. Can you tell me if he is here yet?"

"Good afternoon, madam, welcome to the Intercontinental. Let me have a look for you."

She scanned the screen in front of her and looked down at the large leather-bound book that lay open on the desk; her eyes scanning up and down the page as she followed her forefinger.

"I don't seem to have an indication that he is here yet. Would you like to wait in the bar?"

"Yes, please."

"Certainly," she pointed to her left, and Cayenne looked down an exquisite open corridor which was dotted with small seating areas where a mass of leather chairs had been carefully laid out. On the glass tables were bowls of sweets and nibbles and various guests were sitting around and greeting arrivals. Cayenne ignored the stares that she received from some of the tables she passed. She glanced around and noticed that she appeared rather overdressed by comparison which surprised her. She had expected to be confronted with elegantly dressed women dripping with the most expensive jewellery and draped in designer garments and to see stacks of Louis Vuitton cases. She didn't doubt that on any given day that was exactly what she would find, or perhaps it was the evening that inspired most people to turn on the glamour. But today, during this rather ordinary Wednesday afternoon, everyone looked pretty normal and casually dressed.

She found a cluster of seats at the far end of the bar lounge and rested her feet from the torture of the leopard-print-lined kinkiness. Stretching out her legs, she circled her ankles to encourage the soles of her feet to hang on in there.

She glanced at the time and realised that she was a little early. She decided that to remove her coat would cause too much of a stir, even though she was beginning to get hot. A waiter dressed in smart grey trousers with a matching waistcoat approached her with a tray of unwashed glasses from neighbouring tables. He spoke with a strong accent, though she couldn't quite place it.

"Madam, would like somesing to drink?"

"Erm… actually, I think I'll wait for my companion,"

Cayenne was very thirsty, but at this point, she just wanted to relax in the suite he had prearranged and have a drink in more private surroundings. *After all, he'll be here soon*, she thought to herself.

Thirty minutes whiled away whilst Cayenne made several painful struts back and forth to reception in her haste to get the afternoon started. She could feel herself getting more and more agitated.

The fact that she was being eyed up by gentlemen in the bar and stared at curiously did little to placate her.

She rose from her seat for the last time, clutching her bag she stomped back toward the reception area. She waited just inside the door and stared at the waiting taxis that were lined-up outside. She was about to push through the door and ask the doorman to assist her when the flustered-looking stranger suddenly walked in the through the door furthest away. He was in such a rush to make their appointment that he hadn't realised that she was standing there. She watched him walking hurriedly towards the bar, but something stopped her from calling out.

Moments later, he reappeared, his overcoat hanging from his forearm, his bag over his shoulder and a worried look in his eyes.

His pace slowed as he began to register the mood of the seething fox. She was still staring through the glass door waiting for him to select the right choice of words that may prevent her from proceeding through it.

"Am I late? I'm not that late, am I?"

She turned to look at him and then returned her gaze to the posturing doormen.

"Look, I'm so sorry. My boss called me as I was walking from the underground. There was an issue that needed clearing up." He was looking at her intently to see how much he was progressing toward her good books.

"I'm sorry. I didn't realise how late I was. How long have you been waiting?"

Her jaw refused to cooperate and her eyes remained firm and resolutely transfixed on the incoming guests.

"You look absolutely amazing." He reached for her hand. "Come on. Are you hungry? … let's get something to eat."

She allowed him to take her hand and walked slowly beside him, retracing the now well-worn steps back toward the bar. He approached a waiter and asked if the restaurant was open.

"Yes, sir. The Theo Randall Restaurant is serving lunch; would you like me to find you a table?"

"Yes, please."

"Table for two, sir?"

"Yes, that would be great. Can I also have two glasses of Champagne?"

"Certainly, sir, do you have a preference, sir? I would recommend the Piper with today's lunch menu."

"Okay, that's fine, thank you."

He pulled out her chair and offered to take her coat. She turned her back to him to allow him to remove the full-length coat from her shoulders which he did and placed it down on the seat beside her.

It was moments before he could pull his eyes away from her dress with her bosom peering provocatively over the sweetheart neckline. The tight velvet material clung seductively to her small waist whilst allowing for the rounder proportions of her hips and thighs. As she sat down and crossed her legs, the short hemline crept up further still, revealing perfectly toned legs.

She knew that he could tell by the absent panels on the sides of her dress that she had to be practically naked underneath. The very thought of the torture that she was inflicting on him gave her immense frost-thawing pleasure.

"Am I forgiven now?" he asked when she had safely had her first taste of Champagne.

She smiled in answer and helped herself to the delicious olives and crisps that had been placed down with their drinks whilst they waited for lunch.

He hung his head down to join his shoulders and hunched in his chair like a reprimanded schoolboy.

She began to feel sorry for him and softened the harshness of her expression. "I was sitting there for 45 minutes, clearly overdressed compared to everybody here. I was beginning to feel like some sort of …."

He interrupted before she could answer.

"I'm sorry. Look, let's try and have a good time. I can't believe that you were actually going home."

She was certain that he was used to calling the shots and keeping people waiting. There was no way she was going to allow him to think she was desperate.

She continued to pop the olives into her mouth. Chewing slowly, savouring the flavour before washing it down with more champagne.

The waiter arrived with a large tray and placed down a sformato di fontina for her and insalata mista for him.

She wondered whether her mood had affected his appetite as she watched him pushing the mixed Italian leaves with tomatoes, cucumber and fresh basil around his plate.

Cayenne was positively starving at this point, not having eaten in the morning for fear it would affect the silhouette appeal of her dress and heartily tucked in to her baked squash and cheese soufflé with spinach.

"You are hungry, aren't you baby?"

She swallowed deeply. That was the second time he had called her baby.

She nodded and edged her plate towards him. "Wanna try some?"

"No thanks. I'm not that hungry. Seeing you in that dress has totally taken my appetite away. You look incredible."

She smiled appreciatively, adjusting herself in her seat, deliberately drawing his attention to her legs. She wanted to see him sweat.

He loosened the collar of his shirt.

He made a valiant attempt with his main course—Calamari with pan-fried squid and cannellini beans with chopped rocket.

She licked her lips, thoroughly enjoying her hand-made pasta with shrimp.

They decided to share a soft chocolate cake with crema di mascarpone and took their turns spooning it into their mouths whilst staring over at each other. She knew he was struggling to contain himself.

He confirmed it once the elevator doors closed behind them, and she found herself pressed against the mirror.

His tongue hungrily exploring hers, seeking and finding whatever it wanted, and the deep groans that emanated from his throat told her of his need.

She dropped her bag and unabashedly rubbed the front of his trousers, knowing that what lay beneath would respond almost immediately. She cupped him in her hand whilst her other hand pressed his buttock toward her. The urges between her legs caused her to thrust herself forward in a bid to feel his groin through the fabric of their clothes.

The beep signalled that they had reached the selected floor. They pulled away from each other and immediately burst into a fit of laughter as they realised that most of her rose-red lipstick was now smeared over the lower half of his face. Not knowing who they may face in the foyer of their floor, or who they may encounter coming in and out of the other rooms, he grabbed her hand and hurriedly walked towards their door. Her hand momentarily slipped out of hold in his haste, and she gasped when he stopped suddenly, turned around and clasped her hand again, firmly this time, not wanting to lose the connection.

He slipped the card into the slot, and they were immediately given the green light signalling that the door was open.

He stepped aside to allow her to walk in first thrusting a finger up the back of her dress whilst she grabbed his crotch giving him the green light to proceed with his post lunch chocolate. She stepped inside, and her mouth fell open as she took in the enormity and the opulence of the suite. It was the size of an apartment, possibly larger than the one she lived in. She put her bag on the light brown, textured sofa in the living area and put her phone on the polished coffee table. The floor was covered in thick cream carpet, except for the high traffic areas and the bathroom which had a marbled effect woven into the chocolate brown tiles. A room directly to the left was a dining room which was easily the size of a small conference room with two rows of high-backed leather chairs which looked almost like regal thrones. She peered her head around the door of the bathroom, which was a vision of high-end opulence with mirrored walls, wooden cabinets which contrasted vividly with the brilliant white porcelain on the ceiling. The room she could barely wait to see was the bedroom. The stranger was awaiting her there. He looked small against the huge satin-covered bed with an abundance of puffed up pillows and cushions, which Cayenne imagined would take the housekeepers an absolute age to prepare every day.

He rose to take her. Hands groping her curvaceous glutes with his index finger teasing the crack, edging further and further forward. A groan escaped as he realised his fingers were smothered in her cream.

The next two hours were a blur of fulfilling the promises they had made to each other. She had never been licked and sucked so much in her entire life.

She had never known a man eat her pussy as though she were an haute cuisine buffet. Tasting and poking and sucking to satiate his obvious hunger. Tasting this and then that and then going in for more.

Good God, what had possessed him.

She watched as he forged between her legs until he struck a chord causing her to throw her head back with sheer delight.

After a while, she could sense his hesitation to give her his full measure.

He was nervous, she could tell. She could almost hear him tussling in his own mind fighting to give himself permission to forge ahead and hoping for dear life that he could hold this time.

There was a moment when he lay over her, sheathed at the ready, poking her entrance one last time as he stood at the cliff edge.

He looked down at her waiting, moistened pussy as it throbbed and pulsed with desire at his promise. Deliberating again for a moment, he suddenly surrendered, "Who could resist this?" and then he jumped, diving head first into the vaginal abyss. He could hold back no longer. His conscience abandoned up ahead. She felt him pulse deeper and deeper into her as though unloading a heavyweight that he had carried around for far too long.

She opened wide, using her hands as stirrups, to support the elevation and allowed him to take her on his ride at his pace, as his wings unfurled and carried him deeper still.

He paused for a moment, spinning her around until she was on all fours. After sinking his teeth into her glutes, making her release an agonisingly satisfying groan, he grabbed her hair which she was pleased she had secured with precision. He entered her again from behind, using his grip to pull her back from the ricochet of his thrust.

Without sound, she could tell he was unloading. She tried to imagine that it was pouring into her as opposed to the rubber constraint that embraced him.

When he pulled it off, it was almost half-full of him. Together they watched as the last drops filtered in.

She lay back enjoying the sensation of her pussy feeling alive again, but yet, the yearning for more was unrelenting.

Somehow, he must have sensed her dissatisfaction. She hadn't come, and this seemed to frustrate him.

Aggressively, he scrambled beneath the covers, lifting her buttocks off the bed and pulling her towards his open mouth. She sighed deeply knowing that she was climbing. Momentarily, she toyed with the idea of delaying her satisfaction, but the sweet sensation was far too moreish. The tension was building deep inside her. She was silently willing him to take her right to the edge. She needn't have worried. He was valiantly whisking her to the heights he had just encountered. Determined to show her the sights and sounds from another altitude, and there was no more hesitation as she careered off the precipice.

Chapter 28

"Hello, I'm here for Ocean's annual review." Cayenne peered over the extra-high circular counter that formed the reception desk at Ocean's school.

"Errr, okay, if you would like to take a seat, I'll let Assiah know that you're here."

"Thank you."

Cayenne retreated to the small seating area with its spindly grey sofa. She looked up at the artwork on the wall made from what looked like papier-mache and bits of coloured fabric, depicting a Phoenix rising from the ashes. She considered how apt it was, as it represented a school that took children with learning difficulties and developmental restrictions and helped them arise from the limitations of their challenges to reach their full potential.

Assiah, a mixed race lady with blonde, tinged spiral curls appeared at the glass security door at the other side of the reception desk. Using her fob to operate the door, she stepped forward to greet Cayenne warmly, chatting away in her usual animated fashion as they made their way up in the padded elevator to the fourth floor of the newly built block.

Awaiting them in the informal meeting room was the head of the year, Mrs Catherine Baker. A formidable black woman who Cayenne was slightly wary of. She seemed pleasant enough, but Cayenne had caught her with one sarcastic expression on her face too many.

"Hello, Ms Richards, lovely to see you. Come on in and take a seat. The teacher has just gone to get Ocean; he'll be here in just a minute." Mrs Baker was beckoning for her to position herself on one of the two blue chairs facing the door. It was obvious that there was no love lost between the two women. The only difference being that Cayenne was not the type to put on a fake smile for anyone.

Cayenne knew that her son didn't particularly enjoy seeing his mother in school. He much preferred to keep the two worlds separate.

Moments later, Ocean arrived carrying a selection of various aids and bags and accompanied by Susie Johnston, his speech therapist. A short lady clad in youthful street apparel, sporting a spiky blonde '80s hairstyle.

Her face dropped when she saw her son who was fiddling mindlessly with what was referred to as 'his transition aids' to assist him in travelling around the school and supposedly help him regulate his behaviour.

Cayenne couldn't help but wonder, how it was that Ocean didn't seem to need these attachments when travelling around at home or to the local park or superstore or indeed anywhere else that they chose to take him; and if he did, one look from his mother had proven to regulate his behaviour with immediate effect. One of his aids was a cubic-mirrored object. The kind of item that babies fiddled with when teething, which he intermittently placed in his mouth. Cayenne wanted to be sick. At home, she wouldn't have allowed him to put objects in his mouth. She wondered how they intended for him to succeed the need for such aids. Would he perhaps require more advanced travelling aids to help him progress from these travelling aids? It was a constant challenge for her and Diego to relay to the school the importance of discipline and boundaries for Ocean.

Cayenne tried to take into consideration the fact that the school environment was unique and perhaps Ocean was responding differently as a consequence. But deep down she knew that they simply didn't feel confident in exerting such authority and implementing her standards, even if it was what he needed.

She knew that Ocean harboured a mischievous nature; and once he sensed that he could get away with pushing the boundaries, he undoubtedly would, often to the extreme.

"Ocean, do you want to press the screen so that Mum can see the work you've been doing this term?"

After a few prompts, Ocean responded and touched the whiteboard on the opposite wall.

A selection of pictures uploaded, showing him engaging in various activities in and around the school such as gardening, reading, painting etc., which he proceeded to point at and name.

Cayenne looked on proudly and inwardly thanked herself for having the courage to leave their previous home on the South Coast to move to London in search of an appropriate school for him. They were now reaping the rewards. Ocean and his therapist were excused at this point, probably owing to his short attention span, and he was returned to his classroom activities.

Together with his class teacher and head of year, they perused his report and began setting and affirming goals to attain going forward in the term ahead. Cayenne took this opportunity to reinforce that Ocean should be encouraged to take responsibility for his choices; as those behaviours that they seemed so happy to overlook, were to her mind, his definite choices which to her mind, should be followed by a consequence.

Assiah escorted her back to reception, and soon she was strolling back towards the main road and contemplating whether or not to nip into Westfield again when her phone buzzed immediately upon turning it on.

"Bet you look casually gorgeous."

"That's right."

"Can you meet me in Chanel at midday?"

Cayenne was still rather peeved by the events of earlier in the week when the stranger had invited her to the newly opened bar on the 30th floor of the recently refurbished Novotel. A beautifully constructed open-plan restaurant bar that was spread over two floors with an outdoor terrace, overlooking the River Thames, with panoramic views of the city.

They had met for a quick drink, but he had insisted on showing her the refreshed décor of one of the new suites. Quickly their clothes had been discarded as they rolled around on the immaculately laid bed. The tour had ended the moment he held her in his arms, feeling for her panty less ass before instantly dropping before her as a sign of devoted pussy worship. Smelling and nuzzling into the softness of her pubic strands, using the tip of his tongue to stroke the centre of her in delicate pursuit.

She had placed her cosmopolitan down on the bedside table whilst he kept hold of his glass of Jack Daniels. Using his free hand, he pressed her to lay on her back and lifted her legs one at a time into the air. She closed her eyes and studied the freshly coated ceiling as he supped the remaining dregs of J D from the lobes of her cunt.

She tugged at his belt and unleashed his hardened cock, which protruded to form a triangle in his underpants. He had aroused her to the point of desperate hunger, and she needed him to answer the call.

He had been willing, most certainly. However, his hunger caused him to malfunction, and any promise she may have desired him to fulfil was now deposited elsewhere as he struggled to maintain his composure.

"Sorry. I think I wanted you too much." He had offered remorsefully.

She knew she ought to be sympathetic as she battled with her own disappointment.

As she made her way to meet him, she knew that he would be full of disdain for yet another poor performance.

Usually, they sat opposite each other; but today, he opted to slide in next to her in the booth at the far end of the shop. That way he could slip his fingers beneath the table whilst in the midst of conversation and strum harmonies on her pussy, watching her eyes glaze over as she struggled to contain the evidence of her arousal.

He had bought them a cappuccino and a selection of sandwiches that he thought she might like. All of a healthy nature which she considered very thoughtful of him. It took all of her concentration to finish her lunch whilst being simultaneously finger-fucked.

"I'm going to be smelling of your juice throughout my meeting this afternoon."

"Good. I hope every intake of breath delivers the incense of dripping chocolate pussy juice. My essence will be the silent participant. I want you to harden whilst battling to concentrate. Pity I couldn't crawl under the board room table and unzip your gold exec cock and suck it dry."

As usual, they continued the conversation via email as they parted company.

"Bad bad girl... Keep going... I'm not really taking much notice here, wishing I was still using my gold benefits."

"It's such a damn pity that our liaison was so brief. You certainly haven't left me with the impression of delivering a gold-executive fuck. Whilst very enjoyable, I'd say it was most definitely a three-star which equates to a bronze.
How I wonder what a gold-executive fuck feels like... or better still, a premium fuck. My deflated pussy has now arrived home. It's dejection weighs heavily on me.
Any interesting bitches in that boardroom?"

"I wish it was that interesting... I'm trying to assess whether I can come back and see you."

"I bet you secretly obsess over their parched pussies, don't you?
You secretly like the dryness, I suspect. Probably have to carry around lube in your attaché case. I bet you are inwardly pleased that your cock slips easily into their enlarged cunts. That's why you left me dripping... because you don't really want tight, hot black pussy, do you?
Do you realise how frustrating it is to have a fucking starved pussy?
Where oh, where can I find a premium fuck?"

"The greedy executive is aware he was selfish today and just took what he wanted. He wants to make amends..."

"Not sure you deserve another opportunity. Who walks away from moist hot pussy?"

"You're right, it was fucking insane. I'm sorry I got arrogant.
The toy got arrogant after he got blacked—he thought he knew it all, that he had it all sussed. Stupid white minion."

"On that note. Au revoir.
You just ran out of chances. Guess the gold card doesn't get you everything."

"Oh dear, the white fuck toy now desperately wants to revert. I was only joking. I was trying to make you laugh."

"I trust your next minority conquest will be suitably impressed with your gold status."

"Can just imagine you smirking as you utterly torment me. This executive needs to remember his place. That he is his Queen's toy. His arrogance needs to remain in the boardroom. He must remember his mistress is royalty. Any threat of exclusion from her regal chocolate pussy would mean starvation and destruction.
I am going to book the Westbury Queen suite for her majesty… details to follow."

Chapter 29

She stood for quite some time staring up at the discreet polished entrance of the Westbury. It wasn't quite what she had expected. Somehow, she had envisaged a huge grand entrance and had even worn comfortable, yet still sexy, high-heeled platform boots, just so as to navigate the lengths of the gravel driveway that she had prepared herself to encounter. She was all but ready to take in the landscaped grounds and the sophisticated lighting guiding its guests into its luxurious lair.

She approached the narrow car park at the front of the building and stepped past the attendant and the doorman—who were both dressed immaculately with tall top hats, with a black velvet strip around the base which coordinated perfectly with their thin silk black-and-gold ties and straight leg trousers with seams that could cut through paper.

At either side of the glass doors were four large windows, each framed with white stone panels which set them apart from the granite stone of the rest of the building. Vibrant assortments of shrubbery were delicately dangling to the ground underneath the windows, giving the appearance of a large decadent private home rather than a hotel entrance, except that the grand glass-panelled canopy overhead, with extravagant lighting and various flags protruding above, rather gave it away.

She stepped into the grand hallway where the glass-panelling theme on the ceiling continued on the inside; the only difference being its colour was a deep bronze to match the golden hues of the interior.

The reception area was dotted with large marble-clad columns creating discreet seating areas, with luxurious accessories and elegant free-standing vases bursting with fresh flowers providing a pop of colour in the sea of marble.

The reception desks, two mahogany planks set back on one side of a wide-carpeted corridor, which boasted antique-looking leather chairs with striped cushions in sets of two, as far as she could see, was bustling with people coming and going. There was so much activity, that at first, she didn't know which way to turn; her rose-gold sunglasses perched on her nose impeding her vision further.

At that moment, the stranger arose from one of the discreet leather chairs. He had been waiting for her. He strolled towards her in his blue trousers and crisp white shirt, and she dipped her glasses to allow her to peer over the top to make sure it was indeed him.

His face broke out into a warm appreciative smile as he reached out his arms for an embrace.

"Crikey, did you get lost?" He glanced at his Rolex watch feigning irritation.

She hadn't realised that she had clearly spent too much time flitting around Mayfair, stopping to take a selfie outside Liberties to show the children and marvelling at the exclusive boutiques that lined the back streets, that never seemed to have enough people in them to warrant their existence.

"Sorry. Am I very late?" It made a change for him to be the first to arrive.

He looked at her with mock exasperation and guided her hurriedly towards the Michelin-starred Alyn Williams restaurant that he had waxed lyrical about in his emails.

He had pre-booked one of the many small round tables which were covered in expensive white silk cloths, complementing the cream velvet chairs either side.

As usual, they found themselves seated in a discreet corner.

Living up to the high praise and effusive build-up regarding the high-end European cuisine, together they tucked into the pumpkin soup with foie gras and chestnuts with grilled mackerel and black radish—her choice—and the poached halibut, braised cumbrian beef with cucumber swede, which was his preference, complemented with the finest Prosecco on the menu. As usual, he barely touched his. She would have quite fancied a dessert after eyeing up some delicious fromage blanc and pear meringue being served at the neighbouring table, but she could sense his impatience.

The way he had watched her eat, as though taking note of precisely how to devour her once her restricting thongs were removed. At times, she could feel his eyes narrow behind his glasses as though willing her to hurry up. Desperate for another taste. She knew that had she ordered dessert, it would have been a stroke too far. He stood little chance of being able to sit idly, salivating as she licked the coconut ice cream from her spoon, when all he wanted to do was recapture her own authentic coconut essence.

She could feel the pinch of his insistence as he cupped her elbow and steered her toward the elevator. There was no hope of her being allowed to digest her food in the ambience of the world-renowned restaurant. Once he had placed her leg on the metal railing and waited for their ascent to the Penthouse, he nuzzled so delicately amongst her vaginal shrubbery that she really didn't wish to complain. His free hand mercilessly pinched her hardened nipples, as if to punish her for delaying this moment. She was quite certain, had it not been for the presence of housekeeping as the lift doors opened, he would have happily carried her to the room without removing his tongue from her intimate folds.

She needn't have worried. The vaginal onslaught continued apace; his licks so fervent that she clutched the indigo velvet throw beneath her and held her breath.

With raw passion, she found herself grabbing his hair; his precious hair that wrapped itself around her fingers, pulling him out of her, forcing him to look into her eyes. Having removed his glasses, his eyes were only half-open, waiting for her to come into focus.

Her voice was deep and throaty, "Suck this pussy. Fucking eat the coconut cream, do you hear me?"

Her words infused him with gumption; and before she could even release him for further pursuit, he yanked his head from her grasp, and the force of him pushed her onto her back with her legs in the air. She felt him prize her open using his hands as forceps. He looked longingly into her open cunt, willing her juice to come forth in lashings, yearning to be swathed in her, drowned in her. She let her upper body relax and concentrated her mind on the rumbling taking place deep within the source of her volcanic rupture. His tongue action was so acute, so precisely fine-tuned that it didn't take long for her breath to begin to shorten, and the tension to build. She traced the route of her ecstasy as it crept through the inner workings of her vagina. She grabbed his shoulders to hold him in place in case he adjusted his pace, encouraging him to continue without restraint. Pulling him deep inside, and just as the flow approached the pinnacle, she twisted her torso so that his mouth was directly in line with her parting. She didn't want him to waste a drop.

When she was finished, she lay there. Partly because she had little energy to move, but also to allow his tongue to sup the dregs of her and clear the residue with his lips.

When she awoke, the sky outside was darkening; and the hotel lighting became more illuminated as evening drew in.

She was wrapped in one of the white terrycloth dressing gowns with her clothes folded neatly on the chair beside the desk.

Next to the bed, a glass of Prosecco—now room temperature, had been placed on the bedside table with a post-it note as its coaster.

She could just make out his written scrawl as she squinted her eyes in the semi-darkness.

"Goodnight, gorgeous. See you tomorrow."

Cayenne couldn't deny the injury she felt that he had gone. She supposed she knew he would leave at some point but not like this. She swallowed the wine as her forehead contorted with frustration.

She awoke the next morning to his messages.

"How are you?"

"Okay, you?"

"Did you order breakfast?"

"Yes. Problem gold-card exec?"

"Not complaining—the bill just surprised me."

"Considerably cheaper than Knightsbridge Agent Provocateur I would imagine." Cayenne spat alluding to the lingerie treat he had promised but not fulfilled.

"Now that is a good image. Sipping Champagne whilst you are wearing Agent P…"

"Should have stayed last night then, shouldn't you. Suppose you'll have to introduce me to a platinum exec. Particularly those that are not immune to wet pussies."

"Self-restraint is a virtue. It was a FUCKING challenge I can tell you."

"'How can a man prove he is starving, except by eating', that's a David Niven quote."

"I thought you liked the humour."

"It's your finest quality."

"I appreciate other skills need more practice, teacher."

"I find it almost impossible to teach unless one's protégé is resolutely studious, persistent and determined."

"I'm just remembering the arch in your back."

"Do you want more?"

"What do you really think?

You are so tight which is perhaps why I'm struggling to hold… it's very enjoyable to see how big I look in you…
The contrast lived up to expectation—the image of white disappearing into black hardens me as I write."

"Right now I am very aware of the vacancy of my pussy… the longing…
The hunger within my clit.
What torment now devours me."

"As your toy completes his education his nerves will abate."

"Let us not make haste to the graduation.
For the journey of discovery is to be savoured for fear the truth of learning escapes.
Just supposing you never again encounter the bliss of cocoa genitalia, especially one so deliciously juicy.
Should you encounter such fortune again… you would be prudent to not take it for granted."

"Point made cheeky. Can we be fucking sordid now please?"

"I was imagining earlier, bumping into you in the street accompanied by some pale skank and the very public crotch hold that would ensue. Totally unperturbed by the on-looking colourless hologram… I would continue my assault, and, finally, rub my fingers all over my pussy until infinitely creamed and wipe the remnants all over your pale face and bid you good day."

"The pale skank would have been discarded immediately as the smell of your intoxicating caramel hardens me, and I follow you like a dog on heat.
Perhaps the pale skank could come too and be another bitch toy solely for your use and pleasure."

"Indeed. I'd invite her along to Mayfair… where she would devour the Tapas. I'd wait until the both of you were excited and ready for action (not that Miss Dry Pussy would display any visible signs); then I'd leave you both to your Milky-Way gymnastics whilst I trawl Mayfair in search of sophistication and learned culture, safe in the knowledge that short of a miraculous influx of moisture, your female counterpart can be assured sore disappointment.

"That sounds rubbish. Let's ignore that."

"One must not waiver from one's pursuit of noir exploits. One must be resolute. Is it black juicy pussy you want or not?"

"I will immediately abandon any tolerance of white pussies.
I will no longer give pale skanks the time of day. I am a slave to black pussy juice. I was merely considering my black Queen's pleasure."

"I find your limp-wristed tendency towards indecision, tedious.
I'm inclined to punish you by replicating a white shag experience solely for your comfort… but to consider stretching out and dehumidifying my gorgeously succulent, coconut-lady muffin is just beyond comprehension.
However, I applaud your endeavours to please the Royal Nubian."

"I want to be stiff and hard in your hands… then mouth and then wet cunt."

"Your proposal causes my lady garden to spring a chocolate well."

"I need a drink from that well."

"Remembering the sound of your slurps is causing a juicy reaction. Seeing your head foraging between my legs is such a fucking turn on. I want to pussy slap your face."

"Do you remember how fucking desperate and hungry I was for your black cunt.
Glorious, big long licks of your cinnamon delight with your legs open wide and your chocolate fully accessible.
I rather enjoyed slapping your face with my cock too."

"Oh yes, I clearly remember you demanding for me to look at you. I opened wide and waited in hot anticipation of the warmth of your tongue on the mouth of my tunnel. Stimulating my clit until we were awash with cinnamon cum."

"So much black pussy juice. Liquid ecstasy.
You quenched my thirst and drenched my albeit rubbered cock. We were filth.
I can still hear your moans and smell your juice; I got blacked. Disappearing into chocolate… The way it should be—so said the black Queen as she took her corruption to the next level."

"You'll never forget dipping deep into my sabre-like dripping cunt. For a moment, I forgot my domination as I surrendered to the white cock pummelling me."

"Mmmm, now knowing that turns me on. Mental note—more white-cock pummelling needed."

"Mmmm, drifting in and out of consciousness in the midst of mixed race sodomy. Pummel away, like a drill piercing a log of glossed mahogany."

"I want to be inside. Then you on top. I so wanted your desperate release on me as you rammed yourself down on me again and again.

Taking me as deep as you could, your gorgeous, toned black body, such a breath taking sight as you fucked and fucked."

"You must delve further… for what hidden riches lie within. Oh for more opportunities to straddle your white cock… to find my stride and complete a slow lyrical seduction."

"We were rampant for it… desperate hounds. No one can know the ungodly utterances we spoke to each other, as we crossed boundaries which both hardened and wetted us…"

"Yes, what mind-blowing territories we embraced in passionate abandon. Watching you get immersed in my powerful liberating blackness."

"Free At Last.
The black arrogance hardens me further. My white cock appears to be confirming the truth in what you say… does he only rise for black now?"

"Not at all. The sun will always be the sun. Its purpose is to rise.
However, some days are infinitely more humid than others. Sometimes, the sun leaves the ground relentlessly parched; and on other days, perhaps when there is yet moisture besides… the very same sun causes a wilting lifeless plant to come back to life."

Chapter 30

The gym was strangely becoming a daily ritual which amazed Diego who constantly reminded his mum that she was one of those people that ridiculed gym members and considered that they were being duped out of their hard-earned money when they could achieve the same results at home if they applied themselves.

In actual fact, her views hadn't totally changed about that. She witnessed plenty of people every day that were indeed wasting their membership money. Okay, so they turned up when many didn't, but it was blatantly obvious to her that showing up wasn't enough if you didn't give 100%. Many seemed to just go through the motions, perhaps to appease the guilt of their undisciplined lifestyle. In the few months since she herself had joined, she could even see some people looking more out of shape than when she had first seen them. Then there was the other end of the spectrum—those aggressive women that eyed her up at the beginning of class and walked around posturing with venom in their eyes. She could certainly understand the competitiveness. She had that too. But why the hostility? It made for a very uncomfortable atmosphere.

The glossy videos always made it look like going to one of those high-intensity classes would be full of high fives and shoulder slapping and fist pumping to some R'n'B music. Everybody running out together, as though they were a baseball team, charged-up with enthusiasm after a team bonding session. Everybody looking great and seemingly pleased for one another's success. The reality was very different.

There would be the confident ones standing up front; and the less confident ones somewhere towards the back looking on longingly, hoping that they too would get bodies that exhibited all their hard work.

Cayenne made up her mind that she was going to be competitive, aim to be the best and to push herself harder than anybody else, but she would do it in a friendly way.

Being bombarded with erotic emails had become another daily ritual.

"Let my cock see you...
Or entertain it with some corruptive viewing. Surely I deserve a treat."

For some reason, his demands for videos or pictures always irked her. Especially when offers of his own images were never forthcoming which she was secretly thankful for.

"Viewing must be up close and personal. Within earshot of the moans that they evoke... within smelling distance and within inches of a gaping hungry pussy."

"I want to fill that hungry pussy.
I want to be swallowed.
I want your moans loud and dirty in my earhole.
I want to be your interracial fuck slut."

"I fear the vastness of said hole is beyond filling. Such is the hunger... all juice disintegrates. Only a plethoric waterfall... hot and unceasing would suffice."

"To help slow the tide, would the black Queen in all her generosity allow her interracial fuck slut one localised meeting whilst bigger, more-preferable-to-her-taste plans are finalised?"

"I condemn whatever gave you the deluded notion of such Nubian generosity."

"The black Queen has rightly corrected her toy."

"Let the Queen suffer her hunger, for it is not as though she is unaccustomed.
May her vacant pussy devour her. Render her senseless with frustration.
May the nightmares of white pussy satisfaction shred her nerves.
May she languish forevermore in pussy torment. For no white prince cometh. No. None appeareth on the horizon..."

"Wow… sounds so torturous and unfair. Let me buy you a coffee later in the week."

Reading over their messages later on that evening whilst waiting for her French manicure to dry, Cayenne had to admit that her relationship with the stranger, if it could be called that, was bringing out a side of her she wasn't sure what to make of. Was she so sex-starved that it brought out the Tasmanian devil within whenever she felt the urge?

She had never used language like this in her life, and would probably never have thought to express it out loud.

Was this a good thing? She would probably need to commit to advanced high-intensity workouts to deal with the obvious pent up sexual frustration. Why wasn't she like most normal women who made sure that they got their needs met? Why did she have to be so particular? She imagined that most women had 'go to' people they could call in times of need. A friend here; an ex there. Why was she different? Why did she elect to go without? And what was it about this guy that allowed him to at least peer beyond the veil? At times she felt that she could see the sincerity in his eyes, of what she wasn't quite sure. It wasn't love, but it was sincere.

Then at other times, he would make her feel that she was simply an escape from the mundanity of his corporate world, and his inability to address whatever was making him unfulfilled in his personal life.

And what of her feelings. It wasn't love for her either. But there was something—an electrical charge, a frisson, a spark when they were together that transcended the cringe-worthy actions, and an apparent deep concern for each other's wellbeing.

It feels good for now, so just go with it. Why are you over-analysing it? Maybe that's your problem. Maybe it's not that deep. You always try to make things more than what they are. Maybe this is just about meeting each other's needs, and that's it. She glared at herself in the mirror, studying her reflection.

Her phone vibrated, and she remembered that she had put her phone on silent earlier and forgotten yet again to restore the sound. Diego was always nagging at her about that.

"Muu-uu-uu-uum, why didn't you answer your phone?" He bellowed when she finally answered. After she recovered from the shock of his annoyance, she would smile at the obvious concern in his voice; and the fact that if he didn't get a response immediately, his thoughts were always for her welfare, as though he couldn't rest until he heard her voice.

His was the first message, asking her to get two of his favourite chocolate chip cookies that were actually family size; but he managed to devour them singlehandedly, even though the first thing he would do after opening the packet was to painstakingly remove the majority of the chocolate chips.

Similarly, the second message was another request for chocolate.

> "My white cock needed to go trawling…
> https://www.redtube.com/546d5
> Another innocent white boy turned."

The images that appeared on the screen made her grab for the towel at the end of her bed, suddenly grateful that she had forgotten to put it in the wash. It was needed now to place underneath her to capture the juices that were trickling down her leg.

She lay back to watch avidly as a black woman was sandwiched between two slim, curvaceous Caucasian women who were kneeling in submission and completely at the mercy of the black Queen. Cayenne found herself writhing around on the bed unable to contain the sensations pulsing through her, making her want to climb through the screen and join in. To push the black woman aside and enjoy the service for herself.

> "Fuck. This is fucking amazing.
> I want to follow this, step by step. Never seen the pussy ass swipe before. Hell yeah. I fucking want that.
> I love the adoration. Focused black pussy devotion. I need you to emulate this devotion; otherwise I will find a white minion that does. I want the same hunger all over your face. Desperate for more black pussy and ass.
> I'm going to reward you with the face-fuck of your life. Good boy."

The second video he sent her was of a white man thoroughly enjoying and dominating the chocolate pussy that the title boasted of.

His passion, vigour and intensity were enthralling to her. There was no evidence of the hesitance and concern that often looked back at her during their own encounters. It seemed the stranger was battling inner conflict. Wanting to be a white whore toy but not actually having the courage to execute.

"The second video started well." She conceded. "Love the positioning. The beautiful sight of white on black pussy pounding, FUCKING AMAZING. Fucking black bitch was taking it and loving it. I even liked the dominant and brave white hand on her neck. Hell yeah.
But then I realised that this will never be us."
She wasn't quite sure if she was toying with him here, or indeed where she was going with this. What she was about to say would either cause his face to radiate a healthy pink or drain to a decidedly haunting shade of pale.

"I saw no passion-killing RUBBER.
There was no fear on this fortunate white man's face. No black pussy doubt or confusion.
See how he confidently fucked the life out of his once-in-a-lifetime opportunity.
Black bitch got the full sensation of white cock. Hot and unhindered. He clearly came with the intention to devour his chocolate feast, not simply sit on the side-lines guilt-ridden.
Are you trying to hasten my fucking torment?
I won't have that ecstatically blissful look on my face, will I?
Of all the white execs in Canary Wharf... even in the underbelly... I had to stumble across Worry William who approaches every fuck with extreme caution. Who has to spreadsheet couture cunt.
Thanks for ruining my fucking orgasm."

She clicked off her phone, but then she realised she had more to say. She couldn't move her fingers fast enough as she urgently typed in her thoughts, as though her life depended on it which caused her to mistype some words which added to her frustration.

"You haven't been fully blacked, you deluded white fuck; any more than an immigrant with a temporary visa, does not a citizen make.

That's you all over, isn't it? Delusional Dan. Wanting it but not really wanting it. Saying you do with such corporate bravado, but when it comes to the crunch, you just can't fucking hack it.

Blacked my arse!

Forevermore you can go through life in white suburbia telling your little white friends in your dry pussy gang… that 'I nearly got blacked once'.

I suggest that you go back to the safety of white suburbia and keep your black hunger where it ought to be… In your fucking dreams WHITE BOY."

"Wow. Good day to you too. The Queen's wrath is ruthless considering the delivery was only supposed to give some afternoon pleasure and satisfaction."

"What use is satisfaction that falls below the grade."

"The feeding in video 1 is still making me horny.
PS: Remind me to make sure you're aware of my platinum AMEX status the next time you are in my company."

"Video 1 was amazing. If only I could find a platinum amex hungry white fuck.
Platinum Amex! Really? Wow. Impressive white toy."

"Dirty, dirty black MILF…
Your toy awaits his next command."

"I believe I've made my commands VERY clear."

"Coffee? I'll use my platinum card."

"So if the Mayfair, Westbury and the Intercontinental are merely aware of your gold status… what establishments pray tell are privy to your Platinum Amex credentials?
Claridges?
The Savoy?
Ritz?
Dorchester?"

Chapter 31

"Good morning. Still seething about the ever-present Sheik at the Hilton yesterday that seemed to be as enamoured by your presence as I am."

"Yes, I was just wondering what suite the Sheik may have commanded in return for exclusive black pussy rights.

In fact, from my furtive research… they have been known to hire an entire floor in which to entertain royalty in the style to which they are accustomed. Flying in flowers from Geneva, fresh oysters from France.

I am beginning to fear, dear boy, that this cardinal warfare for black territory is one for which the Arab world is better equipped. I couldn't possibly imagine what a mere city exec, prone to spreadsheets and excessive calculation before action, would need to do to even compete. My heart bleeds to think of you desolate in the womb of the wharf… whilst I am transported to exotic climes for spicy exploits and queendom upgrades.

Where anywhere beneath the penthouse is on par with a British basement and jewels other than diamonds are discarded like cheap tapas.

Poor Languid Lee, destined for abandonment. Languishing in milk chocolate sewers for eternity… mourning the loss of moisture, tightness and high-quality caramel.

Whatever will become of Careful Colin? Who, in his immediate circle will ever believe he once dared reach for exotic fruit in the heart of London and got resolutely (half) blacked until his heart was content.

Will he ever forget the memory of the equatorial Queen he once encountered, and finally forgive himself for not meeting the challenge to become a Daring Dan.

In actual fact, he went on to live unhappily ever after with Safe Sally, taking yearly vacations on senior citizen cruises with decrepit wrinkly Caucasians.

I truly hope Evasive Eddie will one day step outside of his comfort zone and live on the edge where real living begins.

Or will Boring Boris forever stroll to Chanel Café at precisely 11:03 to place his usual tab before resuming the order of the day."

"I will never make the mistake of asking you to torment me again."

"So … you can't give me what I want, and now you can't handle torment.

How short-lived this escapade into the dark side turned out to be.

I'm off for a fucking Sheik hunt."

Why did she insist on taking her frustration out on him and toying with his already fragile ego when it was clear he was determined to put a smile on her face.

Yesterday he had been so attentive, almost adoring. The sensitive way in which he looked at her couldn't be denied. She could feel a depth of feeling that didn't come across in their email correspondence. When they sat opposite each other, and she clasped her hands together over the table, he would subconsciously reach for her hands before remembering himself and pulling them away. If a strand of her hair fell over her face, he would instinctively move to tenderly push it aside and then look bashful as though he hadn't meant to.

This was all becoming quite confusing. Hadn't she been the one who had stipulated that she had just wanted a bit of fun? That there was no need to reveal too much about each other. So why was she now pondering silently the circumstances of his personal life? What of the fact that they were yet to exchange telephone numbers or addresses. Was this something she should question. She was certain there was somebody in his life, although there was no evidence of them on his Facebook page. Admittedly she had browsed it once or twice, but she justified herself that he was the first one to reach out to her Facebook page during the three-month hiatus when she had cut him off.

Why did she now find herself wanting more? Not much more at this stage. Just a little more. An invite to his home for lunch perhaps. The odd direct phone call.

What did he want from her?

She remembered their encounter at the Intercontinental when he lay looking at her intently and almost absentmindedly admitted that had she not had any children, he really would be in trouble. He clearly wanted children. Why had he left it this late in life? *It's alright for you, you've already got your brood*, he had mockingly chided on another occasion before asking her whether her children were black, and whether it was a conscious choice.

She recalled the smile of admiration on his face as she had passionately expressed how important it was that her children look like her and carry the intrinsic features of her heritage.

Her child-bearing days were surely in the past. Hurtling towards her mid-40s, albeit in the best shape of her life, was no time to contemplate adding to her little herd. She had promised herself that she would never do it out of wedlock again anyway.

She fantasised occasionally about getting married, not the dress and ceremonial aspects so much as the day-to-day and having that knowing that you are in it together. Properly married. Not just settling for someone but finding someone exceptional to enhance an already full life, who, in addition, would now have to be an exceptional stepfather.

That morning she had received confirmation by email from E-Quip that her position as playgroup coordinator had been confirmed, and that further emails would follow detailing the terms and conditions and requiring her to e-sign the necessary documentation.

When she had informed him, she could feel the pride in his written voice.

"Hey, that's great. Well-done, you. I knew you'd do well. We must have a celebratory cup of tea."

Somehow despite a packed schedule of meetings at the office, he was determined to see her. His urgency was palpable.

There was something in the way he made her feel. As though she was the only person there, or at least the only person who held his interest. They looked at each other longingly, their eyes communicating words that could not be spoken. The silent conversation continued as they strolled towards the opposite side of the quay so as to delay their parting. Their matching, long winter coats aligned, so that passers-by would not be privy to the furtive touching going on beneath. Her hands would appear as though they were simply stuffed deeply into her pockets, seeking warmth from the chilled conditions as they stood facing each other, hips pressed together as though about to render a choreographed, intimate rumba. Her outstretched fingertips, hidden within the confines of their full-length fabric lining, were stroking his rapidly lengthening cock, slowly and seductively. He momentarily rested his head back and looked skyward enjoying the pulsing of his blood flow. He glanced around tentatively, relieved that his altered profile was hidden from view.

She looked up into his face and whispered without coyness "Touch me."

She needed him to know that there was nothing to separate his touch from her soft, moist intimacy; and that under her skirt, the satin finish of her cocoa-buttered skin was without constraint.

He read her eyes and answered the call with immediacy. His fingers reaching inside her belted coat, slipping within the inner folds and curving under her mini-dress, hastening the short distance to the source of heat that emanated towards his hand.

One finger, then two. It only took one stroke, and his hand cupped to catch the soft silk dribbling into his palm.

A gasp escaped them both almost at the same time. He brought his mouth down to meet hers which was parted slightly, waiting for him.

She knew that if they hadn't happened to be standing in the middle of a lunch-seeking crowd, that he would be on his knees, burying his head inside her coat and sucking hungrily on her Queenly labia, salivating as each enriched pearl moistened his tongue.

If they had been alone, she too would have surely beaten him to the post, gladly and temporarily abdicating her deity, kneeling before him, mouth agape, his own jewels encircled, devouring and tea-bagging away, oblivious to the dull lunchtime hubbub.

They pulled away, reluctantly, adjusting their coats to protect evidence of spent passion. They stood momentarily staring at each other and then almost in sync, as though performing part of their own unique swansong, they backed away a couple of steps before turning around in opposite directions and walking away without saying a word.

Chapter 32

"Did you see the way he rose for the Queen?"

"So sexy."

"It felt good being blacked in public…"

"Indeed, white Sheik. I wish I was sitting opposite you with each leg sprawled on two separate tables with no panties on, gyrating on the boardroom swivel chair and clenching and releasing my cinnamon clit.
You would soon abandon your spreadsheet and crawl over to the source of my spice mix aroma, tongue hanging out.
Lick away, white Sheik. Lick away."

"I only wish I could. I'm so very thirsty. My mouth is so dry."

"I'll be sure to store up extra juice for you.
Could have sworn I've just felt the sensation of white cock wedged in my vagina. I opened my eyes and was alone.
My pussy must have been experiencing muscle memory.
How it longs to be ravaged in a terroristic onslaught. Until there is a massacre of cunt juice and pussy debris all over the crumpled sheets. An array of drenched towels discarded around the room as the white Sheik slumbers after his princely feast."

She was turning herself on again, yielding herself to the consequent bout of pent up frustration that followed.
"I'm so fucking white-cock hungry."

"Such a dirty bitch… hardening at my desk."

"I think I'm done with busy execs who are more turned on by a conference meeting."

"I'm not more turned on by a conference call—I'm turned on by your greedy filthy need for platinum, and what I have to do to keep the status…"

"I'm turned on by your black hunger and your white cock."

"Show me that delicious, tight, wet black cunt that has utterly corrupted me and fucked up such a nice innocent good boy."

"You think you've seen corruption?
By the time I've finished with you, you will need blackberry juice as part of your five-a-day.
My eventual absence from you will evoke terror, like a Jamaican man on Father's Day.
Panic like an immigrant denied indefinite leave to remain. Discomfort like a so-called platinum executive seated in an actual authentic haute cuisine Tapas restaurant."

"That's made me laugh. Thank you. You do make me laugh."

Several days passed without a word. Cayenne was annoyed with herself to realise that she was actually missing the messages. The urgency and hunger that satisfied her so much.
Usually, she made sure to wait until he reached out to her, careful not to be the first to text.
Today her emotions got the better of her.

"All okay?"

"Serious executive stress… left the wharf estate in the company car service at 2:00 a.m. My sore eyes need something."

The video she put together for the stressed executive was worthy of an Academy Award. After much painstaking trial and error, she managed to position her phone, leaning it strategically against the velvet-buttoned foot of the bed ensuring that the camera was trained resolutely on the vaginal samba taking place between her legs.

There was no formal routine to the dance, but every motion of her hips produced an effect on her exposed pussy as she adopted a kneeling, downward, facing-dog pose, hips and fanny elevated to the sky. The clenching and releasing producing an open coconut image on her screen.

Several miles across town, a hungry exec excused himself several times to the solitude of the marble-clad men's room of his executive offices, whilst all around were dutifully busying themselves with their daily tasks to fulfil the latest mandate submitted from head office in New York. One hand clenched in-between his teeth to stifle the groans threatening to escape from deep within his throat, whilst desperately attempting to steer his relief into an imaginary funnel. His eyes closed in a drunken stupor as he rested his head back and leaned against the inside of the cool cubicle door.

"Damn, that woman. What is she doing to me?"

Peering around the door for fear the words had actually escaped his mouth, he washed his hands and stared at the reflection of the man he no longer recognised in the row of mirrors. The steam from the hot water faucet drifted upwards until it almost obscured him from sight, making him look as though he was getting lost in the foam of clouds. Funnily enough, that was exactly how he was beginning to feel inside.

Chapter 33

Cayenne pulled up the collar of her jacket to block out the howling wind circling around Mudchute Park. The surrounding trees were swaying violently, like baying crowds watching the action, as fallen leaves and morning strollers battled the winter elements. She wondered why she hadn't given more thought to what coat to wear, chastising herself for not giving much consideration beyond what matched the generic E-Quip uniform that she had received by post a few days earlier, consisting of a black polo shirt and black pullover, which were to be matched with black trousers or a skirt of her choice.

The park was a shortcut to Manchester Road, an area which starkly contrasted the relatively tranquil order of life on the island. She remembered when she had first moved to the area, some two years before, when she would hear people refer to 'the island'. It took several weeks for her to realise they were referring to the Isle of Dogs, an area in the East End of London that is bounded on three sides by one of the largest meanders in the River Thames and upon which her apartment block was situated.

The park and adjoining farm were an unexpected attraction amidst a mass of iconic skyscrapers, which Cayenne considered a hidden gem in the middle of a built-up district. Set in 32 acres of countryside, her and the children had whiled away many hours there to get a feel for their new area. A large expanse of green formed the main part of the park, an oval-shaped field with a running and cycling path and adjoining dog-walking trail forming the perimeter. The middle of the green was occupied most weekends by rugby, football and cricketing teams interspersed with joggers and fitness enthusiasts vying for space. At the far end stood an enclosed basketball court with light-blue-painted railings, just before the Island Gardens Light Rail Station. On the rare occasion that the local teenage ballers left the basketball court unoccupied, groups of elderly Chinese Tai Chi practitioners performed an array of synchronised routines that belied their advancing years. It was a magnificent sight. The elegant motions, swords in hand, locked in their own world, arms and feet dominating territory, directing energy both away from and towards them with commanding motions to the light refrains of soft eastern music.

Cayenne couldn't help but stop and watch; no matter how late she was for wherever she was going, the aura was so compelling as though it was trying to teach her something.

After a few moments, she continued past them conscious that she would be expected to arrive early for her first day of work.

She was told to report at 9:00 a.m. and leave at 4:00 p.m., even though the holiday schedule on the leaflets she had been given stated a start time of 8:00 a.m. and closing time of 6:00 p.m. As it was out of term time, she guessed that she wouldn't be going through the main entrance. She wandered around the back of the building and still it wasn't obvious where she was supposed to enter the building. On closer inspection, she noticed an intercom unit with a button next to it. She pressed the button tentatively and waited for a response. She tried again and still nothing. The corner of her eye caught sight of a shadowy movement behind one of the windows. She squinted and peered intently and made out the large figure of a young man gesturing with his arms and beckoning her towards him. A clipping sound released the catch on the metal gate, and she pushed it open and followed the path towards the large glass sliding doors. The lights were dimmed, but she could just make out a semi-circular unit which she presumed was the reception desk, and a wide reception area which seemed to recognise it's out of term redundancy. Clive stepped forward from around the desk and introduced himself as the E-Quip manager. He looked to be no more than 22 or 23 years old, and the lack of formal introduction skills confirmed the culture of his youth. Cayenne had expected a firm handshake, direct eye contact and a managerial disposition.

Clive, a tall black gentleman, was unkempt in his appearance. His hair reminded her of the style that many black men adopted in the 1970s when combs were not considered a necessary requirement outside of special events. She observed him from behind as he had asked her to follow him along the main corridor. In tribute to his 70s forefathers, his head clearly hadn't seen a comb in days and probably resisted any form of styling or conditioning judging by the white flakes highlighting the mass of black fluff, that were cascading down onto his shoulders with every movement. She wondered why nobody had noticed and thought to mention it. An area manager perhaps, an observant flatmate or a concerned patron or parent worried that these same flakes would season their little Emma's jam sandwich. He walked in a way that documented his poor self-image, shoulders slightly hunched, a dipped head and a downward gaze. His head appeared small compared to the large expanse of his girth, which the E-Quip uniform department had clearly underestimated. She followed Clive down an empty corridor, passed several empty classrooms and closed doors, eventually turning left into a large assembly hall.

She imagined that during term times, this room was occupied for formal assemblies and school productions and multi-tasked as a dining hall during lunch times. Today, there was a row of tables along each side with a different assortment of toys on each one. In one corner, a separate cluster of tables formed the impromptu lunch area judging by the multicoloured array of cartoon lunch satchels and water bottles.

Around 40 children, ranging in age from four to twelve, were running around in various groups, some kneeling in corners sorting through buckets of toys whilst others were sitting colouring and making full use of the stationary laid out on the tables. A couple of the older boys were tossing a basketball around with one eye trained on Clive, hoping that the lady they hadn't seen before in the black uniform would keep him preoccupied for a little longer.

"This is the main area where we will be working most of the day," Clive was showing Cayenne the general routine. She noticed that he was almost well-spoken, and there was a slight effeminate edge to his voice.

"This is where you will sign in when you come in each morning," he pointed at a blue felt register with a pen wedged into one of the pages. "This is the children's register." He picked up an A5 ledger with the children's names listed, and several columns where they were to be ticked present or absent when the register took place twice a day. It seemed some of the children were dropped off at 8:00 a.m. and others arrived later at 10:00 a.m.

"When the children come in, direct them over here where they can take their coats off and put their bags down."

He wandered towards two rows of low-level benches which already had a stack of coats and scarves thrown in a heap in no particular order. She wondered quite how they were supposed to keep track of which coat belonged to who, but it was a great example of why lost property was such a large part of primary school life.

"We have a snack break at 11:00 a.m. and then break for lunch at 2:00 p.m. We always remind the children that it is snack time first, so they should only grab a small snack." Clive covered his parched lips with his hand conspiratorially, "We've had a few incidents where we've turned around, and some of the kids have eaten all their meal during break, and then at lunchtime they've had nothing left," he chortled heartily making a snorting noise and revealing teeth caked in days' worth of plaque and a thick furry-coated tongue. His eyes crinkled in the corners where yellow crumbs resembling cornmeal gathered in clumps.

He continued to run through the routine. "I've taken the liberty of assigning you to a group. There are four of us coordinators, and we are all responsible for a group each. I'll show you your group in a moment."

It was all Cayenne could do to stifle her excitement.

"We generally swap around. In the morning, your group might be inside, so you will be leading them in an exercise. I'll give you some ideas. Then in the afternoon, after lunch, you'll most likely be outside where you'll do a fun outdoor game with the children. There's no formal routine though, so sometimes we will all go out together and do a large group exercise."

Cayenne tried not to let the surprise show on her face. She had only just walked in the door barely 15 minutes before, and now she was responsible for a group already? She had expected to perhaps shadow for a day or so and casually assist with a more experienced coordinator until she found her feet. It seemed she was expected to find her feet almost immediately. She didn't even bother to ask Clive to give her some ideas for the exercises. She got the distinct impression that he could hardly wait to offload the stress he was obviously experiencing himself. As they sat in the prop room, a kind of staffroom-come-abandoned-accessories room with a row of wooden cupboards that looked like the result of a woodwork experiment, and a dirty sink in the corner which was covered in hard dried paint and clearly used to wash paint and glue utensils from the arts and crafts classes, Clive removed a stack of files from one table making room for them to sit and talk. "I've got all that paperwork to do later," he sighed rolling his eyes towards the removed pile and looking heavy with disdain.

"You've got some paperwork to do as well I'm afraid. As I pass them to you, just read through them quickly and sign at the bottom. Sorry about this, but the head office will expect me to have it done today."

"That's okay," she smiled pleasantly and sat opposite him taking one of the biro pens that were strewn across the untidy table. She deliberately took the seat slightly to his right on the opposite side of the table, as she knew that sitting any closer to the permeating odour, that she suspected was coming from the beneath his bulging jumper, would arouse a bout of acute nausea. She rested her forehead against her hand, as she leaned on the table, partly to shield the horror on her face that this young university student had been appointed a manager of a children's out-of-school programme, when it was clear looking after himself was a constant, precarious challenge. Either that or the sadness in his eyes spoke of a deeper issue to such an extent that he had lost any interest in his day-to-day care.

Pen poised over her paperwork as though she was pausing to think of an appropriate answer for the numerous mundane questions that lay before her, she screwed up her face in confusion as to how his appearance had gone unnoticed. This wasn't simply a case of bad odour or bad breath or the usual traits that one would come across in a work environment. As far was completely evident to her and any normal person, this guy was seriously neglecting himself. Particles of food had hardened onto his work jumper that had the audacity to boast manager on the back. It was as though he had fallen asleep somewhere the night before, perhaps the last two nights, and simply woken up and ran out of the door in the way one would expect a student to behave or at least someone with a less responsible position, such as collecting glasses in the local boozer for extra cash. Not a representative of a reputable children's company that was subsidised by the local government.

Before she could finish her list of autographs, he was openly confiding in her about the pressures of his position. He had been promoted the previous year from senior coordinator to manager of the St Edwards Primary placement which ran several programmes throughout the year.

"How long have you been doing this now?" She looked up at him and smiled, deliberately attempting to soften her eyes and not alert him to the way in which he was startling almost all of her senses at once.

"Three years now. I'm studying business management at Coventry University, but I've been doing this in the holidays to earn extra money." He rested his head on the heel of his hand and closed his crusty eyes momentarily.

"It's getting too much now. All this paperwork for one and the area managers don't help. They just turn up and expect me to have it all done." He was gazing towards the other side of the room with a faraway look in his eyes. She knew he wasn't focusing on anything in particular. She wondered why he seemed so lost.

"There was supposed to be someone else here as well. There was supposed to be two new people starting today. You and someone else. But they haven't turned up, and the two people that were here last term," he snorted and wiped the end of his nose in an upwards motion exposing two caked nostrils. "Gone," he flicked his hand to suggest they had disappeared into thin air.

"It's not that bad, is it?" she laughed thinking how she could lighten the mood.

"It's alright. Some of the kids are a bit…" He screwed up his face as though suddenly catching a bad smell. She wondered whether he had finally gotten a waft of his own armpits.

"Some of them just don't want to listen and are such hard work." It was clear to Cayenne that Clive wasn't exactly following his passion with this job. She was prepared to hazard a guess that even without the perceived pressures from senior management, that Clive would not be the most motivated, energetic person to be around. She could certainly understand his lack of enthusiasm, as she wasn't exactly drawn to the prospect of working with children either. She often found it amusing that people presumed that she enjoyed working with children, or that she would be suited to it. Most of the time she barely thought she was even suited to parenthood, and that was with her own children. There were aspects that she enjoyed. The responsibility of guiding them through the challenges of life and preparing them for the obstacles that lay ahead; helping to cultivate the mindset that a good foundation will see you through almost anything—that was her forte. That was where she felt she thrived. The day-to-day routine, not so much. She was enjoying that her children were mostly of an age that they could engage in great conversation, and their own personalities were showing through—obviously it was different with Ocee. The conversation was limited, although she often questioned whether she had helped set that limitation herself and perhaps should have challenged him more. All of the children had been late developers with their speech. More than likely because she was always in her head and should have been more vocal with them from an early age. Most expectant mothers began their dialogue with their child the moment they knew of their existence. Cayenne barely saw the point until they were at preschool age. The age where she could expect a decent response. Perhaps therein lay the problem. Obviously, she hadn't divulged this during the interview process for this job.

She certainly hadn't been honest about the fact that she would much rather rake over 50 acres of land and dig up weeds with her bare hands than spend eight hours with nose-dribbling, whining children whom she suspected had parents that hadn't much fancied it either, which is why they dropped them off at the earliest opportunity and picked them up ten hours later. She was prepared to bet that many of them weren't at work at all but rather sitting at home with a good book.

Shortly after, Cayenne had the opportunity to observe the opening session when all the children were gathered around to sit in a circle with Clive perched on a brave, spindly, wooden chair in the middle with the other two coordinators on duty that day, looking on with bored expressions. Both of the women were of a similar age to Clive. Joanne was a white, wild-haired girl in a stretchy striped jumper, with her E-Quip uniform over the top and holey jeans and purple Dr Martens. Vanessa was black, short and round and looked much older than her 22 years; and again, she was relying heavily upon the generosity and imagination of the E-Quip uniform department.

"Hello everyone." Clive sang with a deliberately cheery voice. "Welcome back. I can see that some of you have been here before. Who hasn't been here before?" Clive looked around, to see if there were any hands in the air, taking note to glance at Cayenne to see if she was paying attention. Two little hands were raised, and she later found out that there were a few more in the crowd that had obviously wanted to remain anonymous.

"Can anybody tell me who else is new in the room?" A few cheeky fingers pointed in her direction.

Cayenne obliged with what she hoped was a friendly winning and engaging smile. A smile that said, 'Yes, I really want to be here, and I can't wait to spend time with you all, and I don't mind at all that you may wipe snot on me and tap me on the arm with no regard for the combination of paint and glue wedged between your fingers.'

"This is CAYENNE. Can we all say a friendly 'hello' to Cayenne and make her feel welcome."

"Hhheeeeeeellllllloooooooo," came the loud chorus. She waved at a few faces that caught her eye and wondered how long she could keep up this smile without her cheeks aching.

Clive proceeded to invite the children to say their names and to tell everybody something about themselves. Whether they had a brother or sister, what their favourite cake was, what sweets they hated, how much they couldn't stand vegetables etc.

Several group activities followed until snack time, after which Cayenne was thrown into her first assignment. She had been assigned to the blue group according to Clive's programme, which meant that she would have to take 15 of the children outside and entertain them for 45 minutes.

She tried to ignore the panic threatening to build-up inside. "Come on, it can't be that hard," she scolded herself and took a quick look in the store cupboard whilst the children were eating to see what was available to her. She looked longingly at the tennis and badminton racquets but immediately ruled them out, as most of the children in her group were too young to grasp the game with such short notice, and they weren't exactly team sports. She spotted a leather bag, with what looked like plastic hockey sticks inside, perched in the corner of the room behind a sack of basketballs. Managing to climb over an assortment of objects to reach for the sack, she rooted inside and found some plastic balls. She quickly formulated a plan in her head. Something simple and straightforward. She would need some plastic spot markers, which luckily, she found behind the door; and once she led her team out of the double doors at the end of the hall, she noticed there were dozens more scattered and abandoned around the large enclosed playground looking decidedly worse for wear.

"Okay children, follow me." Cayenne elevated her voice injecting as much enthusiasm as she could muster. Raising her arm in the direction of the large playground, the children filed along behind her.

Clive followed shortly afterwards to see how she was getting along. If he was displeased at all, it didn't show.

She lined the children up along the wire mesh fence whilst she demonstrated what she wanted them to do. They watched with excited anticipation as she placed the spot markers to form two long lines, one for each team, spacing them out with enough room for a little person to meander around, long stick in hand.

She then retrieved two sticks from the leather bag and two plastic balls. Placing one of each on the floor, she held the other stick in front of her poised next to the ball. Nudging the ball gently with the stick, weaving in and out of the markers right to the end of the line and then back again.

"Once you've managed to get back to base, you then hand your hockey stick carefully to the next person in your team, and then it's their turn. The first team to finish is the winning team. Okay? Does everyone understand?"

"Yeeeeeaaaaaaah."

She divided the group into two teams, soon realising that they were one team member short. "I will have to join your team," she exuded pointing to the team with one man down.

She was surprised to see that the children grasped the game very quickly and were remarkably skilled with the ball, even with southeasterly winds to contend with.

Clive looked pleased with what she had done, and Cayenne was relieved when the time was up, and they gathered up all the materials and marched back to join the others in the hall. She was even more relieved that when she looked at the clock, there were only 15 minutes to go until she could leave. All thoughts of wanting to work maximum hours, when she had first considered the job, were quickly abandoned at the end of her first day. She tried her hardest not to literally run out of the door when the clock struck 4:00 p.m.

Retracing her steps from her journey to work that morning, she returned with none of the gusto which had carried her there, skipping over the morning dew. She stumbled home almost in a daze feeling as though she had had the life force sucked out of her. She hadn't expected young children to be so demanding. She certainly hadn't remembered her own children being this hard work. Despite the fact that she had seemed to career through the day with relative ease, it wasn't until she had walked out of the door that immense fatigue hit her. She felt the effects of every last call of her name which had ranged from Caym to Caymen, whilst some gave up using her name altogether and simply tapped her on the arm to get her attention for the slightest concern that they had, ranging from broken or missing toys to detailed descriptions of the contents of their lunch box.

When she finally walked through the door of her apartment, she couldn't remember ever being so appreciative of her own children and their self-sufficient stages in life, confirmed by Sugar removing her coat and bag and beckoning for her to sit, so that she could assist in removing her trainers; and Diego putting the kettle on, reaching for the Jamaican Wray and Nephew 100% proof rum to infuse her Earl Grey after folding his tired mother into a warm embrace.

Cayenne lay down in the middle of the living room floor, still fully clothed in the E-Quip uniform. The last thought she could remember when she awoke the next morning was the sensation of a quilt being thrown over her and vaguely listening to the sound of the kettle boiling and hearing the children pottering around to prepare her hot beverage.

She could have sworn she heard the cheeky giggle of her daughter in the kitchen whispering, "A little bit more rum."

Chapter 34

"You're back then?" Clive seemed genuinely surprised when he buzzed her in via the intercom the following morning.

The first part of the day was spent playing with the children in their chosen activities. Cayenne knew that this was going to be the hardest part. Structured play she could handle. Having to sit and engage into their four-year-old minds whilst they played games or drew pictures suddenly seemed like an uphill struggle.

She was relieved when Clive called her into the staffroom again to complete some additional paperwork. She would quite happily spend all her time in there completing all of Clive's paperwork, as long as it kept her away from anybody under 11.

Cayenne glanced discreetly at Clive whilst he rifled through the pile of files in front of him.

It was obvious, and not only by his stale odour, that he was wearing the exact same uniform that he had worn the previous day minus the washing machine cycle in between that it so desperately needed. The same embedded stains in the same places. His hair still hadn't been terrorised by a comb, let alone any form of moisturisation. She could have sworn the crumbs in the corner of his eye sockets were the exact same ones as the day before, and she daren't inspect the teeth. How could this happen? Where does he live? Didn't anyone happen to mention over breakfast that it might be an idea to glance at the shower? Surely he wasn't homeless. Was he? He reminded her of those black children in the '70s who were adopted by white families—families with the best of intentions that had all the love in the world to offer this child but with absolutely no foreknowledge of the child's heritage and culture. The ones Cayenne came across always seemed to boast National Health Service glasses, displayed dry skin and uneven hair, in a unisex but slightly boyish and doubtless, manageable style. After several years in their adopted environment, you could almost identify them in a crowd. They were black on the outside, but it was as though someone had sucked the very soul out of them leaving an overall impression that something was missing.

She silently wondered whether Clive had been adopted and culturally starved. His flaking lips cast her mind to the image of Saturn on Sugar's bedroom wall, whereas some of her earliest memories entailed having Vaseline slapped unceremoniously onto their lips as children before even thinking of walking through the door. It wasn't long before their conversation turned to his emotional state.

"One of the kids this morning," he paused and glanced towards the door. "Do you know the one that's around 12, one of the older ones? His name's Connor. The one that never wants to join in with the group activities."

Cayenne pretended to be searching her brain running through an imaginary list in her head. Twisting her mouth and wrinkling her nose until she felt she had given the search sufficient attention before confirming, "No, I don't think I know him," as though it wasn't only her second day on the job.

"He came in this morning in a mood. He doesn't like coming here, but his mum's gone somewhere, and he's staying with his aunt. That's the woman that brings him here. I told him to stop throwing the basketball around, and he didn't listen. So I told him again. I mean there are little children around." Clive looked at her, eyes wide, desperate to see if she agreed, though she knew that it was most probably his pride that was sore and less to do with any health and safety concerns he may have had.

"Yes, of course, surely he knows it's not allowed indoors." She offered.

"He still wouldn't listen, so I said, 'Connor, if you don't stop, I'm gonna have to call your aunt to come and get you'. And he said 'I don't care; call her, you fat sod'." If Cayenne had the inclination to laugh, it soon disappeared when she saw the injured look in his watery eyes.

She tried to adopt a compassionate expression, "Oh no."

"They can be so cruel, and the managers don't help. All they care about is the paperwork, and I've got so much to do already because we are short-staffed. I've asked them to send someone else and sent loads of emails. They just ignore it." More tears welled up in Clive's eyes.

Cayenne's maternal instincts kicked in. "If it's all getting too much for you, you must say something. There's only so much you can take …" She was aware that kids could be cruel; though she half-wondered whether the comments he was relaying were a rather parred down version, for surely there was much more they could have said.

"I'm gonna do one more term, and then I'm leaving."

"Really. You're not enjoying it anymore?"

He shook his head solemnly. Scratching his scalp causing a smattering of snow dust to decorate his shoulders. "I'm going to America this summer to take part in a summer camp out there." Cayenne nodded approvingly. She sincerely hoped he would find whatever he was looking for, notably some kind of makeshift family, preferably with some running water; and that he wasn't simply trying to escape anything. Something told her that a change of climes wasn't quite the answer.

Chapter 35

Walking into body conditioning class was always an interesting situation in Cayenne's mind. She would evaluate the others in the class, as though they were taking part in a state championship. As though they were her fierce rivals competing for the ultimate reward. Admittedly the real contenders often caused her to have a nanosecond of doubt. She would groan inwardly as she saw them limbering up or running into class at the last minute, and she could see the exact same emotions on their faces whenever she turned up in her latest gear showing off her newly developed abs or curved biceps. Diego had begun to taunt her, "Mum, you're taking it too far now; you're beginning to look like a man."

She knew he was exaggerating. She didn't particularly care whether she was beginning to look masculine. The feeling of being strong was too intoxicating to stop. Every time she had to push herself beyond her current limits, she knew she was developing her mind, and that that would affect every area of her life.

She could see the exact same emotions on the faces of her opponents. "Oh no, she's here. Why did she have to come today? I wanted to feel like winning today."

She totally understood. But she also knew she needed them to push her. Even though she would say outwardly, I'm only competing with myself which was only partly true. In class she would position herself in the same spot towards the back in the left-hand corner of the studio where she could face herself fully in the mirror, not necessarily to correct posture as advised by the instructors, but so that she could stare herself in the eyes menacingly and will herself through the pain, will herself to keep pushing, jumping, pressing until the last count and perhaps one more for good measure.

Marcia, today's instructor was tuning the sound system, adjusting knobs and tweaking wires trying to connect her phone to the speakers. This was a different Marcia to the one you would see walking around the gym in her capacity as assistant gym manager.

Outside of class you would find her in sleek, fitted black trousers, showing off her curves, matched with the black and green tops that the staff wore. She didn't need much makeup as she was a naturally pretty, strong, tall African lady. Her sleek black flowing wig complemented her look to perfection. Cayenne almost choked on her water, the first time she actually attended one of Marcia's classes. The sleek wig was presumably left hanging in her managerial locker as she now stood at the helm of the class with her natural hair tucked into a skullcap. A skullcap that, had she taken the time to read the label would have advised her, STRONGLY, possibly in huge, bold, neon flashing lights with an accompanying thronging symbol; that it was specifically designed for use UNDER a wig, not to be seen EVER. To be used with the utmost care and discretion. Do not expose to everyday folk (particularly white folk).

Cayenne didn't know whether to applaud her bravery, accept her practicality or to lynch her for her betrayal.

"Hello ladies, my name is Marcia. I'm you're instructor today. I hope you're here to work 'cos I'm gonna push you."

Marcia clearly loved her music, and her classes were so loud and vigorous that she could scarcely be heard over the pumping R'n'B tunes that she blasted out between instructions.

Cayenne looked herself in the eye and silently warned her conscious mind not to dare to give less than 100%. The warm-up had begun, and the group of 15 women obediently followed Marcia's lead of three rounds of push-ups, star jumps, walkouts and burpees.

Marcia would demonstrate the exercises in her broad East-London accent. Cayenne always smirked whenever Marcia said 'here' as the East End dialect, at least for the black sector of the East End, caused it to sound like 'hair'—the irony.

Cayenne would pace herself at this point. Her competitors would be going all out already. She admired them for that, and she too executed with precision, paying particular attention to technique and to the muscle they were targeting at that given moment. Without even a glance, she knew that others were focusing on winning already. Doing more push-ups than anyone else, doing it faster than anyone else at the expense of their technique. Surely this was setting them up for difficulty later on. At this stage of life, Cayenne knew she couldn't afford to do that. She had to take care of herself, to minimise the risk of injury. One particular competitor had a new injury every week. She couldn't be more than 28, 29 years old.

So the warm-up for Cayenne was just that—warming up the muscle, preparing it for the onslaught to come.

Marcia divided up the group into three sections and demonstrated to each group what she wanted them to do.

The first group had to jump onto one of the four blocks that she had set out and accelerate upwards, landing in a deep squat and repeat. The middle group had to have a dumbbell in each hand, jump down into a plank position, pull up the dumbbells one by one and then jump forward into a low squat and then stand up and into a shoulder press. "You're hair, ladies." Marcia hollered as she executed a deep squat with a dumbbell in each hand, rising up and pushing them into the air. "Then hair. Okay, you're hair."

'No, Marcia, where's your hair?' Cayenne directed her thoughts back to the exercise at hand. The third group had to run from one end of the far wall to the other as fast as they could. Sprinting over and over again until the one minute was up. Then the groups would rotate.

Cayenne knew she could do these exercises with aplomb. Some of the others could too. Most would attempt a few and then stand with their hands on their hips, allowing their overprotective mind to dictate what they could do, with pained expressions on their faces, looking at Marcia with longing in their eyes willing the one minute to be over; only moving again in response to Marcia's barking.

"Come on, ladies. I see you, Cayenne, well done."

Marcia rarely took part in the actual exercises. Few instructors did these days. They simply demonstrated and then focussed on their charges with military sharpness. Cayenne often wondered whether they spent so much time instructing that they lost sight of their own personal goals. But if your job is to instruct others, shouldn't you also be leading the way by maintaining your own goals? She would ask herself. Cayenne didn't underestimate the power of subjecting herself to the right people for effective inspiration, although sometimes it was a case of, needs must if her favourite instructors were unavailable. In Marcia's class, the exercises were demanding and effective, so she made more of a determination to push herself with each task.

After each group had attempted each task, Marcia gave the group one minute rest whilst she reset each station.

The block section now had to jump from one side of the block to the other with both feet together. Cayenne would need to pace this one but go after it to the end. The middle section now had to pick up a barbell of their choice from the assortment of different weights and clean and press for the entire minute. The third section had to mountain climb their way to the countdown.

"Okay ladies, let's get after it."

The jumping was hard on the legs. Hard on the breathing. She concentrated her efforts on keeping her breathing at a comfortable regular pace and willed her legs to respond. Zoning out the voice of her mind that said, "Rest…rest and then restart." She answered it firmly…
"No. Keep going. Don't you dare stop till the countdown."
Cayenne chose the heaviest barbell. Not to show off but to challenge herself. To face possible failure. She knew at that moment, she would want to stop. Her mind would be pleading, her muscles in total agreement with 'rest a little'.
The look she gave herself in the mirror silenced her insistent mind. She knew her mind feared her resolve. One look would make it quiver with doubt. The piercing stare would always win.
The last section was a breeze. Mountain climbers were tough on the breathing but relatively easy compared to the other tasks.
"Now we are gonna change the pace ladies." Marcia was pushing the equipment to the side of the class, out of the way, to make room for the next stage. Everyone stood around watching her lug the heavy equipment whilst explaining the next step. Cayenne rushed over to the dumbbells and put them aside and moved the few remaining mats over to their stand.

"Thanks, Cayenne.

Okay now, we are gonna do three sets of each of the following exercises. First, we are hair ladies, hair."
Marcia was demonstrating jumping squats, accelerating high up into the air and landing into the inevitable deep butt-shaping squat.
The last task before the cooldown was Cayenne's favourite.

"Lastly ladies, we are gonna finish off, jumping up as high as you can with high knees. We're hair, okay? Hair."
Marcia demonstrated jumping with both knees in the air, touching both knees with her hands. She would pause at the bottom of each jump before accelerating up again, after a count of two.

Cayenne smirked inwardly. Knowingly. This was her forté. She knew that this would propel her around the bend and down the last 100-metre stretch to the finishing line. That her competitors would fade away in her wake. That she would be inwardly posturing, like Usain Bolt, during the cool down.

Admittedly, after the jump squats and the star jumps she was a little winded, but there was something about the knee-high jumps, and her assurance of her ability to do them that caused her to override any fatigue. It was as though she would go into another dimension, and she wouldn't feel the pain until the end. This was when she soared. When everyone around, either directly, discreetly or trying desperately to avoid it, couldn't help but stand in awe that this 40-something woman was able to do this.

Cayenne didn't look at them. That would be cruel, not to mention brazen. She would be staring at the woman in the mirror, who was in the best shape of her life, who was somehow executing age-defying high-knee jumps, one after the other, without pausing and saying to herself 'YOU ARE UNSTOPPABLE'.

Chapter 36

"TITLE: getting what we need.
How is your calendar for next week?"

"Still awaiting my schedule…I should be getting it later today."

"I will try to come by Chanel today if you're around. I've just been looking at the video you sent me… nice hard platinum fuck—a good thirst-drenching."

"I'm only free between 12:00 and 3:00."

"What are you wearing/how's that tight black cunt?"

"Deciding what to wear.
Still… BLACK
Still…TIGHT. I'm due for a getaway.
It hasn't quite been an Annis Horribilis, however, one certainly feels the onset of a much-needed stint at Balmoral.
I have barely started my hiatus from lady-of-leisure status, and I'm already somewhat weary. I could certainly benefit from some significant cunt-cuddling.
By the close of my two-week sentence at this play scheme, the slightest touch of my vagina will cause a Niagaral outpouring."

"Good. I need a drink."

"I'll render you helpless in a drunken stupor. Pussy juice galore."

"Your white suburban fuck needs his fortnightly feed…
He's looking forward to being the Queen's secret toy and getting on his knees to please before becoming the arrogant platinum exec and fucking her hard in a number of positions.

He particularly wants to see the Queen on all fours…

He's going to be a disgrace—hopefully, these suburban streets will never know the interracial shenanigans he will indulge in next week.

The nerves and procrastination have gone. His white cock simply needs a dirty chocolate release.

He needs blacking."

"Your words fill me with exuberance. I like it… the Queen rightly takes pre-eminence… she will need complete subservience to satisfy both hers and the pussy's hunger.

Your thirst must be unprecedented, for the flow is unceasing.

Once the Queen is satisfied and emptied, she will await her replenishing as the Wharf knight drills her with pent-up executive stress. And she will take it. All of it. Momentarily denouncing her throne to submit to desperate buggery.

She will allow you to express your masterful Amex authority until she is thoroughly pierced and sufficiently pummelled and drenched in your platinum milk."

"It will be disgusting filth from the moment we are alone.

I am in need of a dirty disgraceful blacking. I will submit to your black chocolate milf cunt, like a whore on heat. My white cock is straining in my trousers—it needs a black pussy juice drenching.

You have made me into your whore—this nice suburban white guy is damned… promise me this secret will be hidden."

If Cayenne was perfectly honest with herself, his request to keep her a secret dented her ego a little. If she was at a place to be transparent with her feelings, she would have admitted that she secretly wanted him to acknowledge her openly and proudly. Instead, she reminded herself that this wasn't the way they set this up.

Instead, she replied… "I have no desire or need to divulge this delicious clandestine eroticism. I have chosen to live my life privately, and it will remain so. I respect my own majesty and your executive status highly.

At any point, you can diminish this aspect of your life. Delete the email and to the fellow strangers in the wharf you will return.

Meanwhile…

Such is the sexual hunger… your clothes will be removed the moment you close the door.

Start licking my pussy in the elevator. Finger me in the foyer. I'll lead you to the penthouse by your cock.

So proud that William has abandoned his worry and Dan his delusion.

Let me blacken you fully. Cast doubt aside. If this is our final encounter… let's have a blast.

Give me an Amex fuck I'll never forget.

Every time we look back on this strange Wharf encounter…let it be full of fond memories."

"We won't be done after next week's pure abandonment, and you know it…

The question is, how fucked up do we want to go…

I do fancy watching you be Queen over some white bitch who has to lick hard… perhaps that's the SWF in me who wants to see tables turned, but would that turn the Queen on or simply bore her?"

Cayenne was silently offended. Offended that he seemed to want to open up their experience to others. Or was he simply asking this as a way of trying to look into her own mind? To see what her objectives were.

"How contrary these Amex executives are.

One moment asking for private exclusivity (please don't tell all).

The next you want to introduce the element of white loose pussy skank with crimson flaps.

How do you suppose to keep it private by introducing another… unless of course you already know someone willing… perhaps my predecessor? Oh, it all becomes clear.

Or else it's your current squeeze… at least that would reduce the hotel fees, and I trust we could eat imitation tapas 'round at your place to satisfy the platinum scrooge in you.

My suggestion:

We enlist one of the black hunks who are forming a trail on my dating app account.

Tall, dark, big black cock that actually holds it's form. You could watch and take inventory to see how a black woman should be fucked… without hesitancy or fucking post slave owner fear. No pausing to muster the courage or dare I say stamina. Just fucking with rhythm and coordination which are admittedly attributes that your sort are hardly synonymous with.

While you ponder my suggestion… I wouldn't bother to reply… It will be automatically relegated to my spam list.

Deluded Dan returns.

Or is your current, suburban, squeeze-the-deluded-one thinking that she is actually being fucked correctly."

"Erm, it was only a tiny suggestion."

"I've had my fill of 'tiny' suggestions from you."

"Fine…settle for low-grade black shit!!!"

Cayenne gasped. Her hand on her chest. Wow. That was harsh. But admittedly her words were harsh also.

He had riled her, she had riled him; though he was soon repentant.

"Obviously, I never meant to irritate. It's not in any way a big idea. Not sure why I mentioned it—apologies for any upset.

Mmmm… I think sometimes you take me too literally. It is a good job I don't do the same :p"

Cayenne placed her phone down to charge and to examine the turmoil spiralling in her mind.

"Hey you. I'm really hoping you've forgiven me for being a complete fool."

She picked up her phone again.

"I am seriously having a bad time at work at the moment. The Queen has too much power over me… I can't concentrate if I'm not in her court."

Cayenne smiled. A warm feeling spread over her, like a comforting blanket, as she assessed his grovelling.

"I need a fucking spanking.
I need to be put in my place.
I need to be taught a lesson.
I need to be tormented and fucking used.

I'm having the executive week from hell. Hope you're okay."

"I've decided to enjoy low-grade black shit."

"I forgot I said that :(
Should never have said that. I'm very sorry."

"Don't be sorry for true colours."

"They are not my true colours :("

The next morning, Cayenne awoke in forgiving mode.

"Good morning, good-looking. Are we friends again?
Only fair since you made it impossible for my cock to rise to white bitches. Let's get back to what we do best."

"Just when I think I know what that is…you persist on wanting to introduce outside agents.
Clearly, we are not on the same page.
Quite a contrary personality, aren't you? Like the true politician that you aspire to be. Entice people with high-end promises, then once you think you have them captive, your words take on a holographic air. Be honest… I know it goes against the grain for you. Do you really want a threesome?"
She was annoyed at herself that she wanted to know the answer.
"No seriously, it's not overtly important."

"That suggests it is a consideration.
How would you feel about a threesome with myself being the only female? And perhaps the only chocolate counterpart?"

"I get your point. Seriously—didn't mean to offend. And no that's a rubbish idea."

"Now now, let's not be hasty. Let's consider this option thoroughly."

"Cheeky :p"

"Let's consider the benefits.

Halve the cost of hotel fees. Provide inspiration if you lack quality culinary choices.

If your cock can't take the heat… our guest could take over and complete the task with efficiency.

If you don't have the quality time, you offered during your underbelly campaign… And have to rush off after the lunchtime hour… our guest can continue to drink from my chocolate well.

You could leave our guest to escort me to Agent Provocateur in your absence.

He could open the champagne whilst you see to your numerous emails.

Now… how's that for a proposition?"

"Ha-ha, cheeky bitch.

Oh, you do make me laugh. Just in time before I get another mauling here in the office."

Cayenne hadn't finished making him pay.

"Wouldn't you like to watch while another man licks my chocolate delight?

You said it would turn you on. Imagine seeing a big black cock protruding into my tight vagina. Ooh, I'm getting wet.

Imagine the screams you'll hear from the other side of the hotel room door that closes in your pale face."

"I can just imagine you getting off on all of this."

Her phone was silent for many hours after that. She was tempted to message him. Wondering whether she had pushed him too far. Confused that he would switch from needing her, to the apparent satisfaction with not having her.

In the early hours of the morning, she was awoken by her message alert.

"Just got in the car service, for the second time this week; Leaving the Wharf at 12:30 a.m. in the morning is becoming routine.

Shame you can't join…

The last week has been tough.

I'd much rather be drinking berry juice… think I need it."

"Pretty addictive, huh?"

"Too tired to be eloquent, but yes, I want your wet black juicy cunt in my face."

"So you keep saying."

"Good night, you. I'm knackered, and the taxi driver keeps kicking off about Brexit."

The next morning…
"Good morning, gorgeous. I have actually had to earn my platinum status these last few days.
Should allow Thursday p.m./Friday a.m. to be good though.
Want to teach me a lesson and make me lick?"

"Should I decide to totally relinquish you from the spam category, then I shall indeed teach you lessons that will elevate you to Palladium-card territory.
Provided a more keen knight, a more responsive knight, a knight who knows a Queen's true value, not pit you to the post.
You do realise, don't you? That now that the Queen is aware that the exec can indeed earn his status with additional nightly hours… her expectations have increased immeasurably. No longer will she accept mediocre pussy-licking and half-fucking at lunchtime.
The white knight's allegiance must firstly be to her majesty. Any executive obligations are merely secondary to her needs if he has any hope of securing cinnamon-cunt rights in the future.

Surely my nutmeg coolie is utterly wasted on an overburdened accountant."

"I need to see the Queen."

"The Queen has desperate urgency also."

"Tell me. Be that filthy behind-closed-doors bitch that I harden for."

"I can scarcely put into words the insatiable hunger brewing within the inner sanctum…where steamy cum juice ferments awaiting its divine milk accompaniment and savoury seasoning.
The lobes of my pussy ache for your touch and your tongue. The arch of my back anticipates your body heat as we intertwine.
Spend quality time stroking the Queen's pussy. Do not short circuit the entangled journey from the depths of her vagina to the peak of her euphoric orgasm."

"I'm going to be your fucking white slave slut. Massage my face with your cunt and then sit on my cock until you fucking release."

"Oh yes. A full pussy facial is in store."

"I can't wait for my feeding and blacking.
Bad, bad Queen milf."

"How fortunate you are… what gods of fortune favoured you the very day you encountered a Queen in disguise in the unlikely location of the Wharf slums.
No greater prize could you have foreseen… black Nubian Royalty harbouring secrets of pussy-licking hunger having long since dismissed any notion of cunt escapades.
How the stars must have aligned in light of our shared passion for erotic culinary delights.
What mercy the Queen has shown to lower her standards to favour a lowly pale city executive over cultural princes and exotic Sheiks.
For their fortune pales into insignificance when she considers the exec's hunger for gateaux cunt and caramel soufflé pussy."

"It's completely deserved :)"

"Oh to stem the flow of a dribbling pussy…
And how to cause it to subside whilst you whisk me through an itinerary of excitement and luxury before our conclusion.
Black British with a Caucasian exec having intercourse on Egyptian cotton, drinking French champagne and sampling

exquisite Mediterranean cuisine, fucking in hedonistic fashion, climaxing in a universal panoramic intercontinental collision."

He promised to amorously reward her poetic prose at their much-anticipated rendezvous.

Chapter 37
March 2017

The unusual entrance to the Park Plaza Hotel in Westminster was accessed via illuminated twin escalators either side of a spiral staircase which opened up into the vast reception forecourt, with its white marble floor and low ceiling. She couldn't help but rest her case down momentarily and stand in the centre, turning around on the spot, trying to take in every last detail. The low ceiling adding to the cosy yet opulent ambience.

One of the many features was an unusual installation consisting of several beautifully handcrafted, painted teacups which looked as though they were suspended in mid-air in a circular formation, depicting a whirlwind frozen in time. It had to be at least 8 feet tall and appeared to be held in place by a succession of wires attached to a stainless-steel frame.

When her eyes were satisfied, she approached the middle of the three white long desks that made up the whole of one side of the space.

"Hello," a friendly voice came out of a short blond woman dressed smartly in a navy blue uniform. Her name badge read, Claire Reading, receptionist. "Can I help you?"

"Yes, is there a reservation under the name Halpern-Smith?"

"Can I take your name please, and I'll just check for you." She peered into her computer screen. "Ah yes, here it is. I'll just get your key ready for you. Will you be having lunch in the restaurant today. Would you like me to reserve you a table? Actually, I can see it's already been reserved for you."

Cayenne waited whilst the receptionist produced the key, watching the staff busying themselves behind the desk and disappearing in all directions to meet the constant needs of demanding clientele.

"There you are, Miss Richards." The receptionist handed her a folded card with pictures of the plaza and details of some of its services and features. Tucked inside was the electronic door key.

"Thank you very much."

Her heart began racing as soon as she emerged from the elevator. It didn't seem as though he was there yet but she couldn't be sure, though he had mentioned that he was likely to get there after her planned arrival due to a meeting at work.

She slipped the key into the slot at the side of the door. It was silent as far as she could tell. When she went inside, the lights were on but remained dimly lit, and the curtains were closed. The room had been designed beautifully. The space was mostly white with a cool grey marble floor, off-white walls and ultra-modern furniture arranged for the convenience of a visiting family. There were even flowers and plants strategically positioned, and she almost felt as though she were intruding in somebody's home. The scene could have been taken straight out of an ideal home magazine. Outside of the large doors that framed the perfect backdrop of Central London, there was a partially decked terrace complete with tables and chairs and potted exotic plants. She glanced into the first bedroom which housed two double beds side by side, a black shiny desk and swivel chair and several framed pieces of abstract wall art.

She threw off her leather jacket and pulled off her boots and wandered into the second bedroom which was dominated by a king-size bed, adorned with silk quilt covers and purple and gold velvet throws which matched the beautifully draped curtains. Orchids stood proudly in a contemporary vase on the bedside table. A decanter of water and two glasses were set on a tray on the desk. She could feel the quality of cashmere carpet between her toes.

She checked the time. It was almost 1:00. He had said he hoped to arrive by 1:30 p.m. She had just enough time to get ready.

By the time, she heard a faint clicking noise on the outside of the door 20 minutes later. She had draped herself seductively at the far edge of the bed and tilted her body towards the door.

She had taken the time to shave her delicate area, and the cocoa butter oil that she had caressed her skin with was glistening in the semi-darkness. This, along with strategic dabs of Chanel were her only garment.

She heard him enter and listened to the sounds of him dropping his bag and coat on the table which echoed the sound of jangling keys.

Excitement mounted as she followed the sound of his hard office shoes tap dancing across the marble floor. The staff downstairs would have alerted him of her arrival. He would be following her deliberately positioned trail. The high-heeled boots by the front door, the coat draped over the high-backed chair, the dress hanging on the bathroom doorknob, and her bra laying across the short corridor towards the bedrooms. Her stockings framing the African wall art, and her thong pinned to the bedroom door.

When he finally appeared, her thongs gagging his mouth, she was relieved to see that he had a more self-assured appearance today. The uncertain, guilty look that usually pierced his eyes had been abandoned. His smile revealed his satisfaction at seeing her there, waiting for him.

Today she needed more. He would give her more today. He had to. It was time.

He sighed, and she could see his shoulders visibly soften. She rolled onto her back and closed her eyes and listened to the sound of him disrobing. She wanted to heighten the sensation, and the anticipation of not knowing which direction he would approach from, and how he would embrace her. Tentatively or aggressively.

She felt her legs being uncrossed and spread apart, then wider apart. Then she felt his hands at the back of her legs, sensitively moving the back of her knees up and folding them outward until she found herself in the diamond position that she practised in yoga. Silence hung in the air. She imagined him standing watching her. She could feel him drawing nearer, or was that her imagination. She could hear him breathing heavily and deeply. Taking full intakes of breath, filling his lungs with the smell of her—his favourite smell. His nose moved up and down her legs, slowly following the scent of her, his tongue joining in the search, licking the cocoa oil from her skin.

He was taking his own sweet time. He clasped both her hands in his until their palms were adjoined above her head. The intensity coursing through both of them.

She lay back, eyes still closed, savouring every moment. After smelling and licking the opening of her treasure, long luxurious licks that threatened to bring her to her fullest joy, he delicately prized her open further still with his moist fingertips and deepened his search, furtive and hungry, the tip of his tongue forging ahead in a single-minded serge to the source of liquid gold.

She gasped and groaned and writhed in ecstasy, the strength of his hands holding her in place, so as not to thwart his expedition. She knew that this part was not just for her pleasure, but for his insatiable need. She opened up voluntarily, allowing him to sup amorously from her well, and he continued there for some time, long after she had been spent. When he let go of her hand, she ran her fingers through his hair, as though stroking a sleeping child. He arose from his feast, invigorated, determined, wanting to please her, to not leave her in lack anymore. To reward her for her generosity, he began thanking her over and over again with forceful thrusts, indenting the walls of her vagina with determined gratitude. Pounding her in complete recognition of his good fortune for as long as he could possibly, humanly, hold. Until the thrusting gave way to his pent-up release. He shuddered over her as their bodies lay entwined, quivering with coordinating tremors.

He pulled her on top of him and swathed her in his mouth as though she were a tantalising dessert, cupping her head in his hands, forcing her to him.

"I want more." Her hunger remained unabated.

"You're gonna get more."

He positioned her over his penis and let the warmth of her harden him again. Elevating her hips before bringing her gently down whilst thrusting himself upwards to ensure she was in the right spot. A slight adjustment saw them collide again, rhythmically, sensually. Her pleasure filling him with contentment. He knew she had needed this for far too long. His Queen could no longer be denied. When she began to tire, he swiftly placed her down on her back and continued the course; his senses overwhelmed as his body took over. His need for her building by the second.

There was noise coming from the streets below. He was almost certain it didn't sound like general traffic noise. Some sort of commotion that sounded unusual, but the maelstrom of emotions whirling inside and around him was dominant in his thoughts.

She thought she heard screeches, somewhere in the distance. Was it in the hallway, or was it outside? She couldn't be sure. The vaginal vortex taking place inside her was far too riveting to give it much thought.

Suddenly, the unmistakable prolonged wail of sirens, and a confused mixture of diverse alarms interspersed with the tooting of vehicle horns pierced the air.

She thought she could hear his phone ringing and vibrating. Then her message ringtone competed for her attention.

He paused raising his head, and they both listened panting and dripping under the covers.

"Is something going on?" She watched resting her head on her propped elbow as he padded out towards his belongings. He returned phone in hand with an aghast expression on his face. He turned his back to her. He was assuring someone that he was okay in hushed tones. He would ring them back when he had the chance.

She pulled back the duvet and reached for her bag on the bedside table. Her phone was sounding again. Quickly swiping the screen with an upward stroke and keying in her security code, the screen uploaded to reveal evidence of several missed calls, texts and WhatsApp messages.

Her phone was ringing again.

She could hear the television switch on without her looking, glancing up she saw his naked body perched at the edge of the bed as the images on the screen flickered into view. The unmistakable backdrop of Westminster peered over the shoulder of the female news correspondent, and Cayenne could just make out the blaring headlines of some sort of security threat when she heard…

"Muu-uu-uu-uu-uu-uu-uu-uu-uu-uum!" Diego's voice permeated her eardrum, like a volcanic eruption. The only time her son shouted at her was when he was unable to reach her, or if her phone was switched off for a period of time, and he was concerned.

"Yes, what is it, son."

"Why didn't you answer your phone, I've been calling you. Haven't you seen the news?"

He carried on shouting as she peered ahead and read the headlines streaming across the screen.

The news reporter was standing with her microphone in hand, and a look of deep concern was etched on her face.

She assured Diego that she was okay and placed her phone down.

He had finished his phone call too. She briefly wondered who he had been reassuring. The look of worry had returned to his face. The look she had grown familiar with.

He switched off the TV abruptly and crawled over to her and held her in a comforting embrace. "Everything okay at home?"

She nodded.

He looked at her as though she were a bird with a broken wing that he needed to take care of. Whatever distractions that had momentarily diverted his attention had been cast aside. For now, he wanted to take care of her again and again, right this moment. Something about this moment was precious. This reminder that anything can happen, that the next moment is not promised, fired his determination to seize the day. She gladly welcomed his epiphany. Forceful and demanding, yet nurturing and purposeful, he maximised the moment with every last drop of him. Desperately needing to ensnare every last ounce of her.

Wrapping her in her towelling robe and fastening it tightly before slipping on his own, he led her by the hand out towards the terrace. Pulling open the sliding doors, they stepped out onto the deck. The enormity of the disturbance engulfed them as the sounds and sights of disarray and bedlam swirled around the streets below.

He pulled her close, directing her eyes away from the chaotic scenes as though wanting to shield her and prolong their harmonious bubble for just a little while longer.

Chapter 38

Cayenne could have predicted what would happen next. She might have known that her heroic, debonair seducer with his confident, self-assured demeanour would most certainly have packed his heroic costume into his office bag and any masterful resolutions abandoned in a miscellaneous file by the stroke of midnight.

The last time they had met up for tea in Chanel, he had taken her hand in his and looked at her strangely as though questioning something, both in her and in himself.

She was aware that she was now more open with him physically. More engaging, allowing him to see the effect he was having on her. That was new for him. Up until this point, it had been him expressing the most desire, and her combatting his advances just enough to keep him interested.

"What's going on here? How come you give a shit about how much time has passed since we last saw each other?" He was smiling with his lips, but his eyes were still questioning.

She didn't know the answer either. What was going on? Was she falling for him? Had he fallen for her? She would need to know that first.

"I think an awful lot of you. I'm just a bit worried that this could lead to ruin for me. I mean I've spent so much money in a matter of weeks. I can barely concentrate at work. This just isn't… sustainable." He shook his head as though trying to convince himself. "It's not sustainable." He shrugged and took a sip of his coffee which was lukewarm by now, as was hers.

When they stood facing each other to say goodbye, he made several attempts to leave her. On the pier overlooking South Quay to the rear of Chanel, for the most part away from prying eyes, he attempted several times to physically leave her but would spin around and walk back to her, holding her to him again.

She was loving this. Seeing the emotion that he was battling with. Watching his not wanting to let her go.

Kissing her again and again, dipping his fingers between her legs as though stealing another whip of cream from a delectable trifle that really ought not to be touched.

Sighing depressingly as his corporate schedule beckoned, and his precarious private life seemed to weigh heavily upon him. Looking deep into her eyes, like an abandoned puppy at a shelter. Willing her to have an answer.

Eventually, they resigned themselves to the inevitable. His deep kiss spoke a thousand words. Their fingertips lingered as they backed away. He turned away first. Head down with his hands in his pockets, she watched as he wandered back towards Canary Wharf. She watched until he merged with the bustling crowd. Until he became almost obscured from view, with just flashes of him dotted in the canvas. Flickers of his blue-striped shirt, a glimpse of his long hair over his collar. His head hanging low. Then she couldn't see him anymore.

He was gone.

Chapter 39

"Ignoring my currently redundant role, I do hope you had a lovely day. Happy Birthday, gorgeous."

"Thank you." Not for the first time, she was touched that he had remembered.

"I'm glad you enjoyed it. You deserve it…"

"Aww, thank you…"

"Can I treat you to a night out as a birthday treat?
Can the Queen confirm next week's diary… her toy needs to compensate for his neglectful behaviour."

Later Cayenne browsed the internet for somewhere special to celebrate her birthday. He had told her to choose wherever she wanted. Immediately, only one place came to mind.

Looking at the pictures of the Shard on the website made her all the more determined that this was the right choice. She had asked him to plan a complete itinerary for her. One of the things she loved about their time together was the fact that she only had to turn up. He would send her a message stating 'details to follow' or 'await further instructions'. It filled her with excitement that he took responsibility for organising everything. She wasn't so naïve as to think that this was totally for her benefit, but it was enthralling nevertheless.

She had always wanted to go to the Shard. Even before they had moved from Torquay, Sugar had travelled to London on a school trip; and one of the landmarks that they were scheduled to visit was the Shard, as well as Big Ben and to embark on a short boat trip along the Thames. Cayenne had been fascinated by the detailed preparation that had gone into preparing to let a hoard of six-years-olds loose in the capital.

On their return, they had been given a project to complete which included a study of the capital city and the task to write small essays about it and draw pictures of the landmarks they had seen. Prior to this, Cayenne knew very little about this world famous tower which had grown from an office block in its 1970s hey-day, to the spectacle it is today, with world-famous restaurants, fascinating installations, and a neighbouring hotel offering some of the best views of London.

Now it was considered one of the top spots for celebrations and family gatherings or romantic evenings with the 95-storey skyscraper attracting people from all over the world to enjoy it's Neo-futurism style of architecture.

Cayenne couldn't wait to experience the bars and restaurants with the panoramic views of London as the perfect backdrop.

As if on cue, an email notification interrupted her perusing.

"Hey, gorgeous. Trying to juggle stuff. I hadn't factored in my boss being out for half-term, so I will be expected to hold the fort."

"Is next week off then?"

"Will tell you shortly. I want to be in a position where I can totally switch off and enjoy it."

"Understandable."

"You alright? Good weekend?"

"Yeah, weekends are currently a blur of gym activity.
I think this was the first weekend of many where your voice was noticeably silent."

"Wow, did you actually miss it?"

"Clearly you didn't"

"Oh really… I still need my fix. You must be looking so toned. Fancy a tea?"

"Provided gym gear is permitted. The schedule continues…"

"Sure. Want to do now or 5:00 p.m.?"
"Either…"

"Cool. I'll see you in 15–20 minutes."

Over tea he had shown her the Shard booking for her birthday treat, and together they browsed the website and discussed the things that they were looking forward to the most. For him, it was the Jacuzzi. For her, the Oblix Restaurant.

It had been another rushed union as he had urgent meetings to attend late afternoon. She hadn't had time to eat the cake he had bought for her, so she had tucked it into her bag to enjoy after her planned cardio class.

"Are you home yet? How was the cake?"

"A tad on the dry side… lacked moisture. But the flavours were there…
Thank you."

"You're summing up the cake and not me I hope. I could feel the rush again on the way back to my 4:30. meeting"

"A familiar tingling resurfaced I must admit…"

"Mmmmm good…"

Diego picked up the leaflet on the kitchen counter as he cast his eyes around the refrigerator in search of a snack.

"Yay, Mummy, going to the Shard, huh? Look at you."
Cayenne smiled unable to hide her excitement. She knew that Diego was pleased for her. He had tried to encourage her over the years to socialise more, especially as he came of age to be able to look after the younger two. Not that they required much looking after.

She appreciated that he had the maturity not to ask too much about the stranger. He would listen to as much or as little as she cared to share, which was minimal, although she was usually incredibly open with her older son. Diego seemed satisfied with the fact that his mother was clearly enjoying herself, and that it was a positive experience for her.

The black and white bandage dress was limiting her pace somewhat, and the platform heels meant she had to pay close attention to each step which was proving exhausting as she made her way towards Canary Wharf station. The single clasp had broken on her full-length coat, and she shivered as a gust of wind flew up from under the underground carriage, blowing her hair across her face.

She whisked the wisps of hair that were attracted to the red adhesive gloss on her lips, back behind her ear and readied herself amongst the herd of urgent passengers, mentally selecting her seat in the approaching carriage from the imminent vacancies.

As the tube hurtled towards London Bridge, she was too excited to concentrate on the book that she had tucked into her bag at the last minute. She knew she would end up just looking at the words but not taking anything in. A lady sitting opposite did a double take as she sat down after the train had arrived at Canada Water. Cayenne smiled at the lady in appreciation of the compliment, even though the lady hadn't smiled or indicated that she liked what she saw. She had simply stared, glanced at Cayenne's clothes and boots and then looked straight ahead only looking again as Cayenne rose on the approach to London Bridge.

Not even the smattering of patchy drizzle could dampen her spirits as the commanding presence of the tallest building in the country came into view.

She had deliberately not checked her phone that day and chose resolutely to be in the moment. To let the day unfold without distraction.

Walking into the immaculate reception area, she was met with an impressive sight. From the dazzling design feature, a vast chandelier which glittered with tiny fragments of crystal all the way up to the 35th floor and the intricately marble-clad lobby. The contrast from the South London Street to this hive of opulence took her breath away.

Strolling towards the reception desk, she switched her phone back to the sound option and glancing at the screen she could see that the email symbol in the top left-hand corner was stacked, indicating that more than one message awaited her attention.

Somewhere in her consciousness, she was aware that one of the smartly dressed ladies behind the desk was speaking to her, or had already spoken to her and was now awaiting a response. When one wasn't forthcoming, she seemed to shift nervously transferring her weight from foot-to-foot and tilting her head slightly as though trying to get Cayenne's attention.

"Erm, sorry. I err…" Cayenne attempted to raise her head and address the woman properly, but the messages she was reading seemed to be scrambling her brain preventing the words from coming out. She knew she had read the words, but somehow needed to read them over and over again whilst her brain slowly, desperately tried to compute the information.

"I…"

"Hello, welcome to our Shangri la Hotel. How may I help you today?"

"I'm sorry, can I just take this call?" Cayenne held the phone to her ear as though she was taking a call and backed away from the desk, turning towards a black leather seating area bookended by two large freestanding antique lamps.

She felt as though she could physically use some bookends to stabilise her on her own feet at that moment and eased herself down into the comfortable chair.

She wasn't quite sure how long she had been sitting there before she became aware that time was passing by. The bright sky that earlier beamed through the floor-to-ceiling glass now seemed to have dimmed to a grey overcast blanket. She shivered slightly and found herself looking around the vast space, as though trying to ascertain the source of this sudden gust of chilly air. She realised that there wasn't one. That the chill was emanating from inside.

She knew she really ought to move. Do something. React. Make a phone call. But she just felt numb as though her mind had temporarily frozen, and the repercussions from the slightest pressure to move it forward to an actual thought pattern may be irreparable. So, she sat. For some time, just sitting. Drifting in and out of her subconscious mind. Taking in her surroundings, watching families and couples arriving. Others leaving. Porters ferrying expensive luggage around on golden carriages. Uniformed staff seemingly a part of a choreographed routine, swaying in and out of action.

Had anybody noticed her, they would have seen a serene smartly dressed woman, poised at the edge of her chair, legs folded beneath, clutching her handbag with a carrier nestled on the neighbouring seat. They would have simply assumed she was waiting for some tardy companion, or perhaps at the end of her stay and patiently expecting the reception staff to alert her of her car's arrival, to carry her on to her next engagement. Something important and official, no doubt, judging by appearances.

Cayenne was relieved to see Charlotte return from her latest quarterly trip to some far-flung destination in search of some deeper meaning to life. Charlotte was exactly as a yoga instructor should be. She was tall, lithe and blond, but that was secondary. Whenever she breezed into a room, she carried the zenness within her. Not all of them had that. It was as though she embodied the very state that she was qualified to guide others into. Cayenne liked her soft, calm voice and her unique way of expounding on the benefits of deep breathing. Earnestly encouraging them to take in as much life-giving force as possible. The virtues of holding it in place for just a few seconds allowing the body to absorb and best utilise each breath, and then the absolute delight, not to mention rewards of letting it all go again. Allowing oneself to become empty and vacant, ripe for something new.

She instantly inspired you to leave your life on the outside of the door as she welcomed you into the heavenly cavity of the yoga studio.

Cayenne had been looking forward to this all week. She had been steeling herself for it. Possibly, subconsciously holding her breath in anticipation of it.

"For those of you who are new to the class, I'm Charlotte, and this is Yin Yoga. It's a unique practice in that the focus is not so much on strenuous poses, but rather it's about looking inward, examining ourselves from the inside out and ultimately letting go of anything that might be causing the build-up of stress and tension. I'd like to welcome you to a simple practice which is an integral part of Yin Yoga, and it's a lovely way to start our practice. I'll talk you through it, and then we will do it together. You may find yourself in stressful situations sometimes; and it's something you can incorporate in your day-to-day life, and it just takes a few moments. You'll often find that the result leaves you feeling calmer, less stressed, and able to simply slow the mind down as often our busy schedules cause our minds to become overwhelmed; and that has a negative impact on the body. So for the next 30 minutes or so, I encourage you to soften and close your eyes as much as possible and be prepared to let everything go. Anything that has been weighing you down or that you've been overthinking. This is your time. Time to connect with your inner self and be restored."

Cayenne blinked as hard as she could so as to forbid the tears from rolling out of the sides of her eyes and onto the immaculate violet yoga mat.

She reached out her hand for the neatly folded blanket that Charlotte had always encouraged the class to have handy for comfort or to aid relaxation. She unfolded the blanket, hooking it under her feet and unfolding it over her body until it covered the length of her, creating her own little cocoon in the semi-darkness.

"So, when you're ready guys, if you can all come to a comfortable sitting position. Feel free to use one of the blocks to sit on if you would prefer. Place your palms together, hands to heart and soften or close your eyes. Sit up as straight as you can. Place your thumbs on your third eye, right between your eyebrows and set an intention for this practice today. It could be something abstract, or it could be something meaningful and specific to you that you want to concentrate on today. Or perhaps there is someone you would like to dedicate this practice to. Perhaps there's someone who you feel would benefit from it.

Now I invite you to take in a deep intake of breath for the count of five, really filling up your lungs and diaphragm as much as possible. Then I want you to hold the breath in for a count of five, and then I want you to release all of the breath until you feel light and empty. Okay? So, breathe in."

The class followed dutifully as Charlotte took in a deep intake of breath and counted for five seconds.

"Now hold the breath for a count of five…" The class fell silent as they retained the life-giving force that was now bottled up in their open, receptive bodies.

"And now I want you to just release… Let it all go…"

Here it was. The moment that Cayenne had been steeling herself for, going through the motions of the week on autopilot, just to get to this moment.

The moment that she could finally let it all go in a safe discreet realm. It wasn't just about him; there were others, from childhood, fragments from previous relationships, but he was the symbol for all of it for the purposes of this moment. For letting it all go.

"Just be a witness to your thoughts and watch them sail by you," Charlotte urged—her voice like a silky balm.

It was as though Cayenne were reading his torturous email afresh for the last time, watching the words float by overhead as she sat poised on her mat with her hands together in a solemn prayer. She read the words as they drifted away; and on every exhale, watched as the sentences slipped helplessly further into the distance, relinquishing their hold over her.

"Breathe in."

"Hey, sorry for the late notice, but I've had a resignation in my team; and I'm now needed to spend a few weeks in Bruxelles of all places, at one of the other branches at short notice.

I am flying out later today. I will be away for a few months at least whilst we try and address the issues that are arising…"

"Nice guys, now hold the breath in for five…"

"So sorry. It really couldn't be avoided.

I promise I'll arrange PANORAMIC (my phone capitalises automatically now) on my return.

Please don't be angry.

See you soon, my Queen."

"…and now I invite you to release… let it all go…"

The End???